The Art of
STAR TREK®

CONTENTS

ACKNOWLEDGMENTS

ILLUSTRATION BY RICARDO DELGADO.

GLOP ON A-STICK
R.DELGADO
7.92

STICK COULD BE USED TO MANIPULATE GLOP SO IT "SQUIRMS"

An early concept of the Promenade's "Glop-on-a-stick," which, interestingly enough, is how writers feel after sorting through approximately five thousand pieces of STAR TREK art.

The size and scope of this book should make it clear that as authors we are little more than chroniclers of the efforts of dedicated collectors, Paramount employees, movie and television professionals, and appreciators of science-fiction television and movies in general, and STAR TREK in particular.

The enthusiastic and selfless outpouring of artwork, time, and effort made available to us by friends and strangers alike was literally overwhelming, though after three years of being observers behind the scenes of STAR TREK, this generosity of spirit should come as no surprise to us. It is the hallmark of those who collectively labor to bring forth the ongoing television and movie adventures of what is justly one of the most popular and successful series of adventures ever put on film. The positive optimism that fueled Gene Roddenberry's first glimmerings of the STAR TREK universe is alive and well in all who expand and extend his dream, which perhaps accounts in part for the phenomenon's longevity and continued growth, and for which we are indebted more than we can say in these pages.

At Paramount, first and foremost we must once again thank Rick Berman for allowing us access to every aspect of STAR TREK's many productions. As Gene Roddenberry hoped, Mr. Berman has become much more than a keeper of the flame, and is boldly charting STAR TREK's new voyage into the twenty-first century.

Herman Zimmerman was a constant source of inspiration and knowledge during the creation of this book, and we are especially grateful for his persistence in tracking down a fabled treasure trove of dusty boxes that contained artwork sealed away at the time STAR TREK: THE MOTION PICTURE was released.

Herman's generosity was matched by all the other members of the

STAR TREK design team on the Paramount lot—Richard James, production designer for six seasons of STAR TREK: THE NEXT GENERATION, who has now brought STAR TREK: VOYAGER to such thrilling visual life; long-time illustrator and technical consultant Rick Sternbach, who deserves our highest praise for saving and dating *all* his drawings, and who turned up many treasures long buried on the Paramount lot as well. In addition, we thank STAR TREK:DEEP SPACE NINE's prolific illustrator Jim Martin, costume designer Robert Blackman, makeup supervisor Michael Westmore, and Doug Drexler, Randy McIlvain, Tony Sears, and Wendy Drapanas all contributed to our understanding of the dauntingly broad subject matter of this book, as well as to its visual content.

Voyager's Visual Effects Producer Dan Curry provided such a wonderful range of material. And *Deep Space Nine*'s Property Manager Joe Longo patiently opened the vault to give us full access to his carefully preserved store of props.

At Viacom Consumer Products, Paula Block was invaluable not only in helping us sort through almost thirty years of photography, but also in easing our way through the intricacies of wandering the Paramount lot daily, for much longer than any of us anticipated. Harry Lang, keeper of the keys to Paramount's photography library, earns high praise for his dedication and patience, and for his impressive ability to track down misfiled images.

Most importantly, of all who helped us at Paramount, we are once again grateful for the guidance, encouragement, insights, and friendship of Mike and Denise Okuda. Their impressive STAR TREK reference books—the *STAR TREK Encyclopedia*, written with Debbie Mirek, and the *STAR TREK Chronology*—were invaluable to the identification and organization of much of the material in this collection.

And finally at Paramount, the person most responsible for making sure we weren't swallowed up in the deluge of material we accumulated is Herman Zimmerman's assistant, Penny Juday. Without her in-depth knowledge and enthusiasm for STAR TREK, her organizational skills, and her ability to know just whom to call and when to call them, we would most probably still be sorting through dust-covered file boxes while our editor pounded on the door.

Off the lot, the people who came to our aid were no less responsive and informative. As he has so ably helped Pocket Books in the past, David McDonnell of *Starlog* magazine contributed enormously to the content of this collection. Fred Clark at Cinefantastique, and Margaret Clark at DC Comics also provided their invaluable assistance. Stephen Whitfield, familiar to hundreds of thousands of readers who have savored his magnificent book, *The Making of STAR TREK* (Del Rey), graciously gave us access to the material he had collected from STAR TREK's beginning.

We are also indebted to Jim and Anita Dwyer, Andrea Weaver, and all those others who worked on STAR TREK productions in the past, who so kindly took the time to reminisce for us, and dig through their own file boxes. Special acknowledgment must also go to Greg Jein, whose detailed miniatures and props have delighted STAR TREK viewers for years, and who steadfastly gave us *total* access to his extensive collection of props from *The Original Series,* as well as art from *The Animated Series,* and fascinating, behind-the-scenes photos from the entire history of STAR TREK.

Gratitude to Desilu Executive Herbert F. Solow and *Original Series* producer Robert Justman for their incalculable contribution to STAR TREK's earliest formative years and for their invaluable introductions to key personnel from that time.

Noted aviation artist Matt Jefferies, who firmly established the Starfleet School of Design with his original designs of the *U.S.S. Enterprise* and her bridge, was one of the brightest lights we encountered in our research. Where so much of television design is temporary and quickly dated, Matt's work has remained fresh and intriguing and still serves as daily inspiration to the new generation of STAR TREK designers. Incredibly, many of the drawings which Matt gave us have never been published, and have become a highlight of this book.

Andrew Probert, one of the most important of STAR TREK's second-generation of designers, who took STAR TREK to new visual heights in both *The Motion Picture* and *The Next Generation,* thrilled us, and, we're certain, our readers, by making available to us many seminal illustrations that also have never before been published.

Industrial Light & Magic, which has been such an important contributor to the look of the STAR TREK universe for almost fifteen years, also dug through their files to come up with the seldom-seen images contributed to this collection. We are indebted to Bill George—designer of the *Excelsior*—and Ellen Pasternak of ILM for their contributions despite their own tight schedules.

We are especially grateful for the

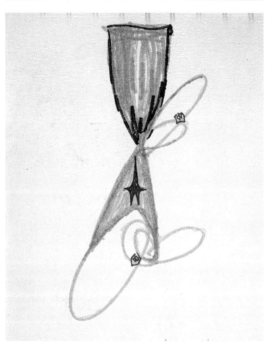

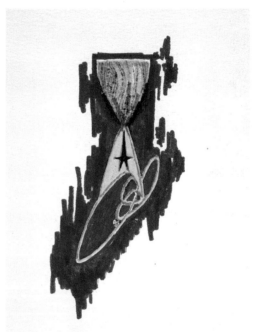

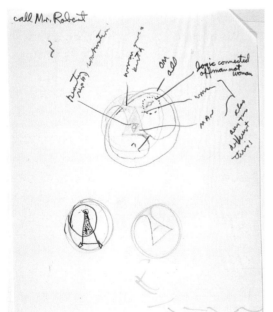

Though committed to the idealism of the twenty-third century, Gene Roddenberry was not blind to the financial realities of the twentieth. Realizing the demand among viewers for merchandise from the STAR TREK universe, Roddenberry worked with William Ware Theiss to create a symbol of Vulcan philosophy, which could also be sold to fans. These sketches by Theiss show the development of two possible STAR TREK medallions which culminated in the IDIC—an acronym for Infinite Diversity in Infinite Combinations. The IDIC was first worn by Spock in the episode "Is There in Truth No Beauty?" and has since been seen as a recurring Vulcan symbol in current STAR TREK productions.

An early version of the *Enterprise*-D painted by Andrew Probert

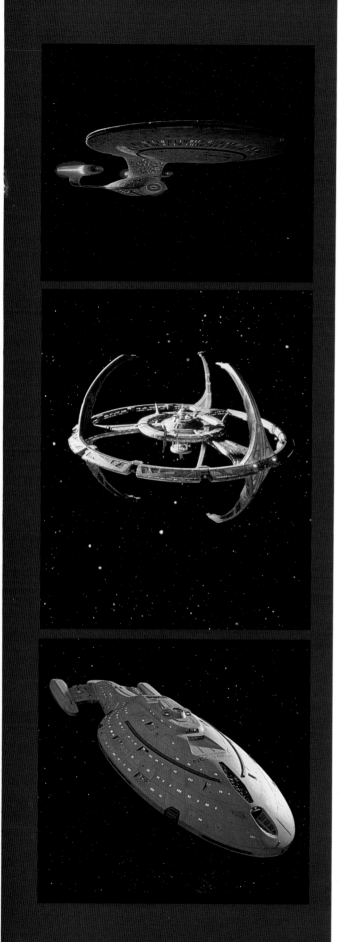

The Art of
STAR TREK®

by Judith & Garfield Reeves-Stevens

INTRODUCTION BY

Herman Zimmerman

POCKET BOOKS
New York   London   Toronto   Sydney   Tokyo   Singapore

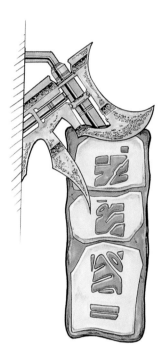

BANNERS

POCKET BOOKS, a division of Simon & Schuster Inc.
1230 Avenue of the Americas, New York, NY 10020

This book is published by Pocket Books, a division of Simon & Schuster Inc.,
under exclusive license from Paramount Pictures.

ISBN: 0-671-89804-3

Book Design by Richard Oriolo
Book Production by Lynda Castillo

First Pocket Books hardcover printing November 1995

10   9   8   7   6   5   4   3   2   1

Printed in the U.S.A.

For Misha, Natasha, Paullina,

and especially Kevin,

who is in every page of this book.

May your future be even brighter than

the one Mr. Roddenberry imagined.

kindness shown us by collector Bob Burns, who provided many of the Mike Minor pieces included in this collection. Mike's legacy to STAR TREK continues to this day, and we are all fortunate that Bob has so diligently kept his spirit and his artwork alive to delight and inspire a new generation of admirers.

The auction houses of Butterfield & Butterfield and of Christie's East were also invaluable by providing transparencies of many of the STAR TREK items they have sold in the past.

On the technical side, once again our photographer, Robbie Robinson, accompanied us on our travels, impressively and inventively capturing many of images taken especially for this collection. And Rick Thomas of Patrick J. Donahue Photography/The Photo Lab was instrumental in the rapid turn-around of Robbie's work, and in producing high-quality copy photography of many of the items loaned to us.

Many others gave freely to us of their time and knowledge throughout this project. Some wish to remain anonymous. Some appear on the credit lines throughout these pages. To any others we've inadvertently neglected to mention as we should, we apologize for the oversight in advance and promise to redeem ourselves in subsequent editions.

Finally, of all who worked so hard on this book, we must give our deepest thanks to the team at Pocket Books—Irene Yuss, Joann Foster, Michael Schwindeller, Tyya Turner, John Ordover, John Perrella, Carol Greenburg and Daniel Truman, as well as Pocket Books Managing Editors Donna Ruvituso and Donna O'Neill, and book designer Richard Oriolo—true professionals who pulled together to smooth our passage through such a complex project. And though it is an oft-quoted sentiment, in this case it has never been more true, than to give our final thanks to our editor, Kevin Ryan, without whom this book would not exist.

Kevin's dedication to seeing this collection in print, his unstinting detective work in tracking down so many collectors and obtaining so much of the never-before-published works in this book, and his many indulgences to two wayward writers goes beyond mere appreciation.

Our thanks to all. We're looking forward to the next round.

J&G REEVES-STEVENS

Production Designer Herman Zimmerman in Stellar Cartography and the impressive new *U.S.S Enterprise* set he designed with his production team for the seventh motion picture, STAR TREK GENERATIONS.

INTRODUCTION

On the evening of September 8, 1966, I, along with ten or twelve million others, tuned in to NBC to catch the premiere episode of a new television series called STAR TREK.

That first evening when William Shatner's voice intoned, "Space, the final frontier...these are the voyages of the *Starship Enterprise...,*" a great many of us were, to say the least, enthralled. From its inception, STAR TREK captured our imaginations and gave us two things: exciting adventures in space, and a close look at a dazzling hi-tech future world. In sharp contrast to the predictions of doom and gloom and the realities of the cold war we found in the daily news, we were taken each week to the farthest reaches of the galaxy and given a chance to explore the stars. That particular fall evening, STAR TREK and its hopeful view of the future beamed into our lives for the first time. It has in the years since consistently entertained us and even today continues to breathe life into our dreams of things to come.

I was, in 1966, an almost totally inexperienced assistant art director, coincidently working for that same NBC network, learning my craft and designing sets for the first year of a new soap opera called *Days of Our Lives.* In the late 1960s, no one at NBC or at Paramount Pictures could have, guessed at STAR TREK's enduring popularity or its eventual status as an icon of pop culture. From that first televised STAR TREK episode, "The Man Trap," I was hooked. Thereafter, for as long as it was on the air, I raced home to see the next

installment of what was for me the best show on television. Captain Kirk and the crew of the *Enterprise,* presumably operating some three hundred years in the future, took me and thousands of other fans with them, voyaging each week in the awesomeness of space to distant planets, to "seek out new life and new civilizations."

The creation of strange new worlds and alien life-forms became a hallmark of STAR TREK. And as each new planet and each new alien civilization was invented, our imaginations were exercised fully. We were awestruck by those real-seeming visions of the future. Those early images of the *Starship Enterprise* traveling in deep space and the fascinating alien cultures its crew encountered along the way were made visible to the motion picture camera through the efforts of a unique and talented team of artists. In the pages of this book, you will be introduced to some of them— talented men and women, intimately involved in creating the future, and also those who have followed in their footsteps, an elite group who have guided STAR TREK through all its more recent incarnations. We are fortunate to have located important samplings of their work, many of which are originals, reproduced here for the first time. (Some of these creations are napkin doodles done at a local Hollywood restaurant that is long since out of business.)

The Art of STAR TREK represents the most comprehensive collection of STAR TREK production notes, plans, drawings, and illustrations assembled to date. I trust that you

will be delighted, as I have been, to review the inspiring body of art that STAR TREK has generated.

But, what, you might ask, is there in these archives to suggest that the often incomplete work of a group of production artists scratching out ideas for a mere science-fiction television show be elevated to the status of art? If we define art as "the activity of creating beautiful things," then STAR TREK's futuristic, alien, often bizarre imagery most assuredly qualifies. For composition, use of color, line and form, inventiveness, unusual use of materials; in fact, using every Art-101 adjective I can remember to describe it, STAR TREK gets an A-plus.

The art in STAR TREK is not just art for art's sake, but art created to visually support a well-told story. And the art told that story with as much freshness and ingenuity as possible, to represent the humanistic philosophy of its creators. This, I believe, has been accomplished consistently and very successfully for upwards of three decades. The moving images created for the screen do service to our dreams and have proved to be as indelible, in their own way, as the paintings of the great masters.

The amazing thing is that there has been such a through-line of artistic continuity from show to show and from series to series. What has emerged is a STAR TREK style attributable, not to a single mind, but to the collective intelligence and vision of many individuals; people who for the most part have not, as might be assumed, worked together

A John Eaves' concept drawing of Stellar Cartography in operation

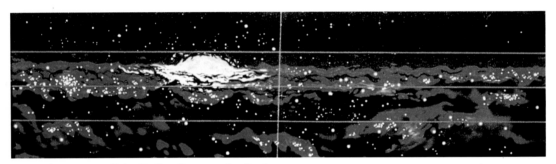

An early concept of the Stellar Cartography display

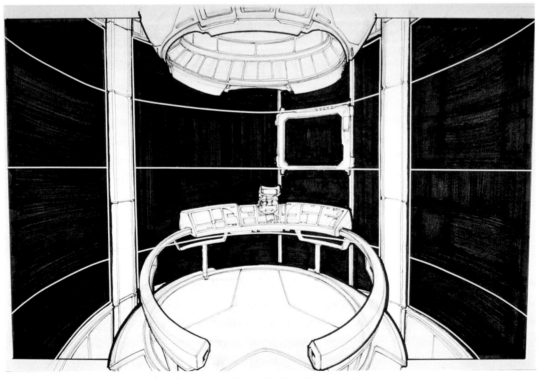

A John Eaves' concept drawing of the magnificent Stellar Cartography set

on a year-in-year-out basis.

But, let's for a moment examine the environment in which the STAR TREK artist must do his or her work. In episodic television, breathing life into the writer's ideas (and delivering on time) requires imagination and the clever use of the things at hand on a daily basis. The filmed-television production team manages to manufacture a quality product at a pace that, more than likely, would not be attempted in any other industry.

A single one-hour episode of a STAR TREK television show represents a staggering amount of labor done by upwards of sixty people who work twelve-to sixteen-hour days on what always seems to be an impossible-to-accomplish schedule. A new episode is begun every seven working days. And while the problems and solutions for today's episode are being dealt with, tomorrow's are hard on its heels. The writer's ideas have to be conceptualized in sketches and plans, the plans approved and budgeted, and the work authorized. Then the sets and costumes and makeup are fabricated and assembled on a sound stage, dressed and lit, and finally, the actors and the director take charge and the drama comes to life in the eye of the camera. Then, under another marathon set of deadlines, the show must be edited; the visual effects, sound effects, musical score, and titles added. All that, amazingly enough, is usually accomplished in three to four weeks.

The fact that STAR TREK has consistently been a visually exciting show, despite the crash-dive conditions I've just described, is due entirely to the talents and dedication of the people who do this stressful work. When you see the finished piece on a television screen, it is as perfect as the production team can make it. There is little margin for error—and there are no excuses.

In what must seem to persons outside the film business to be a panic-driven, insanely intense regimen, the company grinds along, one show after another, until twenty-six episodes are produced. That process takes about ten and a half months. With a five- or six-week hiatus and a two- to three-week lead time on the new first episode, all under the studio's watchful eye, a new season is begun. The producers, writers, actors, and the production unit tighten their belts and do it all over again, always keeping in mind that, throughout each new season, the quality and reputation of the show for fresh ideas and outstanding visual effects has to be maintained, regardless of the short prep time or the constraints of a tight budget.

The creators of the classic STAR TREK series were true pioneers of science fiction television. Those men and women who dreamed up the future on the first series had few precedents to guide them, but nevertheless gave substance to some wonderful and wild dreams of tomorrow. And if sometimes looking backward we are critical of some of the classic STAR TREK episodes, especially in light of the slick *Star Wars* technology available to us now, remember that they were the first. They survived three seasons, producing seventy-nine totally original, history-making hours of television, which can still be held up to close scrutiny today.

Gene Roddenberry told me once that writing a successful television series such as STAR TREK was, for him, comparable to mountain climbing; it's exhilarating while you're at it, and it's wonderful to be able to say that you've done it when you've reached the top. But all the while, deep down, you know that you may not have the courage or the stamina to do it again. Gene, of course, did it again. He was very proud of the fact that with STAR TREK: THE NEXT GENERATION he proved that, contrary to the popular literary adage, you *can* go home again. *The Next Generation* was, for Gene, an even better vehicle for transporting us into his vision of the future. He was very fond of the cast and all the elements of production that built so handily on what he had created earlier. For the record, that series was in production for seven seasons (1987-1994), for a total of 178 hours of quality entertainment.

When a STAR TREK feature film is produced, believe it or not, it goes through many of the same procedures as a television show, if, perhaps, with a bit more money to spend. A feature is usually in pre-production for about sixteen weeks, during which time all the sets, props, and costumes; alien makeup; graphic designs; model making; matte painting; and special effects, both mechanical and optical, have to be invented and approved. Two to four weeks are allowed for the concept and drawing phase and the remaining twelve to fourteen weeks are spent feverishly making things. Concepts, plans, and drawings continue to be worked on after construction has started and the various departments are in crisis mode, trying to make things happen on schedule. Even after the 55 to 65 days of principal photography have begun, the art department is usually still operating in high gear. What drives the production schedule is

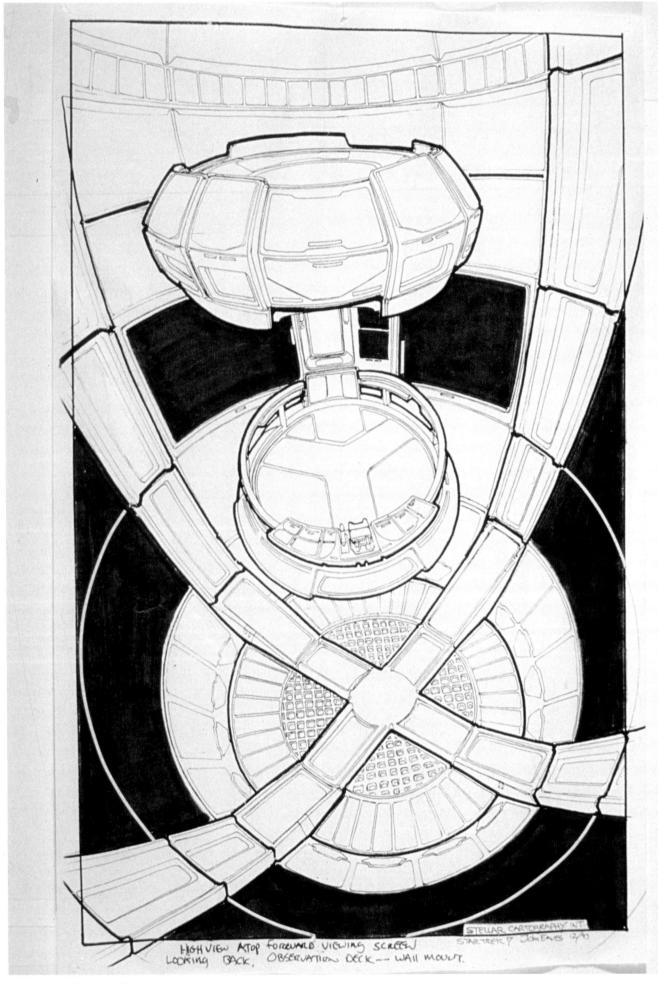

Another angle on Stellar Cartography

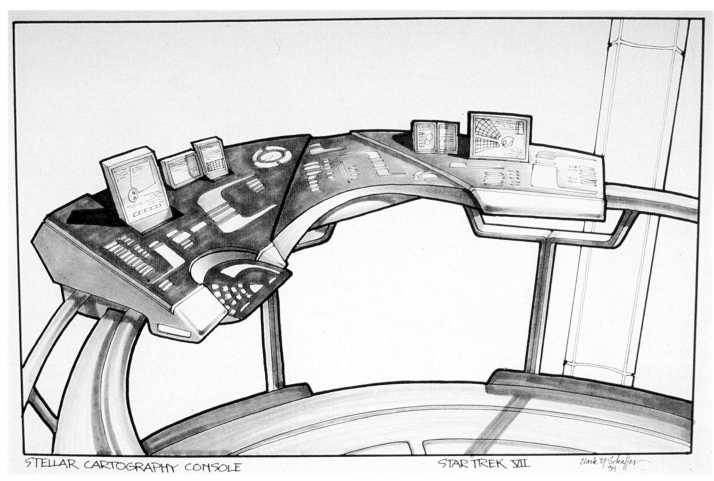

STELLAR CARTOGRAPHY CONSOLE   STAR TREK VII

Getting down to details

the efficient use of the shooting company's time; everything is prioritized backward from the date that the shooting company is due to arrive on each set.

The feature is sometimes in full production when it is discovered that the script is too costly and the whole piece must be reevaluated, reorganized, and in general scaled down. The script changes seem to start at precisely the moment the department head thinks he or she knows what the story is all about and has a workable plan on how it will all get done. Yes, the changes to the script are necessary. Yes, the movie will be the better for having made them, and yes, it is, to say the least, extremely frustrating. Many good design ideas are sacrificed in the process, as some of the sketches in this book will demonstrate. It is a given that the nature of film-

making demands flexibility. The important thing for the design team to remember is not to get stuck on a pet solution to a problem that has managed to go away because of the changes and to remain open to the new inspirations that the new words call to mind. To keep your cool and to remain creative under constantly changing circumstances is an important part of the job.

Designing the environments for a STAR TREK feature means reinventing the STAR TREK universe every couple of years. This is not an easy task. For, regardless of the fact that you are making a $30 million motion picture, the entire design/manufacturing process is mercilessly compressed. Compared to the design and manufacture of something equally difficult in industry, such as a new automobile, feature film designs are given minimal lead time. Work that

would take General Motors three or four years to accomplish must be done in a few months. It has been said that making a feature film is like marching an army of foot soldiers over the Alps. Sometimes, you wish it were that easy.

You have a new director, new writers, a new production manager, and a new script full of production problems to solve. And if you are lucky enough to work on more than one STAR TREK feature, you might think that the next one and the next would get progressively easier to do—a natural assumption, since many of the same key production people may also be involved. However, while I must admit it is never dull, it doesn't seem to get any easier. One always seems to be starting over on the ladder's bottom rung. With regard to all those wonderful things you remember from the last film, you

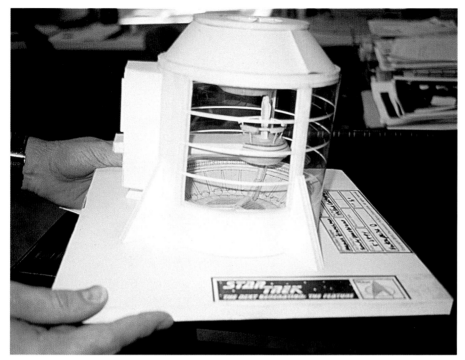

The final check—a foamcore model cut from the set's blueprints

find that nothing much has been saved, and what has been saved is mostly unusable, since it's been stored for several years. More importantly, the demands of the new line of action are always markedly different from those of the previous picture. With a film that is set hundreds of years in the future, everything seen on the screen has to be manufactured. Great attention must be paid to detail; the history of the future, so carefully crafted in all those series episodes and all the other features, must be respected. And the fit and finish of everything must be appropriate to be seen on a motion picture screen seventy feet wide and thirty feet high. It's a lot of responsibility, and it is also a lot of fun.

Production design of a STAR TREK feature is an extremely creative and personally rewarding experience. The team, put together by the producer, sails into the work with great enthusiasm, hoping that the product will be a memorable motion picture and a big box-office

success. In truth, most of us lucky enough to do this work, no matter how much we might grumble while in the throes of production, would be hard-pressed imagining ourselves doing anything else.

Through its many incarnations, STAR TREK has attracted some exceptionally gifted visual cocreators. No more talented and experienced group of cinematic artists exists. From the classic STAR TREK series, the names Matt Jefferies, William Ware Theiss, Janos Prohaska, Fred Phillips, Wah Chang, and Irving Feinberg come to mind.

STAR TREK: THE NEXT GENERATION was visualized by me, Andrew Probert, Rick Sternbach, Michael Okuda, John Dwyer, Richard James, James Mies, Michael Westmore, Rob Legato, Dan Curry, William Ware Theiss, Robert Blackman, and numerous others, most of whom have also worked on STAR TREK: DEEP SPACE NINE and/or STAR TREK VOYAGER.

The STAR TREK features were

envisioned by such well-known production designers as Harold Michaelson, Michael Minor, Joseph R. Jennings, John E. Chilberg II, Jack T. Collis, and another very long list of production personnel.

Through the years it is the imaginations of these artists, the visual keepers of the flame of STAR TREK who have in episode after episode and feature after feature made the writers' visions come to life before the camera. Their names are on the credits at the end of each program, but their specific contributions may not be generally known. Inside the pages of this book, you'll have a chance to meet some of them and to see just how complicated and fascinating the backstage workings of the various STAR TREK production departments can be. STAR TREK owes much of its success to these dedicated individuals—the designers of makeup and costumes, sets and props, graphics and opticals, along with the skilled studio professionals: tailors, sewers, carpenters, painters, electricians, special-effects wizards, matte painters, model makers, and motion control experts; in short, the unsung army of men and women who have been responsible for the art of STAR TREK, people whose work can be seen on every foot of film. We, here, honor their talents and say thanks to them and their peers in the movie industry. The authors of this book and I commend their work to you, that you may celebrate, as we do, their contribution to STAR TREK's amazing vision of the future.

Herman Zimmerman
Stardate: 9504.19

PART ONE

THE FUTURE IN OUR LIVING ROOMS

STAR TREK ON TELEVISION

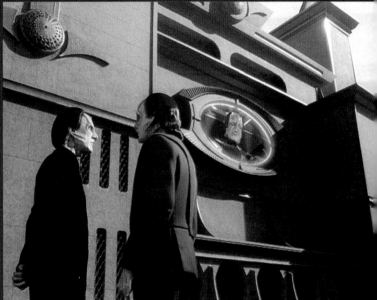

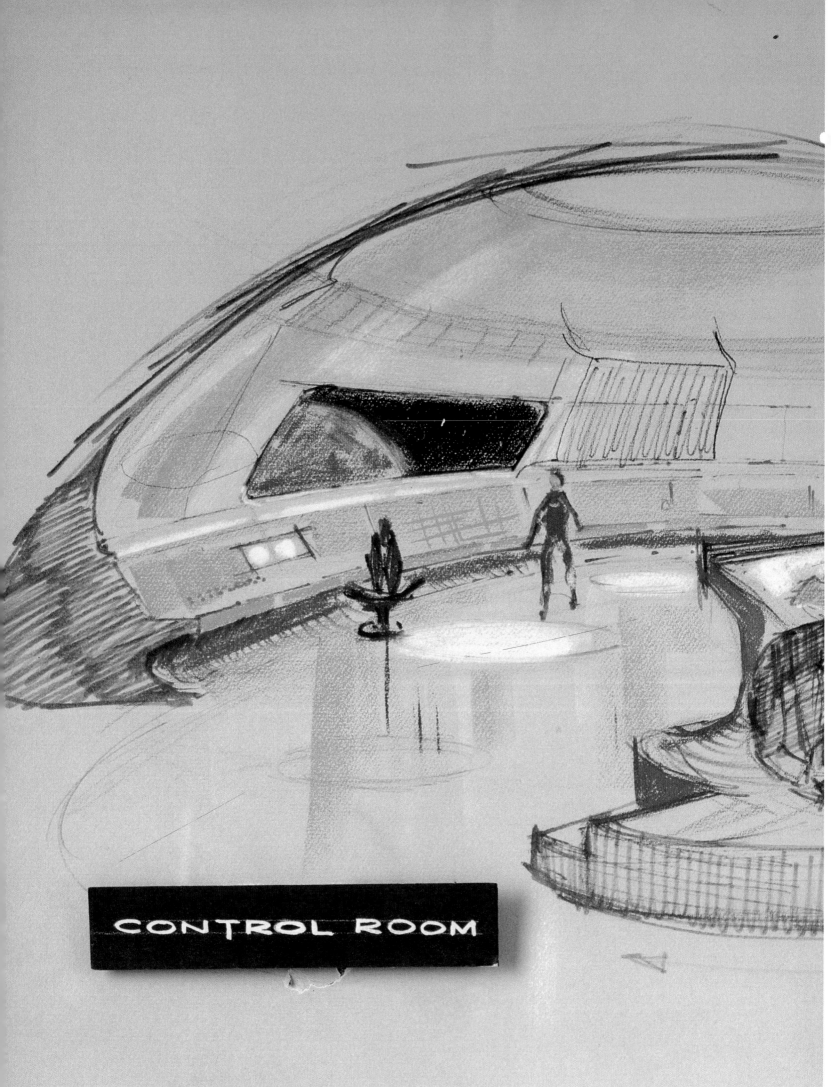

CONTROL ROOM

CHAPTER ONE

A TOTALLY NEW UNIVERSE

"THE CAGE"
AND
"WHERE NO
MAN HAS
GONE
BEFORE"
1964–1965

A classic image from *The Original Series*. Susan Oliver as the Orion dancer, in a trademark William Ware Theiss costume that seems to reveal far more than it actually does

OVERLEAF One of the earliest designs for the *Enterprise*'s bridge, by Pato Guzman

From "The Cage." The first time the words "STAR TREK" appeared on film, though not in the typographic design established for the second pilot

Makeup artist Fred Phillips touching up a STAR TREK legend. Phillips also designed Mr. Spock's makeup in "The Cage."

THE PILOTS

In 1964, everything that would become STAR TREK as it is known today rested in the handful of typewritten pages that had convinced Desilu studios to enter into a three-year television development deal with Gene Roddenberry.

Those pages described the mission of the *U.S.S. Yorktown,* a spaceship with a crew of 203 commanded by Robert T. April. Landing parties would be beamed down to planets by an energy-matter scrambler, stay in contact with the *Yorktown* on their telecommunicators, and protect themselves with "Lasser Beam" weapons.

Though the terminology was still to be refined, the cornerstone of a billion-dollar entertainment franchise was solidly in place. And when NBC committed to ordering a pilot episode in June 1964, it was time to start building that franchise's foundation.

As STAR TREK producer Gene Coon said, "Gene created a totally new universe." Television being a visual medium, the question now was, what was this universe going to look like?

And the moment that question was asked was the beginning of the art of STAR TREK.

Today, STAR TREK senior illustrator and technical consultant Rick Sternbach refers to the "three filters" that stand between any STAR TREK designer and the blank page.

First, and most important from the business side of the filmed entertainment industry, is the filter of *Money.* How much will a design cost to be translated into physical reality—or at least the *illusion* of physical reality—on the screen? Each STAR TREK production must adhere to a budget, and a designer can no more sketch an impossible-to-build prop or set than a writer can call for a scene with thousands of Klingons attacking a starbase.

Second is the filter of *Practicality.* Does a design look as if it can do what it is intended to do? Many artistic judgments come into play here. Does a weapon look threatening enough for the audience to realize it's a weapon? Is an alien machine too alien to understand, or too easy to identify and thus not alien enough?

The third filter is the one to which the audience most strongly reacts—*History.* This is the filter of all that has gone before in STAR TREK. It is the visual continuity, sometimes strong, sometimes almost subliminal, which links the original television *Enterprise* to the *Enterprise*-D and the *Voyager,* and the Klingons of Kirk's era to those of Picard's.

Though hundreds of artists have contributed to the refinement and evolution of this last filter over the past three decades, in the beginning there were two who wrote the first pages of that history: the art director assigned to the first STAR TREK pilot, Pato Guzman, and his assistant, Matt Jefferies.

Guzman was the set designer on *The Lucy Show,* the hit series that funded the Desilu studio, and he enthusiastically took on the demands of designing the interiors of the new series' spaceship, now called the *Enterprise.* (Guzman left Desilu before the pilot began filming in October. Initially, he was replaced by Franz Bachelin, and then by Matt Jefferies, who became art director for the series.)

Matt Jefferies, like Roddenberry, had been a B-17 pilot in World War II, and had earned a reputation for his work on aeronautical designs in

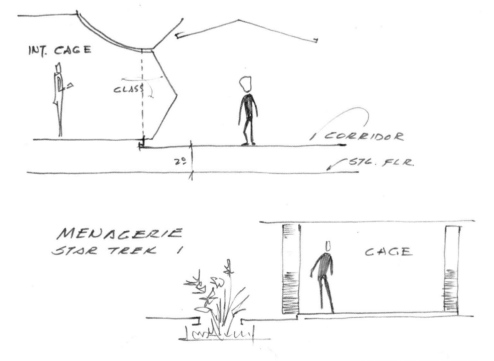

COURTESY OF THE ARTIST

One of Matt Jefferies' first STAR TREK set designs, for the Talosian menagerie. Note the large head on the alien stick figure.

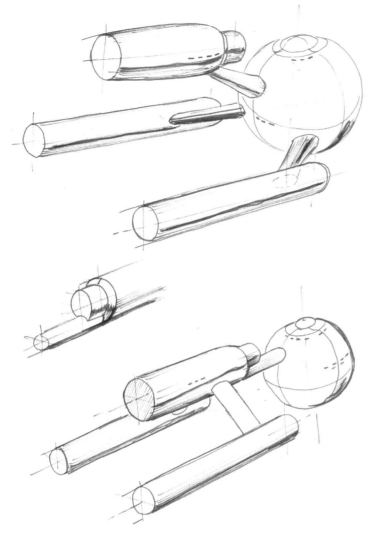

A four-piece body with twin engine nacelles was identified early on as a direction to explore.

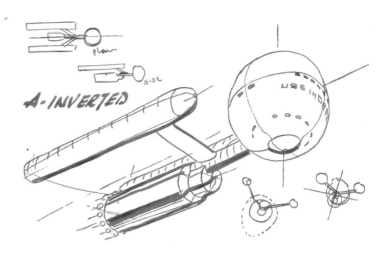

In a further refinement to the four-piece body, here the nacelles are joined to what would come to be called the engineering hull.

Using Matt Jefferies' early designs as his guide, Greg Jein constructed this model of one of the first exploratory vessels launched by the Federation—the *U.S.S. Horizon*, responsible for leaving behind a book about the Chicago mobs on the planet Sigma Iotia II. Though the *Horizon* was never actually depicted in *The Original Series*, this model has been seen as a set decoration on *Deep Space Nine*.

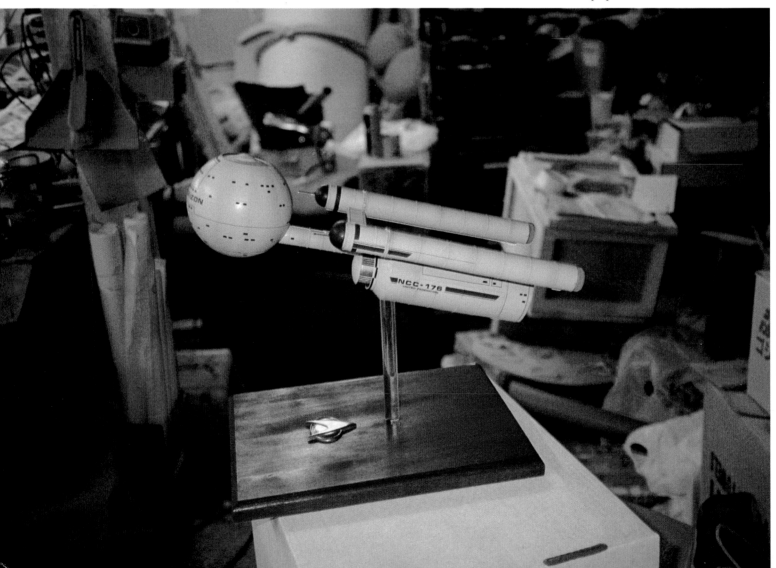

movies such as *Bombers B-52*. As a Desilu employee, he was given the assignment to design the *Enterprise* itself. His only guidelines were Roddenberry's firm list of what he *didn't* want to see, and Jefferies' own background in aviation, which has made him today an internationally recognized aviation artist and historian.

"At first," Jefferies recalls, "Gene had said he didn't want to see any rockets, no jets, no firestreams, or anything like that. So I bought whatever I could find on Buck Rogers and Flash Gordon and pinned it up on the wall and said, 'That we will not do.' At the time, I had been a member of the Aviation Writers' Association for almost ten years, and I had all kinds of mailings from Douglas, and Lockheed, and Boeing, and NASA. So I put all of that stuff on the wall and said, 'We won't do this, either.' So now, at least, I could begin to define some kind of envelope."

The "envelope" to which Jefferies refers describes the boundaries of possible designs for the *Enterprise*. It couldn't look like a classic, and thus dated, science-fiction rocketship. But neither could it resemble anything on NASA's drawing boards, because that would too quickly date the design. Somewhere between the cartoons of the past and the reality of the present, Matt Jefferies had to arrive at a design of the future.

The familiar shape that he eventually devised, after hundreds of drawings and feedback from Roddenberry, the Desilu sales staff, vice president in charge of creative affairs Herb Solow, and a technical advisor from the RAND Corporation, became the inspiration for virtually all other Starfleet vessels created since. Jefferies' "envelope" for starship design had become the first, and strongest, component of the STAR TREK history filter.

Jefferies' practical, engineer's approach to design also helped define another key element of STAR TREK design—the bridge. Pato Guzman had given it its circular shape, central viewscreen, and two-level construction. Jefferies came up with the design of the workstations and control layouts by the simple means of sitting on a chair by a blank wall, holding out his arms in comfortable positions, and having his brother mark the resulting angles on the wall.

All the control-surface and display-screen angles on the bridge were established in this matter-of-fact manner, based on Jefferies' less-than-favorable view of most military vehicle designs.

"If you've spent any time around ships or aircraft, then you know that every time a new piece of equipment comes out, you're going to bump your head on it," Jefferies says. "You've got to duck here and duck there, and if a piece of equipment goes out, then whoever's working with it has got to get out of the way and shut the thing down while they either fix it or replace it. I felt this was kind of stupid, and asked, why don't we change it from the back? Unhook it, pull the thing out, shove a replacement in, and never make the guy have to get up out of his chair."

This no-nonsense approach to modular design was also reflected in the *Enterprise*'s exterior appearance. As Jefferies remembers, "This was probably one of the few areas I ever had arguments about with Gene. I wanted the exterior of that thing just about as plain and smooth as we could get it."

Jefferies' concern was, again, practicality. "To me, the most dangerous possible environment is outside a spaceship. And as Mrs. Murphy says, sometime or another, anything that people make is going to break. So why have equipment outside of the hull that they're going to have to work on? Keep it inside."

Just as Gene Roddenberry developed a network of trusted scientists and science-fiction writers to review his words and keep his vision of future technology at least partially grounded in real science, Matt Jefferies brought an equal element of nuts-and-bolts practicality to the STAR TREK universe which continues to this day.

Though the first pilot, "The Cage," was not accepted by NBC, the network did take the extraordinary step of ordering a second, "Where No Man Has Gone Before." That second pilot, with the introduction of William Shatner as Captain James T. Kirk, was the final foundation stone in STAR TREK's development.

But as far as the art of STAR TREK was concerned, "The Cage" had already set the visual stage for the next thirty years, and beyond.

A STARSHIP TAKES FLIGHT

The evolution of the original *Enterprise* took place over several months and several hundred drawings. Pato Guzman and Matt Jefferies would present a batch of drawings to Gene Roddenberry, who would pick out elements he liked, which would then be used to generate another series of sketches.

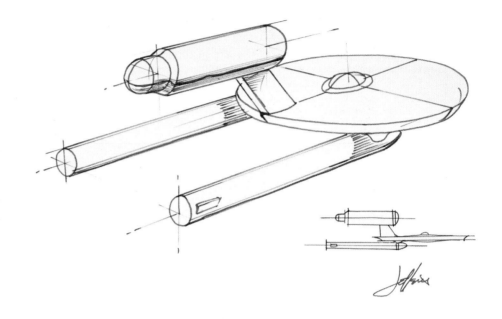

The saucer makes its first appearance, replacing the sphere.

Moving closer. All the parts are present and the orientation has been reversed, with the engineering hull at the bottom. Now it's a question of proportion and connection.

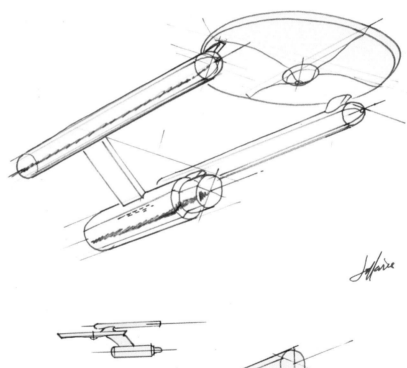

Almost there...

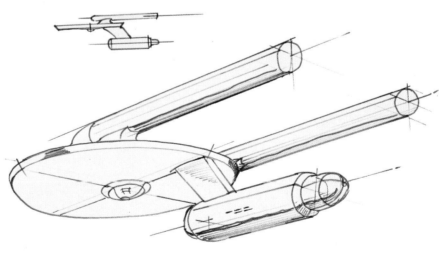

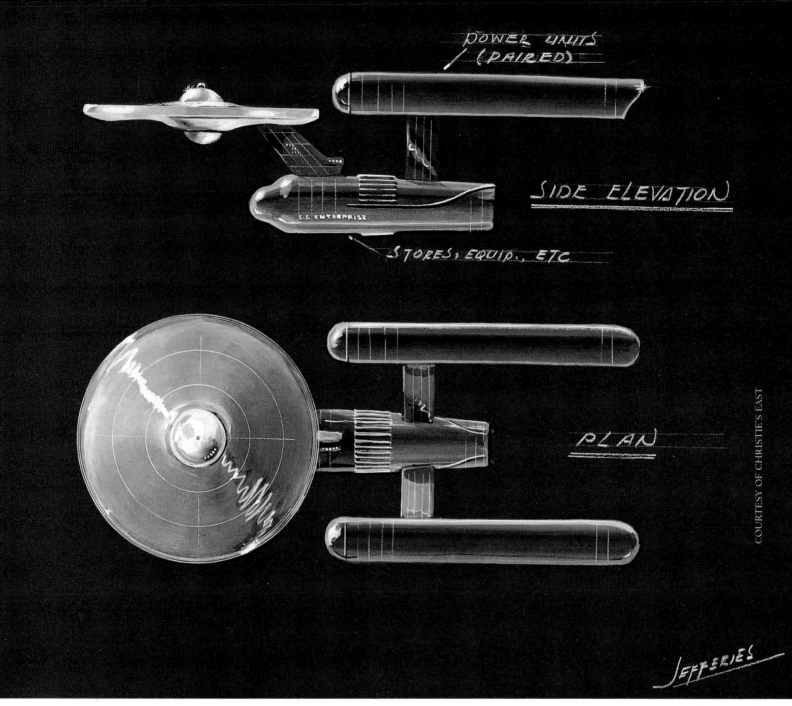

POWER UNITS
(PAIRED)

SIDE ELEVATION

S.S. ENTERPRISE

STORES, EQUIP., ETC

PLAN

JEFFERIES

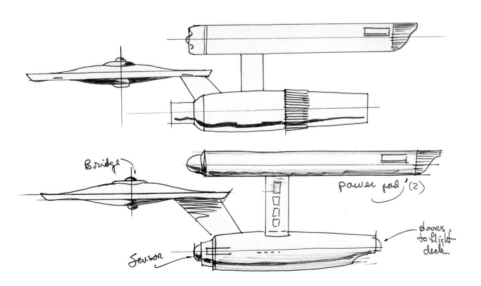

Bridge

power pad (2)

doors
to flight
deck.

Sensor

The first color rendering of the almost final design of the *U.S.S. Enterprise*. The next design stage was the preparation of scale drawings for model builder Don Loos, incorporating the final changes that would turn this into the *Enterprise* recognized by millions.

This is the drawing Matt Jefferies chose to translate into a rough wooden model and present to Roddenberry and Desilu executives on a thread that made it hang upside down. Roddenberry finally felt this approach was on the right track.

LOOKING INSIDE

At a cost of $60,000, the bridge represented the most expensive element of the first pilot. One of its features—the twelve translucent screens ringing the outer walls—threatened even greater expense.

As intended by Pato Guzman and Matt Jefferies, the screens would be constantly flickering with data displays, easily rigged by placing a slide projector behind each screen. However, when the producers discovered that union rules required each of the slide projectors to be operated by an individual projectionist, the screens were replaced with permanent painted panels, except for specific scenes in which the script required a screen to be used.

Other sections of the *Enterprise* were constructed in a much rougher fashion. The conference room was framed by cut-out walls that could be shot from only one angle. A section of corridor, which was later incorporated into the permanent sets, was one of the few pilot sets that could be shot from more than one angle—specifically, two.

The first shot of the *Enterprise* bridge. The monochromatic color scheme would return in STAR TREK: THE MOTION PICTURE. But for the second pilot, it was redecorated with brighter colors in response to the growing popularity of color televisions.

The television set made it into this version of the captain's quarters, but was eliminated from the permanent set designs. Much later, in *The Next Generation* episode "The Neutral Zone," Data reported that television had fallen from popularity by the year 2040, eliminating it from the entire STAR TREK universe.

A section of corridor from "The Cage." Note the resort-wear costumes by William Ware Theiss, illustrating Gene Roddenberry's concept that this was a full community in space, not just a military vessel.

The conference room set from "The Cage." Here the cast sits in unmodified versions of the Burke chair.

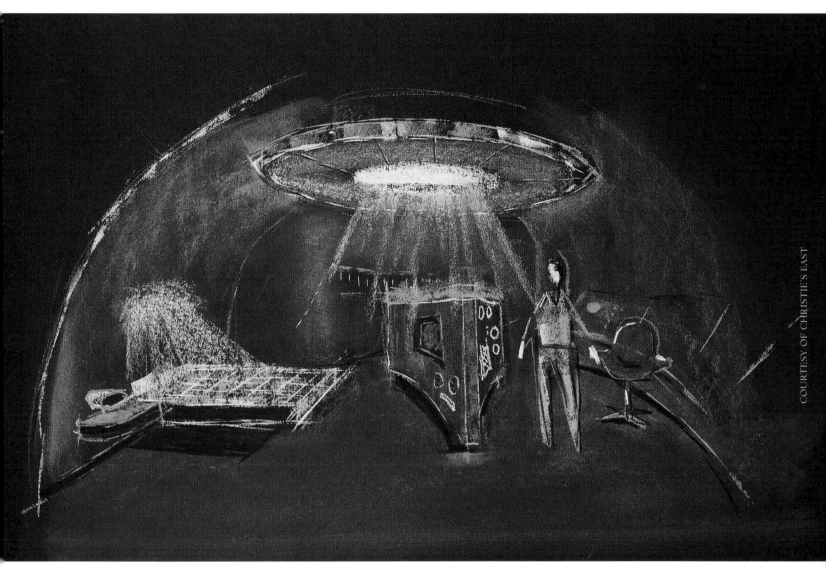

Pato Guzman's sketch of Captain Pike's quarters. Note the television set.

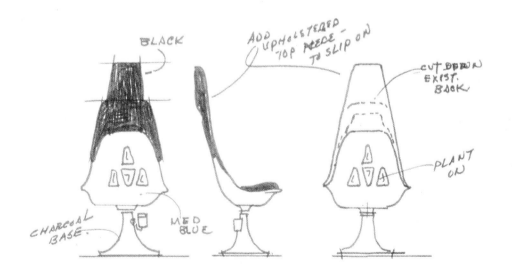

BLACK

ADD UPHOLSTERED TOP PIECE TO SLIP ON

CUT DOWN EXIST. BACK

CHARCOAL BASE.

MED BLUE

PLANT ON

ENTERPRISE CHAIRS
(MODIFIED BURKE)

Matt Jefferies' sketch showing the modifications made to a standard commercial chair to make it a twenty-third-century starship chair. The term "Burke" refers to the chair's model name.

A WAH CHANG GALLERY

One of the unsung heroes of STAR TREK design is the celebrated sculptor Wah Chang. Chang's movie accomplishments range from sculpting the maquette of Pinocchio used by Disney animators in the production of that film to designing and building the spectacular headdress worn by Elizabeth Taylor in *Cleopatra*.

On television, Chang's expertise and inventiveness brought to life many of the monsters and bizarre creatures of *The Outer Limits*, so it was only natural that the producers of STAR TREK turned to him for some of their design needs.

Among Wah Chang's many contributions to STAR TREK are the tricorder, the communicator, the Gorn, the M-113 Creature (aka the Salt Vampire), and the original laser pistols and communicators seen in "The Cage."

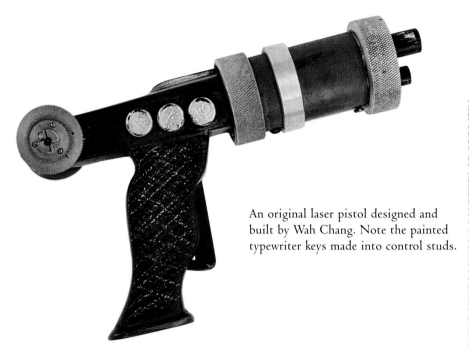

An original laser pistol designed and built by Wah Chang. Note the painted typewriter keys made into control studs.

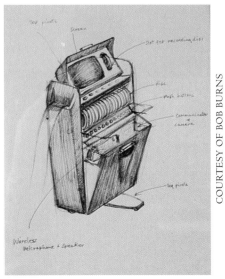

The original tricorder sketch by Wah Chang

Two versions of original tricorders built by Wah Chang's model shop

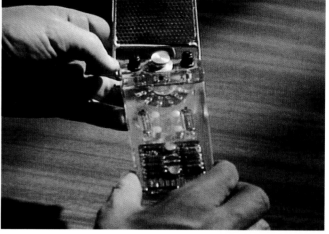

Wah Chang's original communicator design

In the cost-conscious environment of television production, props are typically modified and reused. Wah Chang's original communicator was subsequently reengineered into the device used to control the mindless Mr. Spock in "Spock's Brain."

THE ORIGINAL SERIES

NBC received the second pilot episode in January 1966 and in mid-February placed its order for the series to air in the fall of that year. Two years of effort had paid off. NBC had decided the world was ready for STAR TREK—now the challenge was to make STAR TREK ready for the world.

Technically, in Hollywood there is nothing that cannot be accomplished on film, given enough time and enough money. But in episodic television production, there is never enough of either. It's an on-the-fly environment, driven by an unchangeable broadcast schedule and immutable budget.

Looking back at the first seventy-nine hours of STAR TREK, produced between 1966 and 1969, it's easy to find flaws and be amused by production shortcuts. But it's also easy to find the great strengths of story, setting, and character that transcended the technical limita-

tions of the sixties and fueled STAR TREK's growth as one of the world's most successful entertainment franchises.

Another mitigating factor to apply to the production values of *The Original Series* is that in the sixties, television was a disposable product. Episodes aired once, were rerun in the summer months, and then disappeared. Some series resurfaced in the syndicated market, but generally they were seen by a different audience.

The original STAR TREK episodes some fans today have watched dozens of times were intended to stand up to only one or two viewings. The designers and decorators of any series produced then were well justified in their decisions to reuse props and sets and backgrounds from one episode to the next. Two viewings of an episode were hardly enough for the audience to recognize that the backdrop painting of

Mojave on Earth was suddenly standing in for a city on Planet Q. And who would ever pay close enough attention to an episode to notice that a serving tray on the *Enterprise* one week was inexplicably being used as a wall decoration on a Romulan ship the next, and on a Federation space station bar the week after that?

STAR TREK fans, that's who.

But even as those first episodes were being produced within the limitations of the day, the team that labored on them managed to add precisely the kind of content that actually increased the audience's appreciation of the series with repeat viewings.

William Ware Theiss's arrowhead patches each contained a different symbol indicating to which branch of Starfleet the wearer belonged. Matt Jefferies' small phasers fit perfectly into the larger phasers, and the handles were power

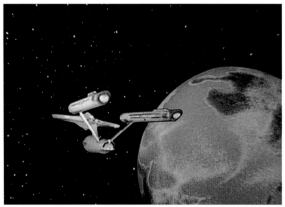

packs of some kind. Romulans were related to Vulcans. The transporter controls were operated the same way each week.

Hour by hour, episode by episode, the telling details mounted, were kept track of, and were reinforced.

With each viewing, it became easier to suspend the knowledge that these were simply actors emoting among plywood sets and papier-mâché boulders, and to accept the illusion that the *Enterprise* existed in a real future made all the more believable by the weight of consistent, functional detail that was presented.

Within this creation of a *detailed,* fictional universe exists one of the most significant reasons for STAR TREK's appeal. Despite the traditions of the day, STAR TREK episodes weren't simply shoot-'em-up diversions intended to pass the time between commercials. Gene Roddenberry *cared* about the future. He thought about it, mulled it over,

challenged himself and others to define the environment in which STAR TREK's adventures took place.

That questioning attitude and desire to know the future attracted others who shared Roddenberry's passion—writers and directors who wanted to *explore* the future instead of just work there for a week or two, and artists and designers who wanted to make that future as real as Gene Roddenberry dared them to imagine.

The universe of STAR TREK created the context for its stories. And in a visual medium such as television, the credibility of that universe and that context were absolutely dependent on the talents of the artists and designers who visualized them both.

The errors made in the production of *The Original Series* are still made today, though not as often. With videotape and computer bulletin boards, woe betide the production crew of STAR TREK:

DEEP SPACE NINE or STAR TREK VOYAGER if they reuse a matte painting from STAR TREK: THE NEXT GENERATION. The fans will know within seconds. And no doubt viewers in the year 2025 will look back at the production limitations of television in the nineties with the same affection and amusement viewers today reserve for television of the sixties.

But the lessons of *The Original Series* have also survived three decades and still guide STAR TREK productions today.

Meaningful consistency—whenever possible.

Functional detail—enough to satisfy the audience through a dozen viewings.

And most important of all— Gene Roddenberry's lasting legacy to his creation—unqualified passion.

For all that has changed in thirty years of STAR TREK, the best things remain the same.

THE SHUTTLE AND OTHER SPACECRAFT

Today, a key model for a STAR TREK spaceship can cost more than $100,000 dollars to build. In the sixties, relative costs carried the same sticker shock, resulting in such cost-cutting measures as Romulans using Klingon ships, and alien vessels that would stay at the limits of the sensors, appearing as no more than sparkles of light.

But when the budget allowed, Matt Jefferies continued to bring his unique vision of future technology to the STAR TREK universe.

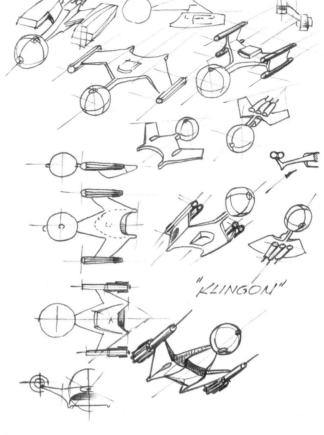

"KLINGON"

Matt Jefferies's development sketches for the Klingon battle cruiser

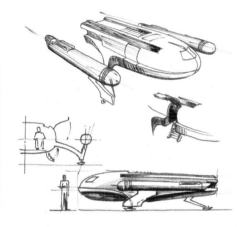

SHUTTLECRAFT

Matt Jefferies had hoped for a more aerodynamically sound version of shuttlecraft in *The Original Series,* but the costs of building a life-size mock-up with a curved hull were prohibitive.

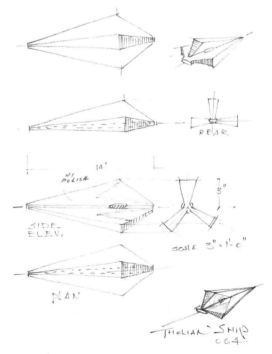

The final, flat-hulled shuttle that was acceptable to the production because the model company, AMT, paid for its construction in return for the rights to make a model kit from it. The AMT kit of the *Enterprise* sold more than one million units.

Matt Jefferies's design for a simple-to-construct (i.e. inexpensive) Tholian vessel

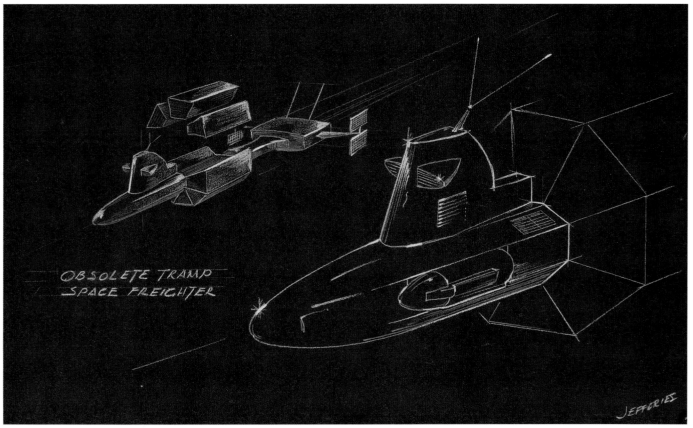

ART BY MATT JEFFERIES COURTESY OF CHRISTIE'S EAST

OBSOLETE TRAMP
SPACE FREIGHTER

JEFFERIES

A final rendering of Khan's sleeper ship, showing the arrangement of the modular cargo containers.

COURTESY OF THE ARTIST

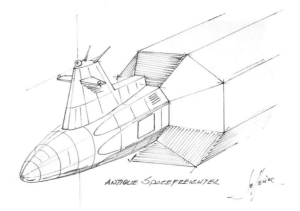

ANTIQUE SPACEFREIGHTER

In designing an antique space freighter of the 1990s, Matt Jefferies was pleased with his notion of modular shipping crates that could be automatically loaded and unloaded without requiring humans to venture into space.

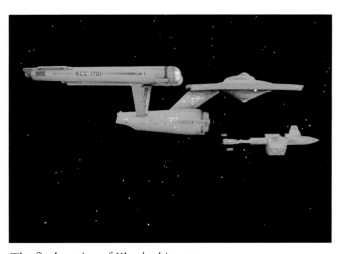

The final version of Khan's ship

COURTESY OF THE ARTIST

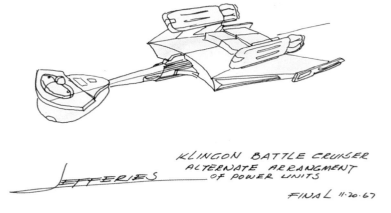

KLINGON BATTLE CRUISER
ALTERNATE ARRANGMENT
OF POWER UNITS

FINAL 11-20-67

JEFFERIES

An early Klingon battle cruiser concept by Matt Jefferies

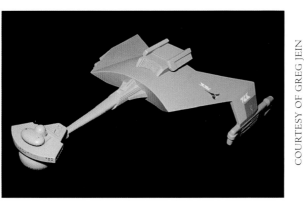

COURTESY OF GREG JEIN

A replica of *The Original Series* Klingon ship

SET DESIGN

All the *Enterprise* bulkheads were the same color…

A mong other limitations, the production budgets on *The Original Series* were so limited that set walls could not be repainted from episode to episode to represent different locations. Thus the series became known for its distinctive use of colored lights to alter the appearance of background walls.

…but were changed by different lighting designs.

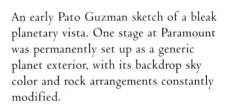

An early Pato Guzman sketch of a bleak planetary vista. One stage at Paramount was permanently set up as a generic planet exterior, with its backdrop sky color and rock arrangements constantly modified.

One of Matt Jefferies's favorite designs—Trelane's manor

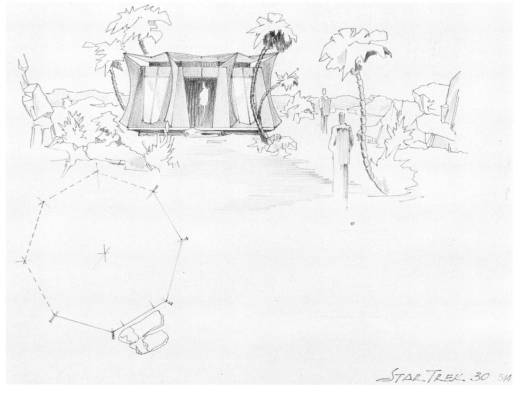

Matt Jefferies's design for the home of Zefram Cochrane

When *The Original Series* went into production, the *Enterprise* acquired a number of permanent sets, including the Briefing Room, which also was used as dozens of other large rooms, from the ship's chapel to the ship's theater.

THE ILLUSION OF REALITY

Another cost-cutting practice of television production is the use of matte paintings and painted backdrops to create large sets and vistas that could not be built as actual sets. In contemporary STAR TREK productions, mattes are sophisticated visual-effects blends of computer-generated imagery and live-action film. But in the days of *The Original Series,* they were literal paintings, matted into film.

In the background of this set from "The Cage" is *The Original Series'* first and only glimpse of twenty third–century Earth—Mojave. Which became...

...a city on Planet Q in "The Conscience of the King."

The mining operation on Janus VI became...

...the underground complex on Triskelion

From the second pilot, this lithium cracking station on Delta Vega was altered to become...

...the Tantalus Penal Colony in "Dagger of Mind."

OVERLEAF The original painting that was used as an establishing shot on Eminar VII in "A Taste of Armageddon," and on Scalos in "Wink of an Eye." Followed by two views of Starbase II from "Court Martial" and "The Menagerie, Parts I and II"

Eminiar VII. Only the wall beside the actors had to be constructed.

A WILLIAM WARE THEISS GALLERY, 1

The key design element William Ware Theiss brought to his memorable 1960s costumes for STAR TREK was his own "Theiss Titillation Theory," in which the degree to which a costume is considered sexy is directly proportional to how likely it seems to fall off.

Many of Theiss's more accident-prone designs began as what he called "doodles" on whatever piece of paper was most readily available, from script pages to restaurant napkins.

A Romulan uniform

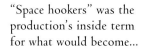

"Space hookers" was the production's inside term for what would become...

...."Mudd's Women."

The starting point for the costume worn by...

...Leslie Parrish as Lieutenant Palamas in "Who Mourns for Adonais?"

The first Cyrano Jones concept...

...from the popular episode "The Trouble with Tribbles." Stanley Adams played the interstellar trader who brought tribbles to the *Enterprise*.

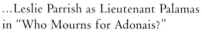

William Ware Theiss's costumes are collector's items today.

Mark Lenard as the first Romulan. John Warburton as his advisor

A WILLIAM WARE THEISS GALLERY, 2

Kara, the Arelian dancer, not to be confused with Kara of Sigma Draconis VI

Kara

The Empath

the Empath

Nona, the *kahn-ut-tu* woman of the hill people on Tyree's planet

Nona

Gav, the first Tellarite

gav

Angelique Pettyjohn as Shahna, the drill Thrall—an example of the Theiss Theory of Titillation.

What might be an early sketch of Shahna, the drill Thrall

Theiss began this sketch during a production meeting.

Two of Theiss's creations for *The Original Series*

GETTING INTO CHARACTER

These photographs record the hour-and-fifteen-minute-long process that transformed Leonard Nimoy into Mr. Spock during STAR TREK's second season. Makeup artist Fred B. Phillips, seen here, had originally worked on the first pilot, "The Cage," while fellow Desilu makeup artist, Robert Dawn, handled makeup for "Where No Man Has Gone Before." When Desilu found itself producing two prime time series simultaneously, both of which relied on extensive makeup effects, Robert Dawn moved to *Mission Impossible* and Fred Phillips returned to STAR TREK, where he remained throughout its three-year run.

The first stage in the process was the application of the single-use foam-rubber ear tips. These were glued to Nimoy's ears with spirit gum. A two-sided tape furnished a strip of adhesive on the back of each ear. This allowed Nimoy's ears to be pressed closely to the sides of his head and remain there.

The next stage was the creation of Spock's characteristic Vulcan eyebrows. This required Phillips to shave the outside halves of Nimoy's actual eyebrows during each makeup session. Phillips filled in the shape of the new eyebrows with an eyebrow pencil, then painted over those lines with spirit gum. The spirit gum was used to attach short lengths of yak belly hair, which Phillips cut from long strands, blending the small tufts into what remained of Nimoy's own eyebrows.

The final stage of the process involved applying base makeup and adding shading to ensure that shadow contours would be seen even under the bright lights of the shooting stage.

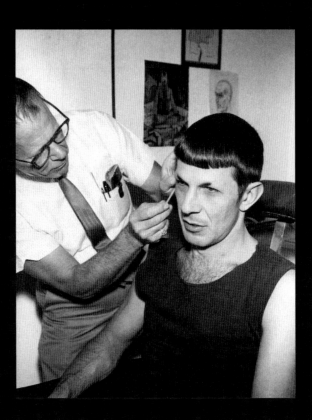

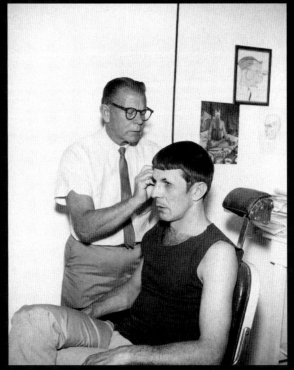

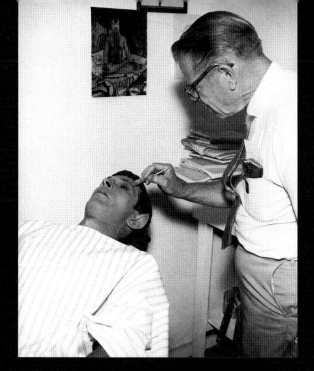

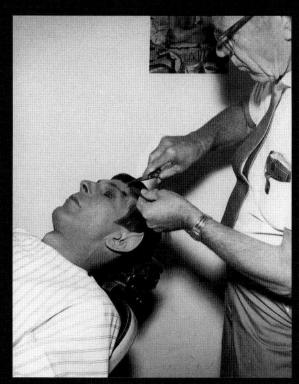

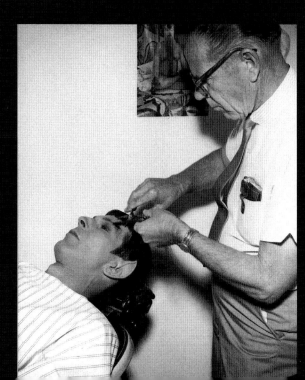

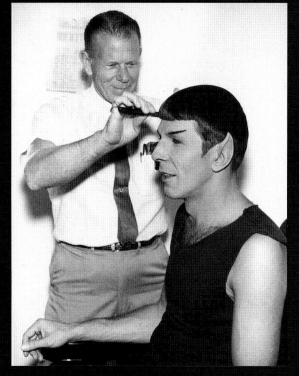

ALIEN LIFE

MGM, the first studio to which Gene Roddenberry had pitched STAR TREK, had rejected the idea in part because of the expense of producing a series with futuristic miniatures, costumes, props, sets, and aliens. However, Roddenberry had already thought of ways to keep costs down, and his practical approach still holds true in contemporary STAR TREK productions.

From Roddenberry's first description of his series:

ALIEN LIFE. Normal production casting of much of this alien life is made practical by the SIMILAR WORLDS CONCEPT. To give continual variety, use will, of course, be made of wigs, skin coloration, changes in noses, hands, ears, and even the occasional addition of tails and such.

As exciting as physical differences, and often even more so, will be the universe's incredible differences in social organizations, customs, habit, nourishment, religion, sex, politics, morals, intellect, locomotion, family life, emotions, etc.

The Gorn, designed by Wah Chang

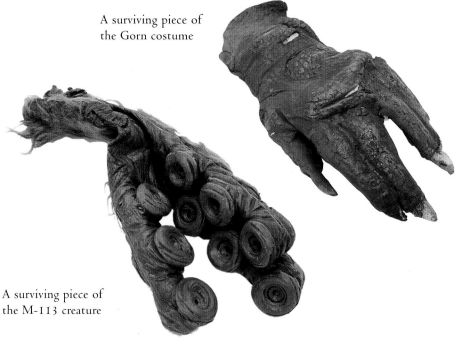

A surviving piece of the Gorn costume

A surviving piece of the M-113 creature

PHOTOGRAPHY BY ROBBIE ROBINSON
COURTESY OF GREG JEIN

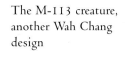

The M-113 creature, another Wah Chang design

An Excalbian, constructed by Wah Chang

John Colicos as Commander Kor—STAR TREK's first Klingon

Michael Strong as Dr. Korby. Humanoid robots were another way of inexpensively, though effectively, presenting science-fiction concepts.

William Shatner as Kirk as a Romulan, designed by Fred Phillips. Romulans were originally intended to be more of an ongoing threat to the crew of the *Enterprise,* but the makeup requirements proved too expensive. Klingons were cheaper.

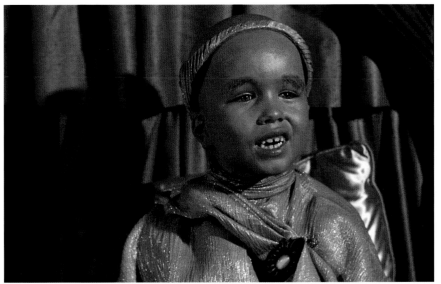

Clint Howard as Balok, an unexpected, effective, *and* inexpensive alien

The science fiction of the sixties has become the Motorola flip-phone of today.

PROPS, PART 1

The props of *The Original Series* were never intended to withstand the scrutiny of the printed page, and only a few were finished with the details that would let them endure a fleeting close-up during an episode. But they are among the first made-for-television science-fiction designs that broke away from the Flash Gordon school of decoration for decoration's sake, presenting a utilitarian and relatively believable glimpse of the future.

Matt Jefferies's design sketch for a Scalosian weapon...

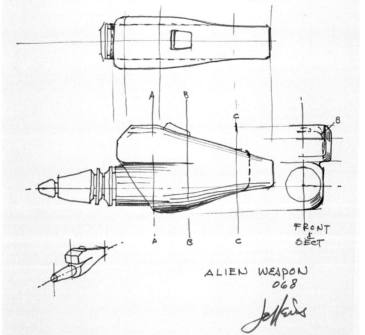

...and the finished prop.

Four versions of phasers, designed by Matt Jefferies and his brother and built by Wah Chang. The white-handled phaser is from the first season. Subsequent models were given darker handles because of the difficulty of photographing a white prop.

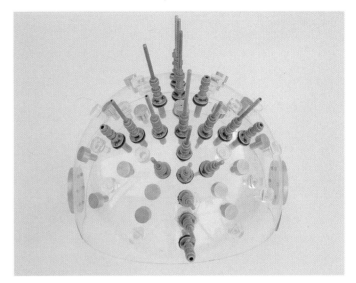

The Teacher's Helmet from "Spock's Brain"

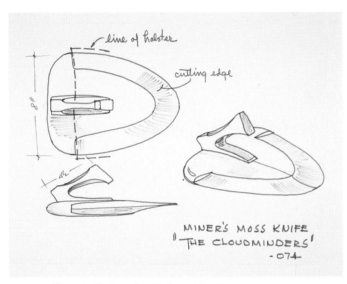

Matt Jefferies's design sketch for a Troglyte weapon...

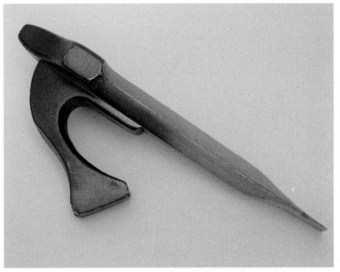

...and the finished prop.

COURTESY OF GREG JEIN
ARTWORK COURTESY OF THE ARTIST
PROP PHOTOGRAPHY BY ROBBIE ROBINSON

The secrets of the tribbles revealed. This large version was powered by a battery-powered toy dog. Other tribbles were operated by squeeze balls and balloons.

PHOTOGRAPHY BY ROBBIE ROBINSON
COURTESY OF GREG JEIN

PROPS, PART 2

This weapon comes with a quick-and-dirty holster made from aluminum foil stiffened by a coating of resin.

The decoration on the first Klingon belt was simply a piece of painted air-bubble packaging material.

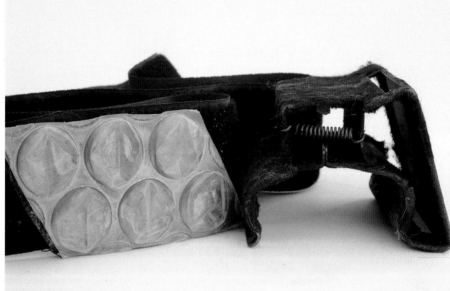

The suede equipment belts made for the first pilot episode were eventually replaced when Velcro strips were sewn directly to the actors' uniforms.

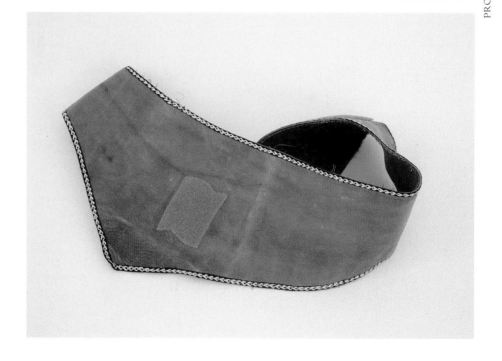

Sometimes the pressure of the production caught up with the designers, resulting in Captain Kirk's using an antique suitcase...

The design team responsible for contemporary STAR TREK productions has taken delight in re-creating this bottle of Saurian brandy for appearances in *Deep Space Nine* and *The Next Generation*.

...Klingons using packing crates made from spray-painted sheets of corrugated cardboard...

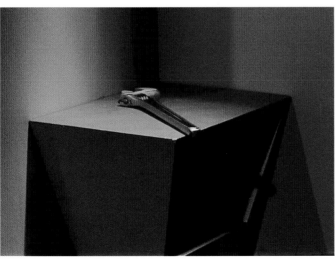

...and the sight of less-than-high-tech tools lying around Engineering.

Some of Dr. McCoy's most sophisticated medical implements were little more than pieces of machined metal and good sound effects.

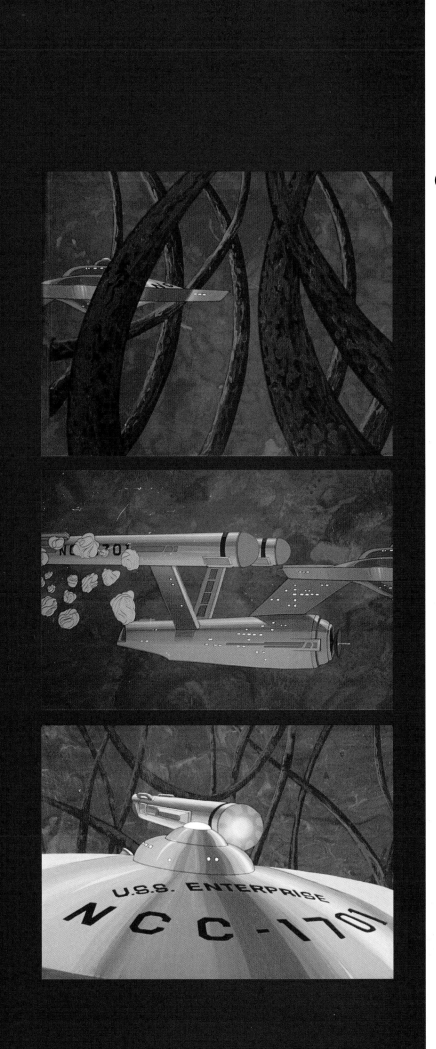

CHAPTER THREE

TAKE TWO

STAR TREK:
THE ANIMATED SERIES
1974

STAR TREK: THE ANIMATED SERIES

A year after *The Original Series* was canceled, Paramount began syndicating the seventy-nine episodes to run in the afternoon and early evening across the United States. As Spock's logic might have suggested, the show that had been killed by a late-night time slot was miraculously reborn by becoming more accessible, finding an audience that had not shown up in the infamous Nielsen rating system of the late sixties.

As attendance at STAR TREK conventions grew and the defunct show's popularity continued to increase, it was inevitable that Gene Roddenberry and the executives at Paramount and at the television networks would start to consider ways of reviving the series. And they did. But as would happen many times in the future, the logistics of the television business disrupted the process.

In 1972, three years after the cancellation, NBC was once again willing to consider a STAR TREK series and was prepared to order a new pilot episode from the studio. However, according to Paramount's calculations it would require $750,000 to rebuild the sets and re-create the costumes and props—an amount the studio wasn't willing to commit unless NBC ordered multiple episodes. The next time Paramount faced this impasse with a network would be in 1986, and it would lead to the studio's decision to make STAR TREK: THE NEXT GENERATION as a direct-to-syndication series on its own. But in 1972, that was not a safe option for such an

Two initial concepts for the animated STAR TREK series called for the *Enterprise* crew either to appear in adventures from their childhood or to be teamed up with young counterparts. These concepts are said to have lasted all of 30 minutes before the decision was made to present the familiar crew as they appeared in *The Original Series*.

expensive show, and STAR TREK was once again placed on hold.

With production expenses being a perpetual roadblock to STAR TREK's revival, many producers came up with the idea of creating a less-expensive, animated version of the show. But of all the animation producers who approached Roddenberry, it was Lou Scheimer and Norm Prescott of Filmation who finally were able to convince him to take this next step.

Despite the above illustrations depicting younger versions of the *Enterprise* crew, Roddenberry said he decided to go with Filmation because the company was the first to say it would keep an animated production true to *The Original Series*, without the addition of such Saturday-morning staples as smart-aleck children and cute animals. But though everyone's intentions were

good, the animated series eventually did fall well short of the mark, and is the weakest of STAR TREK's many incarnations when viewed today.

On the writing side, Roddenberry enlisted Dorothy Fontana as associate producer and story editor. She in turn approached many of the writers who had contributed to *The Original Series*, including David Gerrold, Margaret Arman, Samuel A. Peeples, and Stephen Kandel (who had written the two *Original Series* episodes featuring Harry Mudd, and brought him back for an animated episode as well). Unfortunately, despite everyone's talent and best intentions, the demands of transforming the sensibilities of a one-hour dramatic story into a twenty-four-minute cartoon for children reduced many of the episodes to little more than fanciful action sequences, with no

chance to develop the dramatic texture and character interplay all other STAR TREK series are known for. There are, of course, a few exceptions to the generally lackluster animated episodes, especially Dorothy Fontana's "Yesteryear."

The difficulties of assembling the original cast for *The Animated Series* also brought their own technical problems. DeForest Kelley, reprising his role of McCoy, complained that for many episodes the cast members recorded their lines at separate times in different studios, preventing the actors from having any chance of character interplay. Though Walter Koenig did not return as Chekov, he did write the episode "The Infinite Vulcan."

But it is the technical realities of television animation in the early 1970s that ultimately dates the animated episodes when viewed today. Though at the time the series was one of the most expensive ever produced—$75,000 per episode—it could not come close to matching the quality of theatrical animation, then or now. For example, whereas twenty-four minutes of Walt Disney–caliber theatrical animation might require

more than seventeen thousand individual drawings, Filmation created each STAR TREK episode with between five thousand to seven thousand drawings. Faces, poses, and generic animation sequences of crew members walking or running were extensively reused in order to keep costs down, resulting in an unfortunate repetitive sameness to the look of each installment.

STAR TREK: THE ANIMATED SERIES debuted on NBC in its 9:30 A.M. Saturday-morning time slot, seven years to the day from when *The Original Series* was first broadcast. It was hailed as being part of NBC's most extensive children's programming development, and joined other based-on-live-action-series programs, *The Addams Family* and *Emergency*.

Given the competition and the state of animation at the time, most reviewers praised the series. The *Los Angeles Times* called it as out of place amid the other Saturday-morning cartoon shows as "a Mercedes in a soapbox derby." The *Washington Post* found it "fascinating," while wondering if its story lines were suitably simple enough for its target audience of children.

Cinefantastique, a specialty magazine devoted to science-fiction media, viewed the series with a more experienced eye, complaining that it was lacking "the drama and human interest that made the live-action series so captivating at times." The magazine predicted that children and fans alike would find the series to be "a terrible bore."

Once again, though, in what would become a defining tradition of almost every STAR TREK production, the series confounded those critics who found it wanting. After a first season of sixteen episodes, *The Animated Series* was renewed for an abbreviated second season of six episodes. All twenty-two installments were subsequently released on home video in 1989, coinciding with the release of the movie STAR TREK V: THE FINAL FRONTIER.

Though *The Animated Series* did not represent a true rebirth of STAR TREK, it was a valuable intermediate stage between the past and the future. Clearly, there was still life in the franchise, which even a disappointing production couldn't kill.

MODEL DEVELOPMENT SKETCHES

ALL SKETCHES COURTESY
OF GREG JEIN

With the decision made to keep the characters the same age as they appeared in the series, Filmation artists worked to create simple line-drawing versions of the cast that would remain recognizable, yet be easy to animate.

DR. McCOY

SPOCK

ONBOARD THE NEW *ENTERPRISE*

While many of the basic sets and designs of *The Animated Series* were taken directly from *The Original Series,* some elements of the *Starship Enterprise* were updated. On the bridge, for example, Gene Roddenberry explained that a second set of doors was added in response to all the viewers who had written in to ask "What do they do if the doors get stuck?"

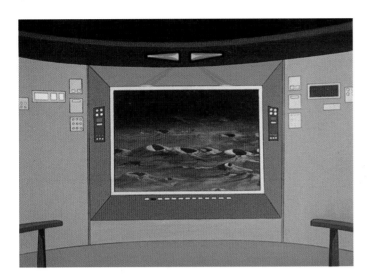

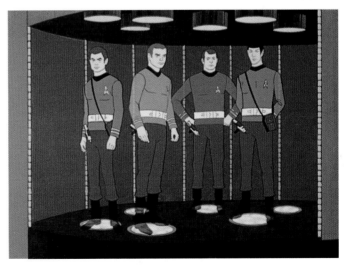

ALL ILLUSTRATIONS COURTESY
OF GREG JEIN

CHARACTERS OLD...

Art director Don Christensen supervised a crew of 38 artists and 36 animators to reinterpret the familiar crew of the *Starship Enterprise* for the demands of animation.

At the time this series was produced, character details as small as the crew service insignia would not normally be included as part of the animator's model. They would add too much complexity to what was required to be a simplified process. However, because Starfleet service insignia were such an important part of STAR TREK's visual appearance, they were redesigned to be larger, and thus easier to draw.

Captain James T. Kirk

Dr. Leonard McCoy

Science Officer Spock. Note the enlarged service insignia.

Communications Officer Uhura. Note the upgraded bridge equipment.

A Klingon commander

...AND NEW

Spock as a young boy. From the moving episode "Yesteryear," by D.C. Fontana

Gene Roddenberry was often asked why there weren't more aliens in the crew of the *Starship Enterprise*. Roddenberry liked to answer, "We always wanted to have more aliens, but there are very few of them in the Screen Actors Guild."

Budgetary constraints were, of course, the real reason. But with no makeup restraints, a new, three-legged alien was added to the bridge crew for the animated adventures.

Lieutenant Arex, the animated *Enterprise*'s three-armed and three-legged new navigator

Dr. Sarah April and her husband, the first captain of the *Starship Enterprise,* Robert T. April. From the episode "The Counter-Clock Incident," by John Culver. April's name was taken from the very first draft of Gene Roddenberry's original presentation for STAR TREK, so technically he *was* the first captain of the *Enterprise.*

SPECIAL EFFECTS

In contrast to live-action set design, it cost no more to draw an alien character or paint a fanciful background than it did to draw or paint familiar humans and sets. Thus the animated series consistently depicted more aliens and alien locales than the live-action series was able to afford.

An animated phaser hit. The glow surrounding Spock comes from his white "life-support belt." This was an addition to the *Enterprise*'s standard equipment during the animated series. It acted as a forcefield spacesuit, allowing crew members to visit a wider range of environments.

Kirk in space in his life-support field

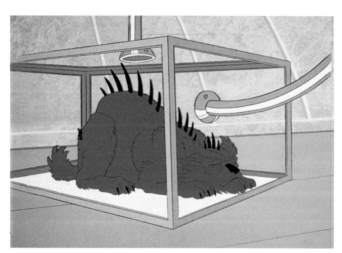

Kulkulkan's zoo-like "Life Room." From the episode "How Sharper Than a Serpent's Tooth," by Russell Bates and David Wise

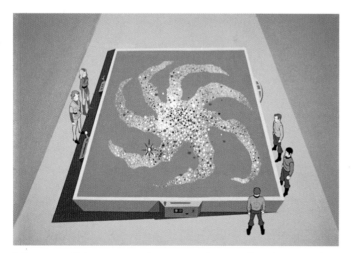

The crew of the *Enterprise* became miniaturized in the episode "The Terratin Incident," by Paul Schneider.

Kulkulkan's city

Alien landscape

Alien landscape

Dramia II and its inhabitants. From the episode "Albatross," by Dario Finelli

The *Enterprise* enters an antimatter universe in the episode "The Counter-Clock Incident."

An ancient astronaut, who was once worshipped as the god Kulkulkan on Earth, transforms from an alien spaceship disguise in the episode "How Sharper Than a Serpent's Tooth."

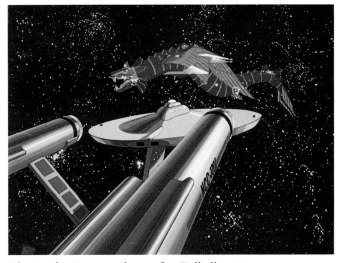

The *Starship Enterprise* chases after Kulkulkan.

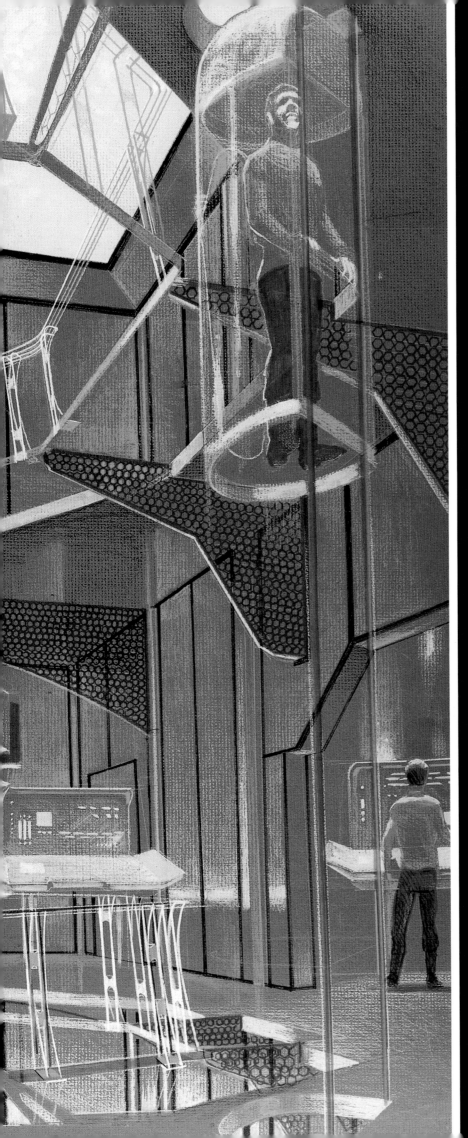

CHAPTER FOUR

THE SERIES THAT NEVER WAS

STAR TREK: PHASE II
1977

A Ken Adam concept sketch of a key location in the Bryant/Scott script *Planet of the Titans*

Ken Adam's concept drawing of a new shuttlebay

A Ken Adam concept sketch of a new *Enterprise,* bearing the unmistakable imprint of Ralph McQuarrie, designer of the Imperial Star Destroyers in *Star Wars*

THE STAR TREK THAT NEVER WAS

After several attempts to bring STAR TREK to the screen (see Part Two, Chapter One), in 1977 Paramount decided to produce a second television series, appropriately titled STAR TREK: PHASE II.

Barry Diller, at the time president of Paramount, had grown concerned by the direction in which STAR TREK had been taken in the latest movie script—*Planet of the Titans*, by Chris Bryant and Allan Scott. After the film had been canceled in preproduction, Diller had gone to Gene Roddenberry and suggested it was time to take STAR TREK back to its original context—a television series.

Just as Paramount would later do with STAR TREK VOYAGER and the new UPN television network, Diller's plan at the time was to use Phase II as the cornerstone of a Paramount-owned broadcast network. The studio's initial commitment was for a two-hour pilot and thirteen one-hour episodes.

In addition to Gene Roddenberry, Robert Goodwin was hired as a producer in charge of production and Harold Livingston as a producer in charge of writing. Jon Povill became story editor, and by July the series was in full preproduction.

Though Paramount was at first reluctant to put aside the development work that had been undertaken for the canceled movie, Roddenberry wanted to reunite as many members of his original production team as possible and start the design process again.

By a coincidence no writer would ever be allowed to use in a script, the designer of the original *Enterprise,* Matt Jefferies, was working on the Paramount lot in the office directly above Roddenberry's. At the time, he was art director for *Little House on the Prairie,* but received Michael Landon's blessing to act as a technical consultant for the new STAR TREK series. In the meantime, Jefferies had his friend Joe Jennings hired as the show's full-time art director. Jennings had been Jefferies' assistant in the second year of *The Original Series,* and had gone on to be the art director for such impressive productions as *Roots* and *Shogun.*

Mike Minor, who had provided many of the wall paintings seen in *The Original Series,* as well as having designed the Melkotian from "Spectre of the Gun," and the Tholian web, part of the Emmy-Award-winning visual effects in the episode of the same name, also returned to contribute to the updating and redesign of the series. Jim Rugg, another veteran from the first season of *The Original Series,* was brought back to be in charge of special effects.

With the Adam/McQuarrie *Enterprise* abandoned, Roddenberry asked Jefferies to update the famous starship to reflect the refit that would be part of the new series' backstory.

Jefferies' redesign changed the engine nacelles from tubes to thin, flat-sided modules, and tapered their supports. He also added the distinctive photon torpedo ports on the saucer connector.

Unlike the first redesign of the *Enterprise,* Jefferies' new version was built this time by Don Loos, who had built the original ship for *The Original Series.* But when Paramount abandoned its plans to create a fourth television network and subsequently transformed the second STAR TREK series into the first STAR TREK movie, that *Enterprise* was packed away as movie director Robert Wise brought in a new art director—Harold Michaelson—who started a second redesign of the ship, essentially keeping Jefferies' new lines, while adding the extensive detail that was necessary for a motion-picture miniature.

Though Roddenberry had endured many frustrating false starts in the eight years since his creation had been canceled, by once again thinking of STAR TREK as a television series and not a movie, Paramount had inadvertently set the stage for the most successful series of movies the studio ever made.

CHAPTER OPENING ILLUSTRATION A Mike Minor concept painting for the engine room of the new *Enterprise*. Many of the elements in this painting were included in the final set for the motion-picture *Enterprise* and the *Enterprise* of *The Next Generation*.

THE SEARCH FOR A
NEW ENTERPRISE

Though these designs clearly reflect the influence of Ralph McQuarrie, the echoes of Matt Jefferies's original concept can still be seen.

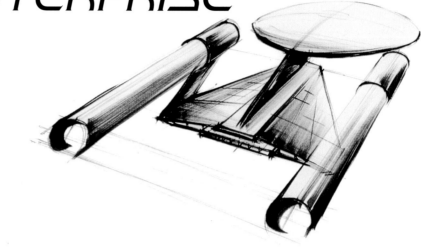

More than a decade after they were built, these concept models found their way into a STAR TREK production when they were photographed as part of the armada devastated by the Borg in the Battle of Wolf 359 from *The Next Generation*.

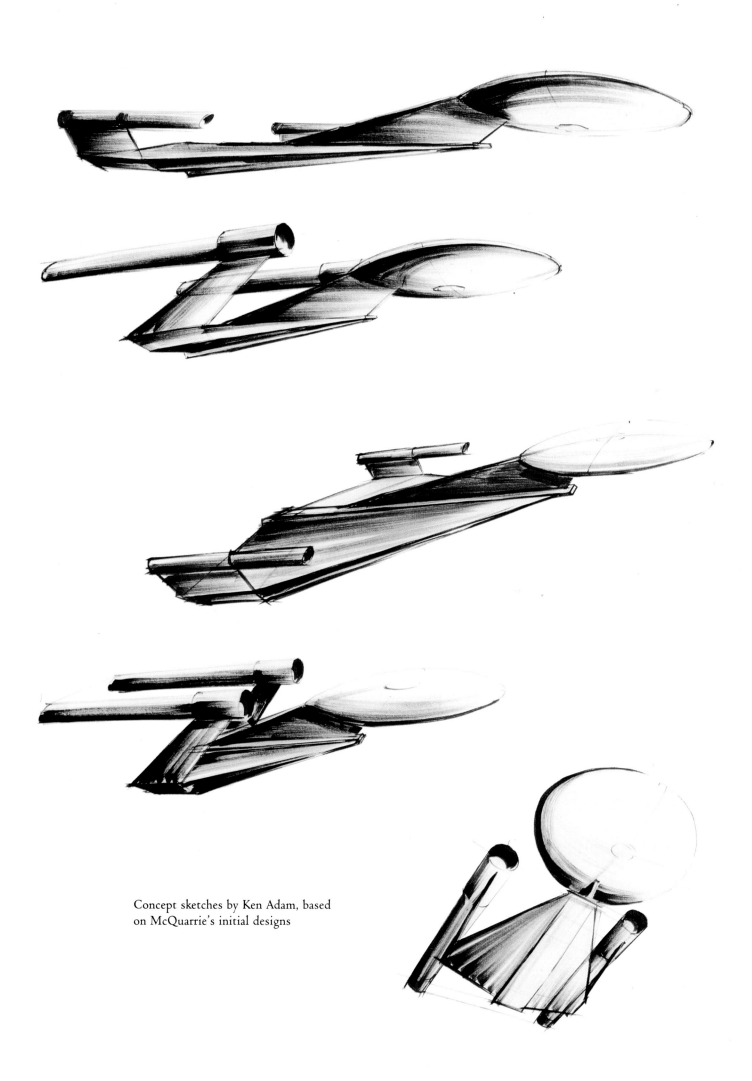

Concept sketches by Ken Adam, based
on McQuarrie's initial designs

A RALPH MCQUARRIE GALLERY

Ralph McQuarrie is best known to the public for his stunning production designs for the *Star Wars* films. His imagination helped guide the final appearance of Darth Vader and his Storm Troopers, R2-D2 and C-3PO, and he also created many of the matte paintings of planets and satellites that appeared in the film.

After *Star Wars* wrapped in 1977, McQuarrie was invited to England to work under Ken Adam to help develop the designs for a new STAR TREK movie, ultimately abandoned to make way for STAR TREK: PHASE II, the television series.

These paintings were part of that process, giving us a glimpse of one possible STAR TREK that never was.

The *Enterprise* approaches a spacedock with a difference—it's carved into an asteroid.

PAINTING BY RALPH McQUARRIE COURTESY OF *STARLOG* MAGAZINE

PAINTING BY RALPH McQUARRIE COURTESY OF *STARLOG* MAGAZINE

Even if this *Enterprise* had made it to the screen, the exhaust shooting out of its warp engines wouldn't have.

ANOTHER PATH NOT TAKEN

Matt Jefferies's updated design of the *Enterprise,* which reached the construction stage, was abandoned when the second television series became the first movie. However, many of his new design elements were incorporated into the next version of the famous starship.

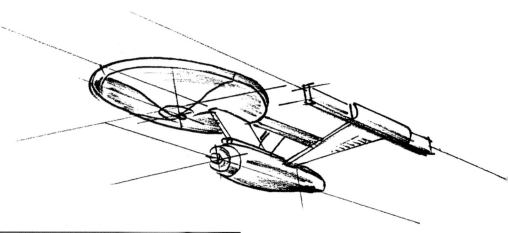

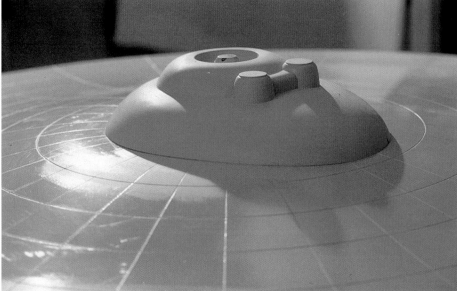

An early Matt Jefferies sketch of the updated *Enterprise*

A lost *Enterprise.* The second television starship under construction

Mike Minor's rendition of the new Matt
Jefferies design

COURTESY OF BOB BURNS

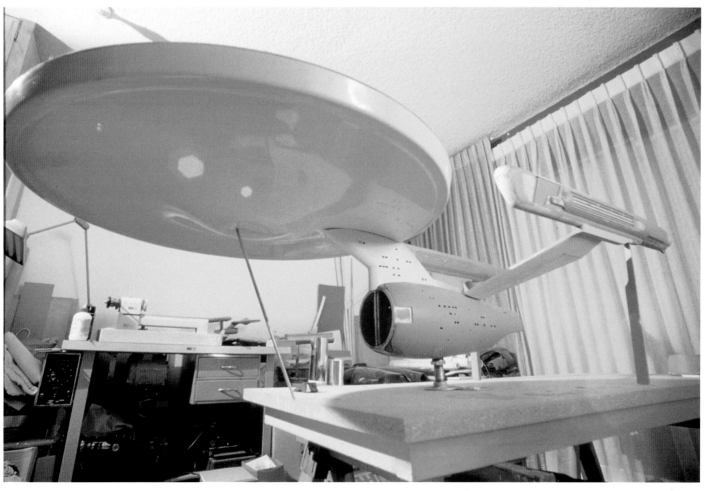

AN INTERMEDIATE
ENTERPRISE TAKES SHAPE

Mike Minor's initial designs for the new STAR TREK series are clearly the evolutionary step between *The Original Series* and *The Motion Picture*.

The bridge-wall control modules survived almost intact to *The Motion Picture*, while the transporter room is essentially a redress of the original set with a more streamlined console and new wall displays.

Note the three-dimensional chess set in the recreation deck painting.

MIKE MINOR. COURTESY OF *STARLOG* MAGAZINE

MIKE MINOR. COURTESY OF *STARLOG* MAGAZINE

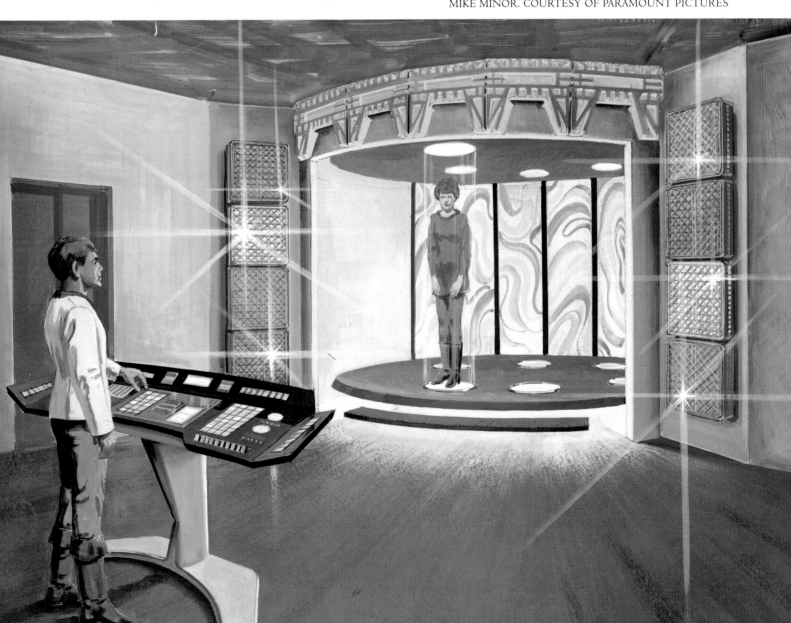

MIKE MINOR. COURTESY OF *STARLOG* MAGAZINE

MIKE MINOR. COURTESY OF PARAMOUNT PICTURES

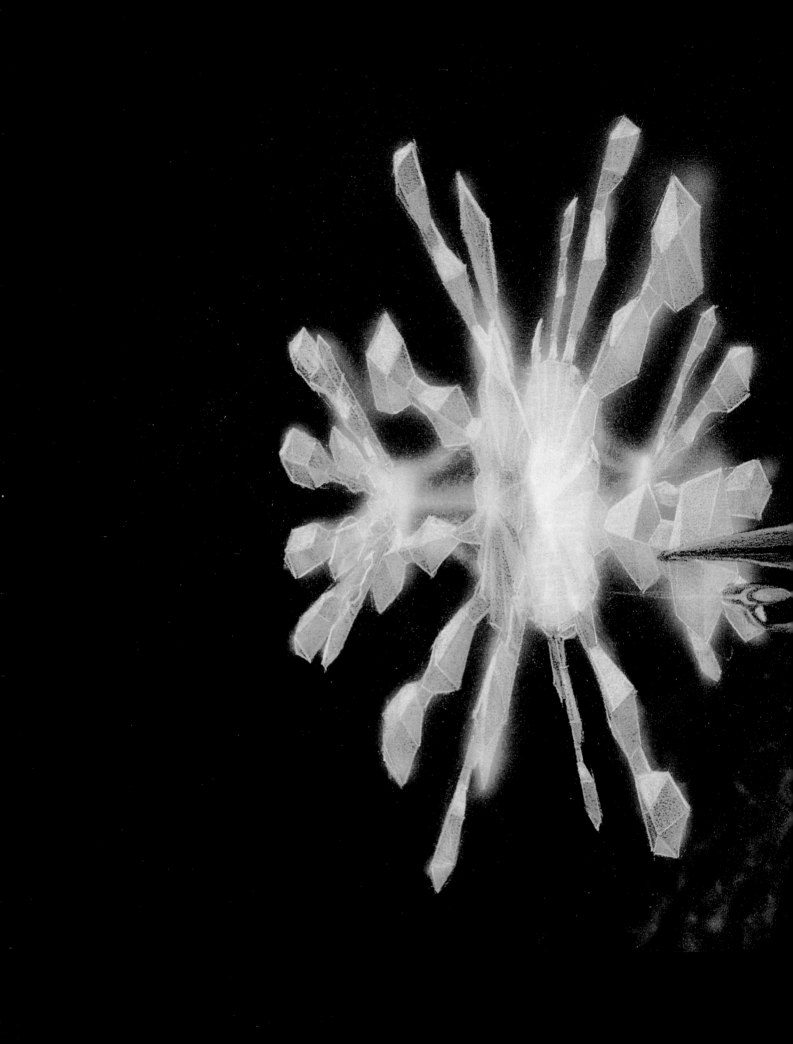

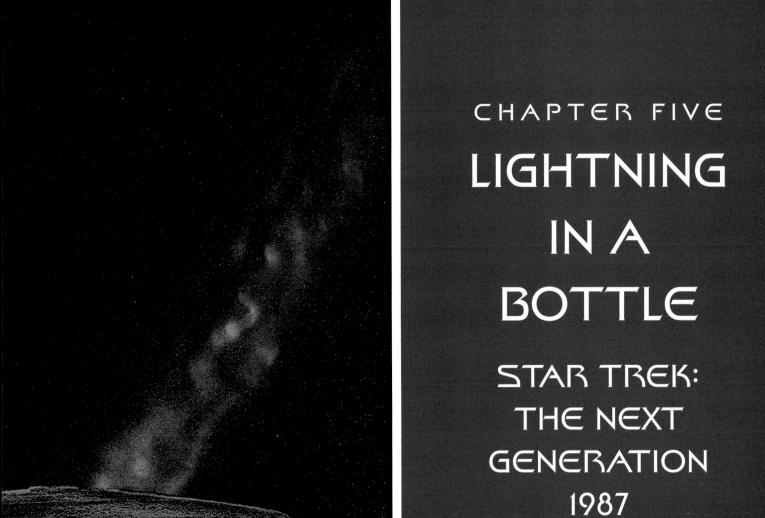

CHAPTER FIVE

LIGHTNING IN A BOTTLE

STAR TREK: THE NEXT GENERATION
1987

OVERLEAF A concept painting by Andrew Probert showing the Silicon Avatar from the episode of the same name COURTESY OF THE ARTIST

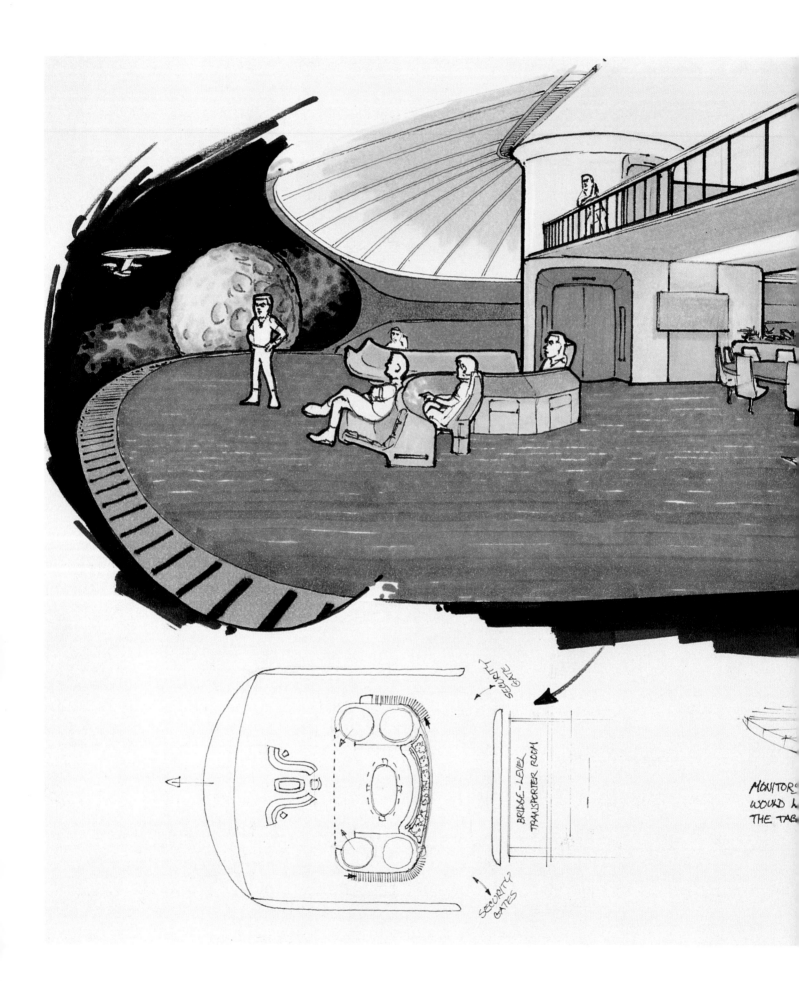

THE NEXT GENERATION

TREK
BRIDGE (9.)

WITH
TIL NEEDED —

Probert 120486

Twenty years ago, the genius of one man brought to television a program that has transcended the medium. We are enormously pleased that that man, Gene Roddenberry, is going to do it again. Just as public demand kept *The Original Series* on the air, this new series is also a result of grassroots support for Gene and his vision."

With those words spoken by Mel Harris, the president of the Paramount Television Group, the long-awaited second STAR TREK television series at last became official on October 10, 1986, seventeen years after the first series had been canceled.

But this time there would be something different in the revived series. The fight to bring back Kirk and his crew that had been waged throughout the seventies was no longer a battle that could be won. The STAR TREK films and the individual careers of the key cast members were too successful for *The Original Series*'s crew ever to be lured back to the weekly grind of episodic television production. So with a grand leap of faith, Paramount had agreed to the concept of setting the next series a century ahead of the first, and going forward with an all-new cast of characters.

At the time, this attempt to "catch lightning in a bottle," as Leonard Nimoy called it, carried considerable risk for Paramount.

The networks the studio had approached with the new series had recognized that risk as well.

One of Andrew Probert's first concept drawings for the bridge of the new *Enterprise*—deemphasizing its operations aspects in accordance with Gene Roddenberry's first thoughts on the updated ship's capabilities

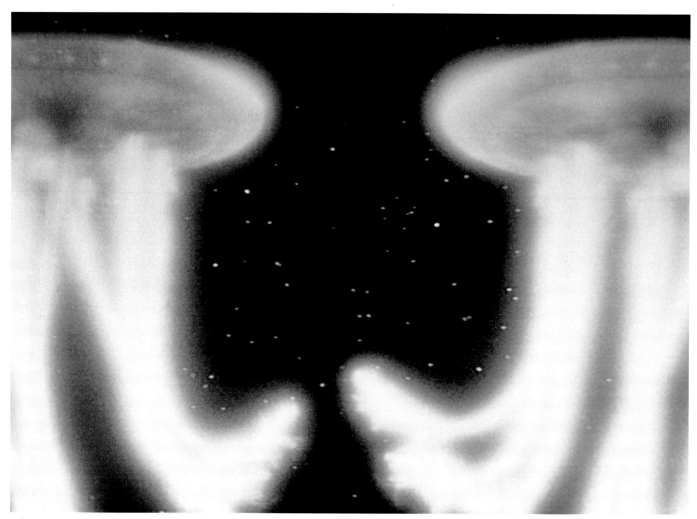

The Farpoint Station creatures as they were realized onscreen

From the pilot episode, "Encounter at Farpoint," an early concept of the Farpoint Station creature drawn by Rick Sternbach

TREK
STATION CREATURE
RISING

Though all were interested in broadcasting an updated STAR TREK series, none was willing to commit to a full-season order. At best, the networks would buy only six episodes. And the potential revenue from only six episodes was not enough to cover Paramount's investment in new sets, costumes, props, and models.

Thus Paramount made the groundbreaking decision to make the series directly for the syndicated market. It had been in the syndicated market that the first series had found its audience, and where it continued to thrive almost two decades later. Paramount executives

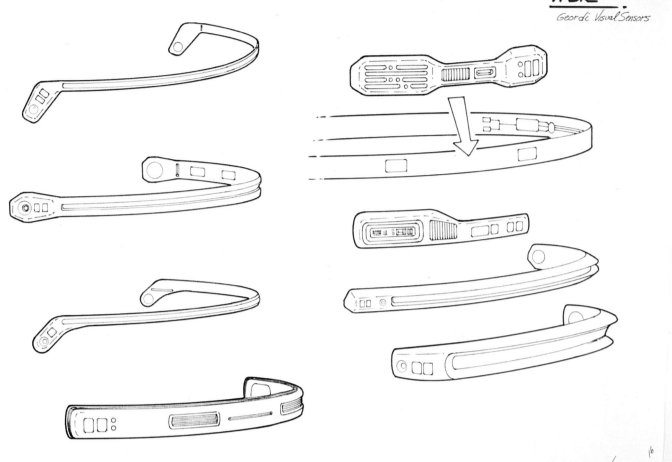

Some of the many Rick Sternbach designs considered for Geordi's visual sensor, until the day...

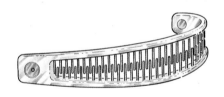

...a 79-cent plastic barrette became the basis for this final Sternbach design. Technically, the device is a VISOR—for Visual Instrument and Sensory Organ Replacement.

ran the numbers and determined that at the very worst, they would end up with twenty-six new episodes, which they could add to the ongoing syndication orders for the original seventy-nine. They couldn't be certain if the series would succeed, but at least they knew the studio wouldn't lose money.

With that critical business concern taken care of, Gene Roddenberry once again began the task of gathering together a production team that would match his passion for the STAR TREK universe, and take it boldly into its next century.

In STAR TREK: THE NEXT GENERATION's first season, its crew of veterans from *The Original Series* included producer Robert Justman, William Ware Theiss as costume designer, set decorator John Dwyer, and special-effects supervisor Dick Brownfield. And

this time, Roddenberry had his own second generation of STAR TREK personnel to draw from—veterans from the successful movies. In the first season, these included makeup artist Werner Keppler, illustrators Andrew Probert and Rick Sternbach, scenic artist Michael Okuda, and the visual-effects wizards of Industrial Light & Magic.

Among the new faces added to the STAR TREK crew that year, production designer Herman Zimmerman, makeup supervisor Michael Westmore, visual-effects coordinators Robert Legato and Dan Curry, and unit production manager David Livingston would go on to make significant and ongoing contributions to *The Next Generation,* as well as to *Deep Space Nine, Voyager,* and the next stage in the evolution of STAR TREK movies.

With the overwhelming and unprecedented success of this new version of STAR TREK, comparisons no longer applied.

STAR TREK had become, quite simply, STAR TREK.

There was not, and there is not, anything else like it, anywhere.

A FASTER ENTERPRISE IN MORE WAYS THAN ONE

PAINTING COURTESY OF ANDREW PROBERT

When it came time to design a new *Starship Enterprise* for *The Next Generation,* history did not repeat itself. Where Matt Jefferies had produced hundreds of sketches to come up with the design direction for the original *Enterprise,* Andrew Probert's main design work for the new *Enterprise* was done before his job even started.

Before the series was announced, Andrew Probert painted the above illustration of a future starship concept, strictly for his own enjoyment. When he went to work on the Paramount lot to design the new *Enterprise,* he brought that painting with him as inspiration and hung it on his office wall.

One day, David Gerrold came into Probert's office, saw the painting, and asked if Gene Roddenberry had seen it.

Probert said he hadn't, and Gerrold immediately took it in to Roddenberry, who approved the painting's design direction on the spot.

All that remained was fine-tuning and filling in the details.

TREK 11/14/86

ENTERPRISE ①

OVERLEAF Andrew Probert's concept paintings of the long-awaited saucer-separation maneuver

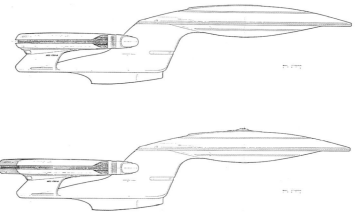

11/2/86

Initial refinement sketches

One of the final refinements to the new *Enterprise*'s design was Roddenberry's request that the engine nacelles be made shorter, as indicated here.

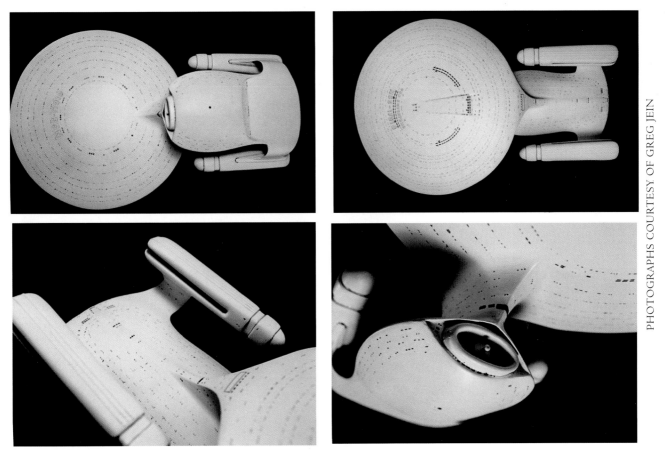

An early concept model showing a wider engineering hull, and different finishing details for the nacelle tips and sensor dish

Though Andrew Probert had originally designed the new *Enterprise* as a single unit, the requirements of the pilot episode sent him back to the drawing board to devise an updated version of a scenario he had originally proposed for *The Motion Picture*.

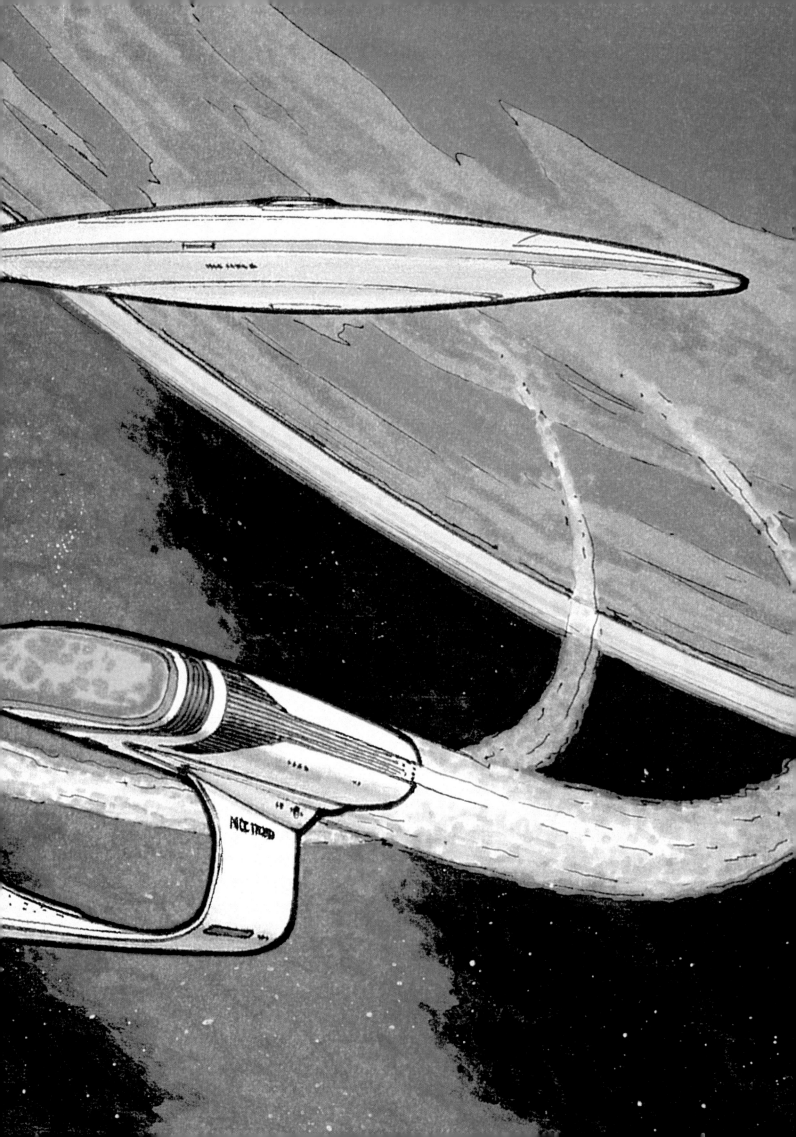

REINVENTING THE BRIDGE

This series of concept drawings by Andrew Probert shows the refinement of the new look for the *Enterprise*'s bridge.

An early writers' bible for the new series described the new bridge as combining "the features of ship control, briefing room, information retrieval area, and officers' wardroom.

In other words, much the same kinds of things happen here as in the old bridge, but with less emphasis on the mechanics of steering the starship." That new, less mechanistic approach can be seen in the preliminary designs featuring viewing couches and a conference table on the bridge.

In the final illustration, note the two design details Probert deliberately carried forward from the original bridge: the starship plaque by the turbolift and the red warning light directly below the middle of the viewscreen, echoing the light that flashes in the center of the combined helm and navigation console.

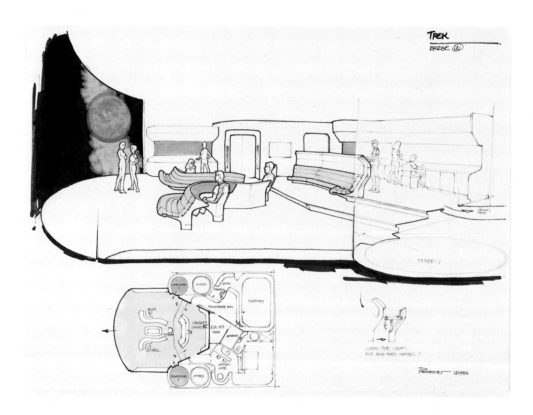

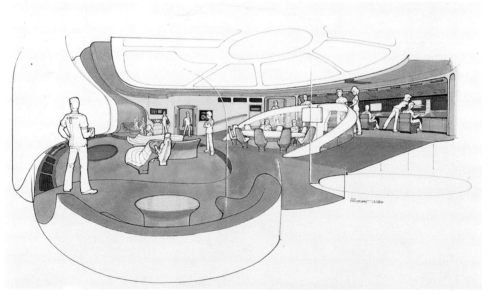

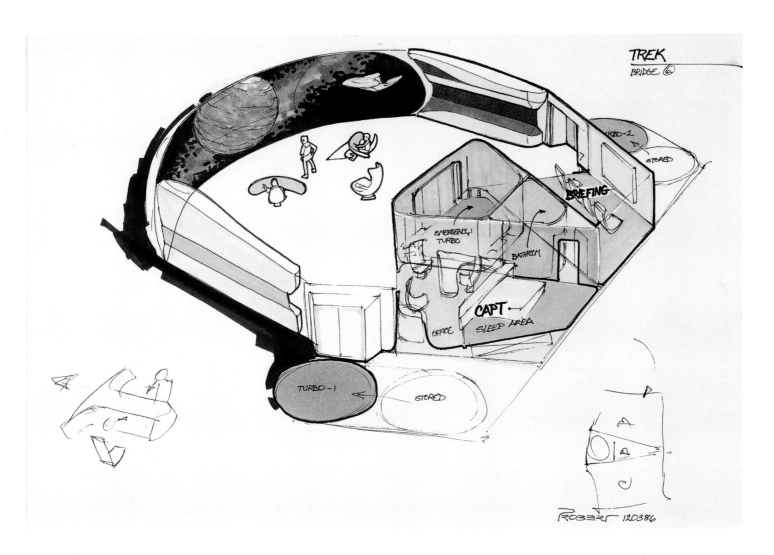

TREK
BRIDGE 6

TURBO-2
STORED
BRIEFING
EMERGENCY TURBO
BATHROOM
CAPT.
SLEEP AREA
OFFICE
TURBO-1
STORED

ROBERT 120386

ALL ARTWORK COURTESY OF ANDREW PROBERT

A TOUR OF THE NEW ENTERPRISE—PART 1
THE NERVE CENTER

Andrew Probert called for this ship display panel as an homage to the design of the bridge of the original *Enterprise*.

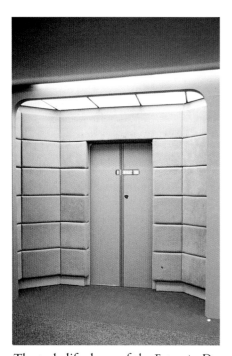

The turbolift alcove of the *Enterprise*-D is exactly the same size as the one on the original *Enterprise* bridge. However, on Picard's *Enterprise*, there were two turbolifts, a design safety feature carried over from the refitted movie version of Kirk's *Enterprise*.

Again echoing the original *Enterprise*, this dedication plaque was created by Starfleet's Advanced Technologies Unit.

Though it appears much larger, the bridge set of the *Enterprise*-D is only two feet deeper than the bridge set of the original *Enterprise,* and at thirty-eight feet wide, the same width. The original carpet colors on the left, selected by John Dwyer, were changed almost every season, each time worn carpet was replaced.

A Worf's-eye view of the bridge. The wishbone railing is left over from some of the earliest bridge designs, which called for a conference table to be placed where the command chairs ended up.

The conn and ops stations, outfitted with Okudagram control surfaces. Technically, the configuration of the controls changed according to mission requirements. In reality, they are sheets of backlit Plexiglas, colored with lighting gels.

A TOUR OF THE NEW
ENTERPRISE—PART 2
BUILDING ON THE PAST

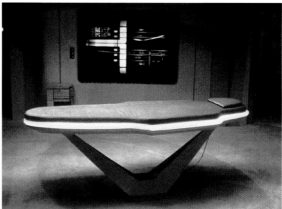

At least as important to STAR TREK stories as the bridge and transporter room is sickbay. Though the finishing details are more refined and intricate than those *The Original Series* could afford, a twenty-fourth-century offspring of Dr. McCoy's medical sensor still rests above each patient's bed.

More than just design elements from the original *Enterprise* turned up in the *Enterprise*-D. The glass floor disks from the original transporter-room set were installed in the ceiling of the new transporter. (And those same disks have found a home in the *U.S.S. Voyager*'s transporter room today.)

The engine room of the *Enterprise*-D incorporated new workstation areas with a two-story warp core installation that was originally built for STAR TREK: THE MOTION PICTURE, based on even earlier designs created by Mike Minor for STAR TREK: PHASE II.

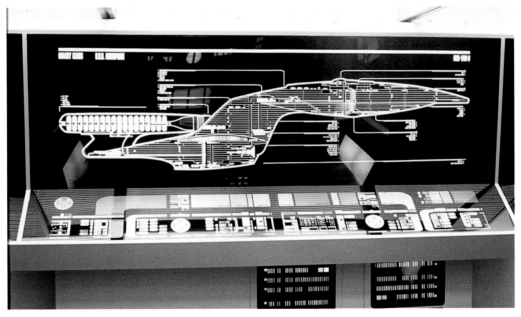

As readers of the *STAR TREK: The Next Generation Technical Manual* know, this wall-size Okudagram in Engineering reveals such secrets as the locations of the ship's giant mouse, the giant duck, and what might be Gene Roddenberry's own WWII bomber.

A TOUR OF THE NEW
ENTERPRISE—PART 3
DETAILS, DETAILS, DETAILS...

With the personal computer revolution of the 1980s, the term "information overload" meant something to the average STAR TREK viewer. With the improvement in television technology to film and broadcast with increased resolution, more detail could be added to sets. Both these trends resulted in intricate additions to what had gone before in science-fiction film and television production. The series' designers' ongoing quest for verisimilitude now resulted in more extravagantly detailed and visually convincing sets.

Seven years after this display of ships named *Enterprise* was added to the captain's ready room set at the suggestion of set decorator John Dwyer, it was pivotal in convincing the producers of STAR TREK GENERATIONS that the never-before-seen *Enterprise*-B should be an *Excelsior*-class vessel.

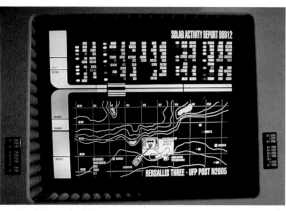

The Original Series had not been able to afford to keep visual information appearing on all the display screens built into the bridge, and had cheated in other sets by generally angling the desk viewscreens away from the camera. But increased budgets and Michael Okuda's relatively inexpensive but impressive backlit designs made the latest *Enterprise* vibrant with computer display screens.

Shuttlebay 1, a seldom-seen miniature set

Just as in the set designs for *The Original Series,* by curving a single corridor so that its end could not be seen, the illusion could be created of an endless string of corridors throughout the new ship.

This distinctively angled corridor will be familiar to anyone who remembers *The Motion Picture.* Many of the set elements of the new *Enterprise*-D were modified or redecorated sets from the movie.

Under Herman Zimmerman's direction, set designers were careful to incorporate wall angles and window shapes that would correspond to those on the miniature of the *Enterprise*-D.

Picard's ready room off the bridge. Note the model of Picard's first command—the *Stargazer*.

The observation lounge off the bridge. Note the PADDs built in to the tabletop.

Ten-Forward was the last major set developed under Herman Zimmerman's guidance as *The Next Generation*'s first production designer.

The microgravity of space is prohibitively expensive to depict for a weekly television series, so the *Enterprise*'s method of dealing with it is seldom made a point of any episode. Signs such as this, however, indicate to careful viewers that the show's production team has at least acknowledged that the ship has artificial gravity.

A NEW DIRECTION

A common conceit of the STAR TREK universe is that all the starships in it invariably approach each other with their "up-and-down" orientations matching. When asked to design a new starship for *The Next Generation* Romulans, Andrew Probert decided to try and free himself from that limitation by building a new orientation into the new ship, making it taller than it was wide.

However, the weight of what had gone before proved too much for this attempt at innovation. Though his basic design was approved, the producers requested he rotate the ship so that it would visually fit in with all the other starships in the STAR TREK universe.

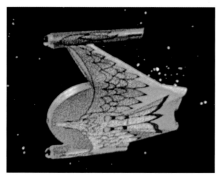

The first Romulan ship—a Bird-of-Prey—from *The Original Series* episode "Balance of Terror"

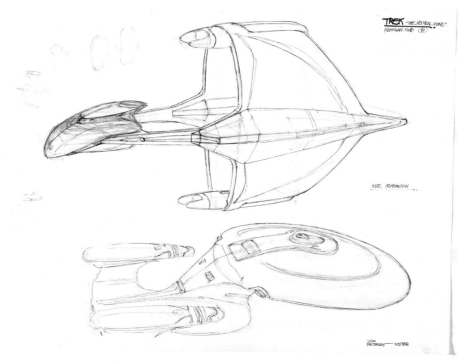

Getting close to the final design, still with a change in orientation

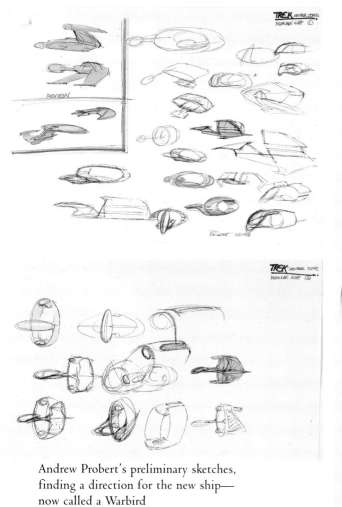

Andrew Probert's preliminary sketches, finding a direction for the new ship—now called a Warbird

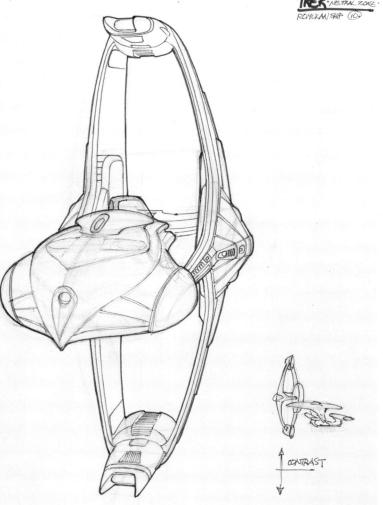

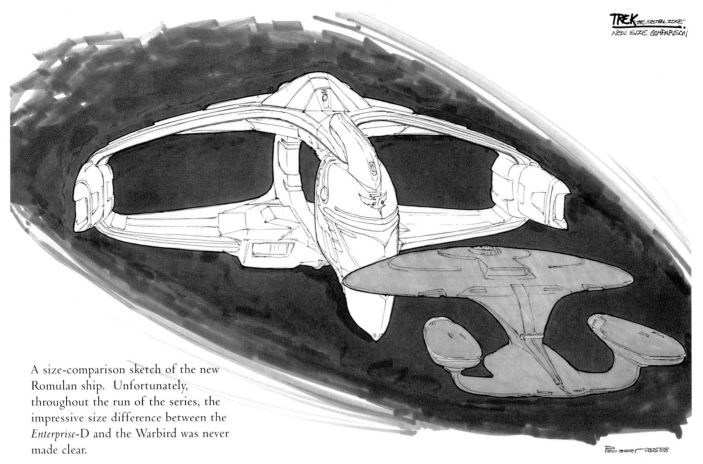

A size-comparison sketch of the new Romulan ship. Unfortunately, throughout the run of the series, the impressive size difference between the *Enterprise*-D and the Warbird was never made clear.

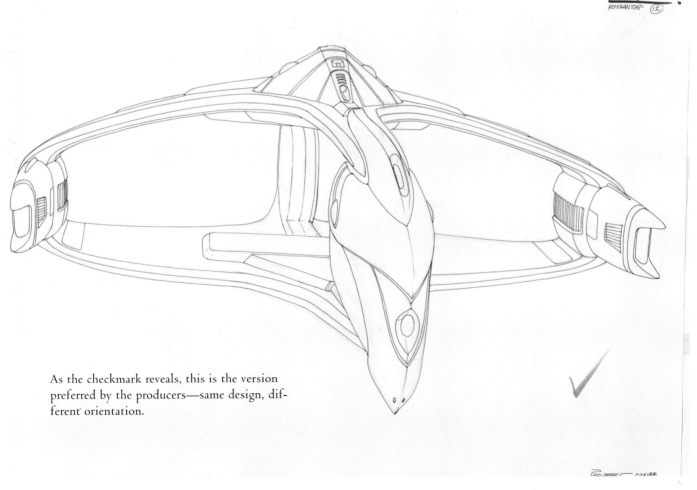

As the checkmark reveals, this is the version preferred by the producers—same design, different orientation.

PAINTINGS COME TO LIFE

An ongoing attribute of those who work on STAR TREK productions is the enthusiasm and talent that leads them to contribute in as many different ways as possible.

Andrew Probert, prolific designer of starships, props, and aliens, also created these matte paintings for *The Next Generation*'s first season.

The shot of the *Enterprise* docked at Starbase 74, from "11001001," was used, with the addition of a photographic matte showing crew members walking through the gangway tunnel.

OVERLEAF The Velara III terraforming station, from "Home Soil," ended up being cut from the final version.

VELARA III
STARFLEET TERRAFORM DIVISION

DEVELOPING
A NEW UNIFORM

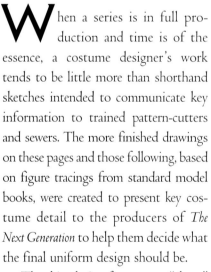

WhenW a series is in full production and time is of the
essence, a costume designer's work
tends to be little more than shorthand
sketches intended to communicate key
information to trained pattern-cutters
and sewers. The more finished drawings
on these pages and those following, based
on figure tracings from standard model
books, were created to present key costume detail to the producers of *The
Next Generation* to help them decide what
the final uniform design should be.

The skirt design for men—a "skant"
—was a logical development, given
the total equality of the sexes pre-
sumed to exist in the 24th century. It
turned up on background extras during
the series' first season. This was not a
first, however, as Chief Engineer Scott
wore a kilt as part of his dress uniform
during *The Original Series*.

ALL ILLUSTRATIONS BY
WILLIAM WARE THEISS

The long frock coat depicted here eventually turned up as part of Starfleet's dress uniform.

This rough sketch on a restaurant placemat shows Theiss's first thoughts on establishing a system of uniform markings to signify rank.

ALL ILLUSTRATIONS BY
WILLIAM WARE THEISS

OLD FAVORITES RETURN

I n the first writer's guide for STAR TREK: THE NEXT GENERATION, Gene Roddenberry included a section titled "What Doesn't Work," warning potential writers what to avoid. Item 9 in that list stated:

> "No stories about warfare with Klingons or Romulans, and no stories with Vulcans. We are determined not to copy ourselves and believe there must be other interesting aliens in a galaxy filled with billions of stars and planets."

An admirable intent, to be sure, but by the time the strength of the audience reaction to the new show had sunk in, Roddenberry and the rest of the staff realized that *The Next Generation* had quickly established an identity of its own. Thus, Worf's Klingon background was explored, Vulcans turned up as supporting characters, and by the end of the first season, even the Romulans had made a reappearance.

The Next Generation wasn't repeating the past. It was forging a new future.

The makeup design for *The Next Generation* Klingons was based on the new look developed by Fred Phillips in *The Motion Picture*. As these first- and fifth-season photos show, the Klingon appearance continued to become more sophisticated throughout the series, matching the complexity Michael Dorn brought to his portrayal of the *Enterprise*'s lone Klingon officer, Worf.

Wardrobe test shots of Anthony James as Subcommander Thei (facing left), and Marc Alaimo as Commander Tebok in "The Neutral Zone"—the first appearance of Romulans in *The Next Generation* series

Series makeup supervisor Michael Westmore gave the "new" Romulans of *The Next Generation* a built-up brow to compete with the Klingons, as shown in this study model.

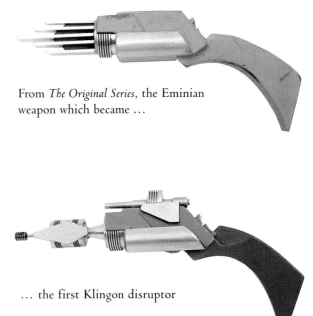

BOTH PROPS COURTESY OF GREG JEIN

From *The Original Series*, the Eminian weapon which became …

The design of Klingon weaponry derives from *The Original Series* episode "A Taste of Armageddon," which has no Klingons in it. The Eminian pistol used by Kirk in this still was later modified to become the standard Klingon disruptor. Both original pistol designs were developed by Matt Jefferies.

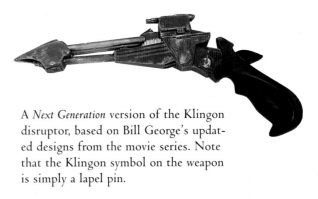

… the first Klingon disruptor

COURTESY OF GREG JEIN

A *Next Generation* version of the Klingon disruptor, based on Bill George's updated designs from the movie series. Note that the Klingon symbol on the weapon is simply a lapel pin.

COURTESY OF ROBERT BLACKMAN

Robert Blackman's third-season design for Worf's *R'usstai* cloak.

THE NEW KLINGONS...ALMOST

TREK
FERENGI RACE ④

ROBERT 050887

With the Klingons no longer a threat to the Federation, a new alien threat was needed for *The Next Generation*—the Ferengi, developed by Herb Wright and Gene Roddenberry.

So fearsome and ferocious were the Ferengi to be, in the pilot episode Riker states that they've been known to eat their business partners. Yet by the time the Ferengi made their first appearance in the first-season episode "The Last Outpost," they had been transformed into what actor Armin Shimerman described as "angry gerbils."

Though the Ferengi eventually became more of a nuisance than a threat to the Federation, Shimerman,

Three approaches to the Ferengi's appearance as imagined by Andrew Probert. These illustrations became the basis for the final makeup design, though the loss of the pointed ears and fangs reduced the aura of danger the drawing so effectively conveys.

COURTESY OF THE ARTIST

who portrayed one of the first Ferengi, in "Outpost," went on to become Quark in STAR TREK: DEEP SPACE NINE, where he has brought a depth to the Ferengi fully the equal of *The Original Series*' Vulcans.

But the Ferengi's failure as effective villains did pave the way for the creation of a truly alien threat—the Borg.

The first appearance of the Ferengi—
Jake Dengel as Mordoc and Armin
Shimerman as Letek

Early test shots of Armin Shimerman in a Ferengi headpiece for "The Last Outpost."
The original design pressed the actors' ears flat against their heads, which, during a
sixteen-hour shooting day, became enervatingly painful. With Shimerman's input, the
new Ferengi headpieces used on *Deep Space Nine* had extra folds sculpted into them to
keep the actors' ears from being crushed.

THE BORG

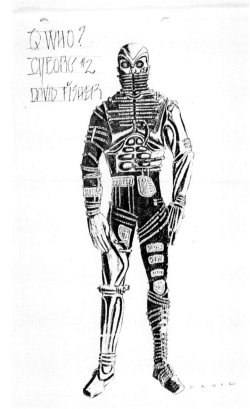

After the Ferengi fizzled, STAR TREK writer and producer Maurice Hurley created the Borg as villains worthy of the twenty-fourth-century Starfleet.

Their name comes from the term "cyborg," which itself comes from "cybernetic organism"—a life-form that is part biological and part mechanical. In the best tradition of science-fiction invaders, the Borg don't just *kill* their enemies, they *convert* them by "Borgifying" them.

The Borg lived up to their promise and became the villains for the two-part episode "The Best of Both Worlds," voted the all-time best *Next Generation* episode in a national viewers' poll conducted at the close of the series' final season.

Rick Sternbach's design notes for the restoration of the Borgified Picard from "The Best of Both Worlds"

Early Borg concepts by David Fisher

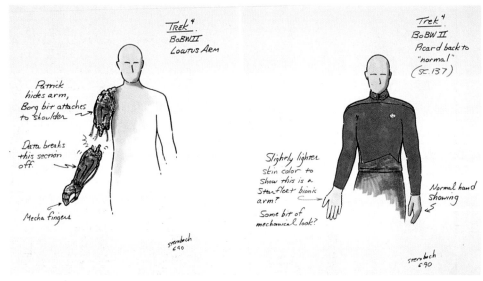

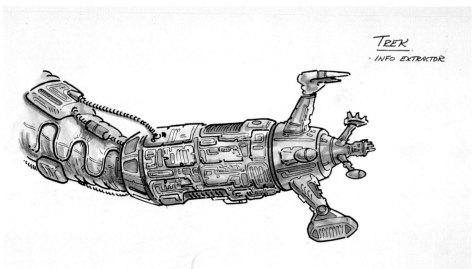

Borg concepts by Rick Sternbach

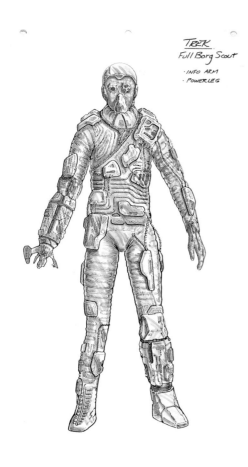

TREK
Full Borg Scout
• INFO ARM
• POWER LEG

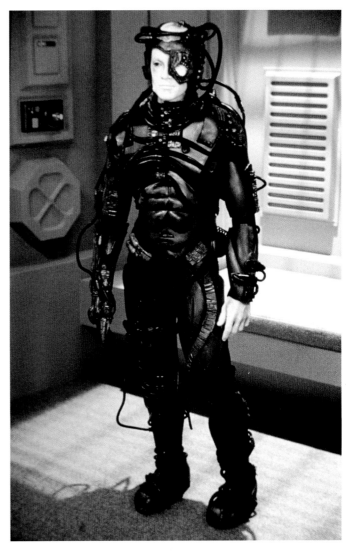

Jonathan Del Arco as Hugh, the Borg formerly known as Third of Five, from the episode "I, Borg"

A Borg

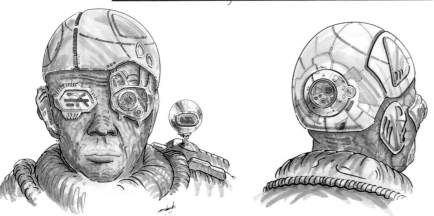

THE ART OF MICHAEL WESTMORE, PART 1

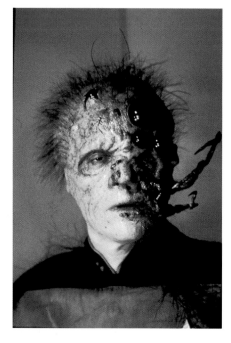

Makeup artist extraordinaire Michael Westmore is the third generation of a Hollywood makeup dynasty, beginning with his grandfather George Westmore, who started work in Hollywood features in the 1920s. He has won an Academy Award for his work in *Mask,* and, so far, almost ten Emmys for his ongoing excellence in make-up design for television.

As the makeup supervisor for *The Next Generation,* STAR TREK: DEEP SPACE NINE, STAR TREK VOY-AGER, and STAR TREK GENER-ATIONS, with his staff of sculptors and makeup artists, Westmore has built and applied more makeup designs than any other artist in the business today.

As these examples of his work so ably illustrate, Westmore's talent and technical expertise are as unlimited as the stars the *Enterprise* explores.

Evolution run amok in the crew of the *Enterprise*-D, from the eerie episode "Transformations"

Sarjenka, an inhabitant of Drema IV

A Pakled

A shapechanging allasomorph in a deadly form

One of the Nausicaans responsible for stabbing Picard and making him a candidate for an artificial heart

WESTMORE, PART 2

Paul Winfield as the Tamarian captain Dathon

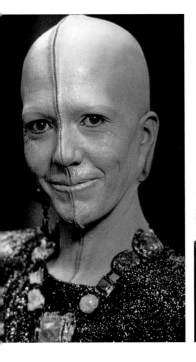

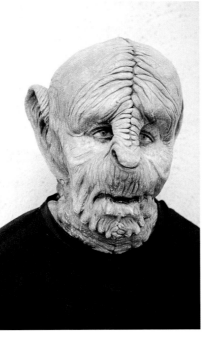

These two shots of the Yridian dealer Jaglom Shrek show how proper lighting enhances the finished appearance of STAR TREK's aliens. On the left is a test shot taken offstage under ordinary daylight. On the right is the same makeup under studio conditions.

VISITS TO THE DARK SIDE

Longtime STAR TREK television producer and director David Livingston agrees with those who attribute much of STAR TREK's success to its positive outlook. Livingston feels that while science-fiction movies such as *Alien* and *Blade Runner* work well in a movie theater for a few hours, not too many people would want to tune in to see such dark visions of the future week after week, the way millions faithfully tune in to the STAR TREK series.

Indeed, the first-season episode "Conspiracy" is the STAR TREK exception that proves the rule. A grim story of an alien conspiracy at the highest level of Starfleet, the episode's graphic portrayal of alien parasites made it stand apart from all other STAR TREK television episodes. Though the story was set up for sequels, the alien-conspiracy plot threads were never revisited, due in part to the negative reaction the episode received.

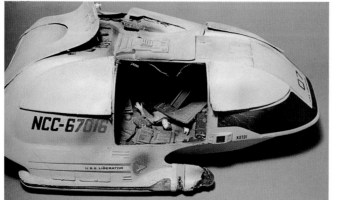

A battle-damaged shuttle and dead crew member from the Battle of Wolf 359. Though the modelmakers might sometimes add this type of detail to the ships they build, none have ever been added to a STAR TREK episode in a form in which the television audience might see them.

The first-season episode "Skin of Evil" marked the death of series regular Tasha Yar—the first time a STAR TREK regular had been killed and *not* brought back to life. Armus, the alien responsible, was described by visual-effects coordinator Robert Legato as "a living tar pit." Here we see one of Andrew Probert's concepts for the creature, and a still from the episode showing the final result.

ARTWORK COURTESY
OF THE ARTIST

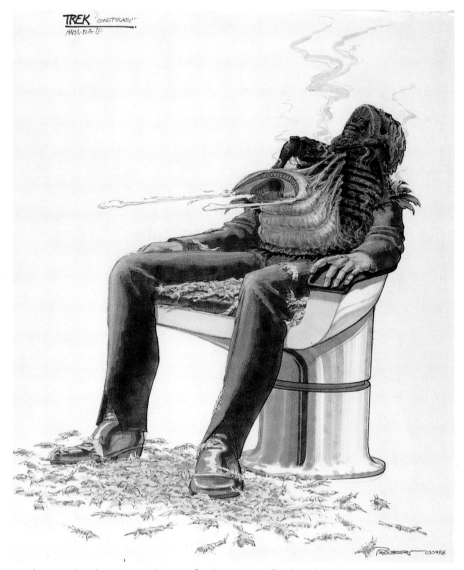

Andrew Probert's concept designs for "Conspiracy." Though tame in comparison to
Alien, this type of story was not typical of what viewers had come to expect of STAR
TREK, and was not followed up.

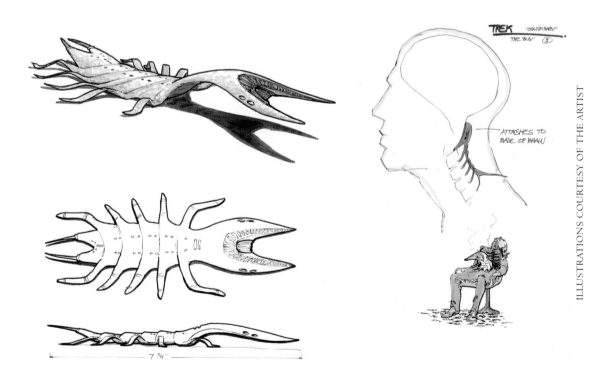

PHASERS, THE NEXT GENERATION

In setting the design standards for *The Next Generation*, Gene Roddenberry was concerned that phasers not end up looking like twentieth-century pistols. He stressed to Rick Sternbach that he should avoid the standard pistol-grip and gun-barrel approach and come up with something new. Since a gun works by pointing it at a target, and since the human hand can hold and point a tool in only a limited, comfortable range of positions, Sternbach was appropriately challenged by Roddenberry's direction, which led directly to the "dust-buster" design eventually chosen as the new shape of twenty-fourth-century weaponry.

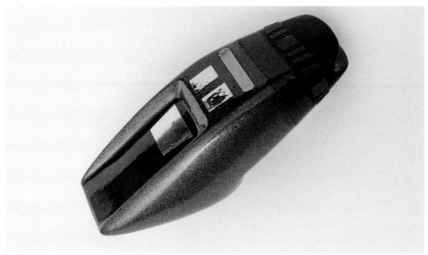

This tiny phaser was Gene Roddenberry's favorite. Dubbed the "cricket," it was less than three inches long, and to Roddenberry illustrated the power of twenty-fourth-century technology. However, it also illustrated the power of production requirements. Because the weapon was so small, it could not easily be seen when actors used it. Dramatically, it added no sense of danger to a scene, and visually, unless specific reference had been made to it, it could appear that phaser beams were erupting from actors' fingers whenever it was used.

The cricket turned up only a few times in the first season, then was abandoned for more identifiable weapons.

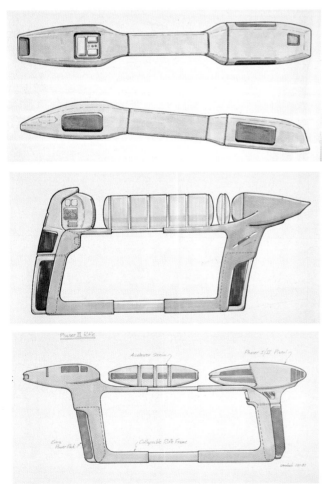

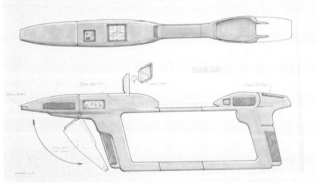

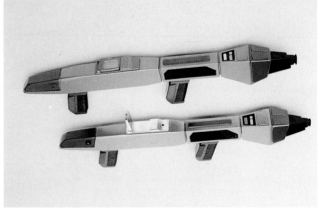

The development of the phaser rifle. Also seldom seen.

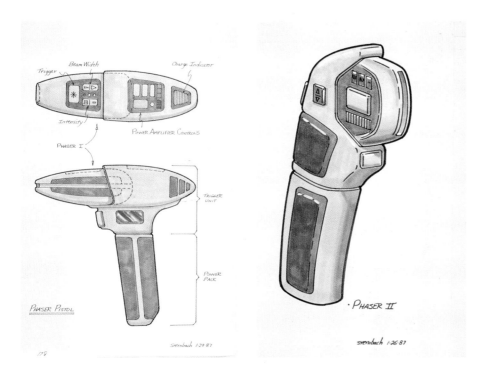

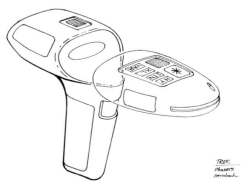

Initial pistol-style phaser variants. Note that Sternbach continued the design feature of the original phasers by having the small Phaser I fit into the larger Phaser II body.

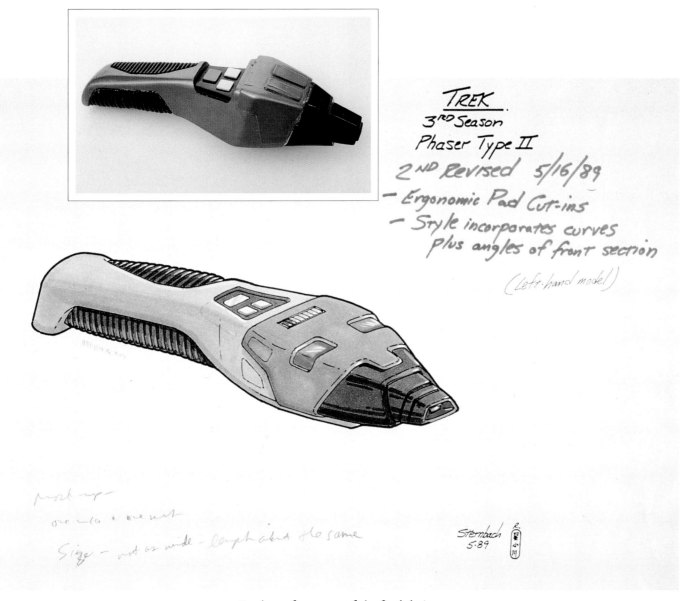

Further refinements of the final design

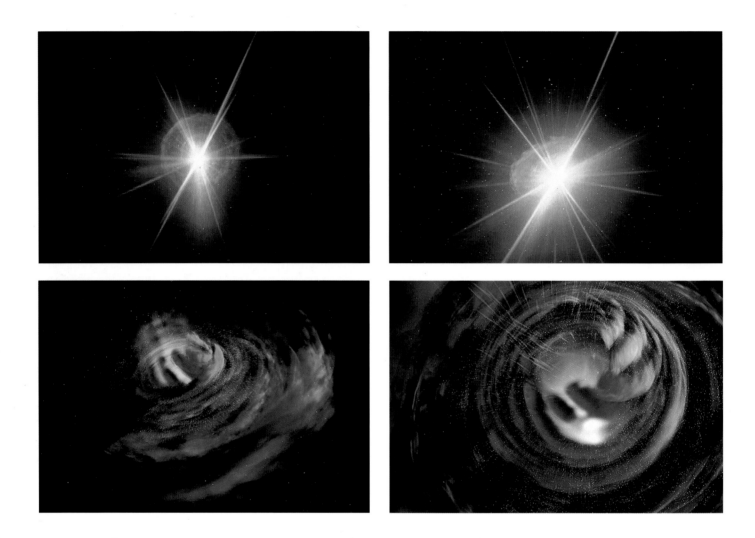

CHAPTER SIX

A NEW DIRECTION

STAR TREK: DEEP SPACE NINE
1993

Deep Space Nine, described in the script
only as "a strange intriguing object in
orbit of Bajor"

STAR TREK: DEEP SPACE NINE

*T*he *Next Generation* had proved the resilience and appeal of the STAR TREK universe—it was not dependent on its famous first crew for its success. The future of STAR TREK seemed unlimited.

But after five years of production, Paramount executives could see that their own future was more constrained. It made little economic sense to continue most television series for more than five or six seasons. Costs invariably increased,

storylines became exhausted, and the syndication market would fill with too many episodes chasing too few time slots. From a purely business perspective, *The Next Generation*'s days were numbered. But everyone's instincts said that STAR TREK still had not saturated its market.

In Paramount offices, the idea of a *third* STAR TREK series was discussed.

The Next Generation had shown that STAR TREK could thrive

without its original characters. Could a new series survive without a ship?

Rick Berman, who was Gene Roddenberry's handpicked successor as the person to guide STAR TREK after his death, and Michael Piller, *The Next Generation*'s most influential writer, created STAR TREK: DEEP SPACE NINE with exactly that challenge in mind.

For more than twenty-five years, one of STAR TREK's strengths

Science-fiction technology had caught up to television production, as these computer-generated final design drawings illustrate.

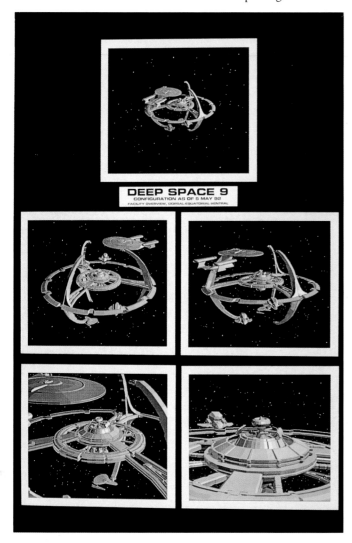

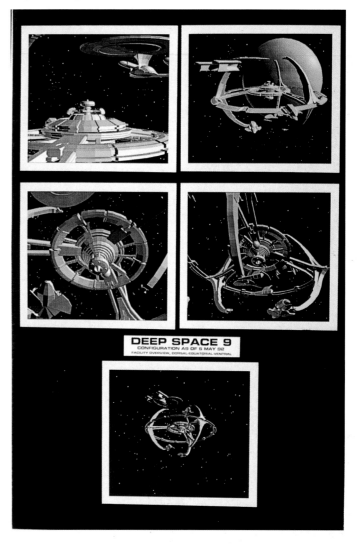

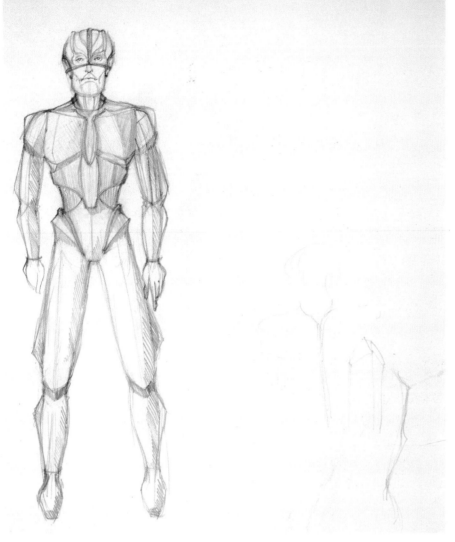

Robert Blackman's original costume design concepts for
Cardassians, first introduced on *The Next Generation*

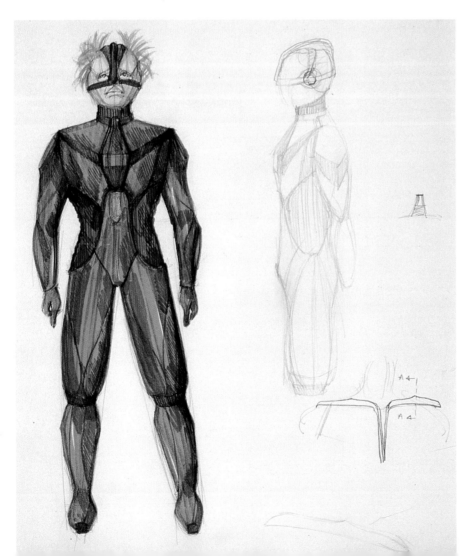

had been the detailed future universe through which the two *Enterprises* had traveled. Now STAR TREK's newest guides decided it was time to venture out into that universe, choose a pocket of it, and locate a new series there.

On the creative side, many of the elements Berman and Piller brought to *Deep Space Nine* had been established in *The Next Generation*: the use of Ferengi, Cardassians, Bajorans, and wormholes provided powerful strands of connection to the familiar universe first established by Roddenberry and since enjoyed by millions of viewers.

On the technical side, Berman and Piller were able to provide the same important connections in the look and feel of the latest series by drawing their key production people from the pool of talented individuals who had worked on *The Next Generation*.

Production designer Herman Zimmerman returned to design the dark and alien sets of the Cardassian space station. Michael Okuda led the art department's effort to come up with an entirely new system of Cardassian control surfaces and data displays. Director of photography Marvin Rush brought a rich lushness to the new sets. Costume designer Robert Blackman refined Starfleet uniforms once again and ably met the challenge of a never-ending stream of new alien races. Michael Westmore faced the same challenges in devising more and stranger alien races for Blackman to clothe. Visual-effects supervisor Robert Legato, along with Gary Hutzel, insured that the same high quality of visual effects that *The Next Generation* viewers had come to expect would be maintained and surpassed on the new series.

Deep Space Nine was the ultimate

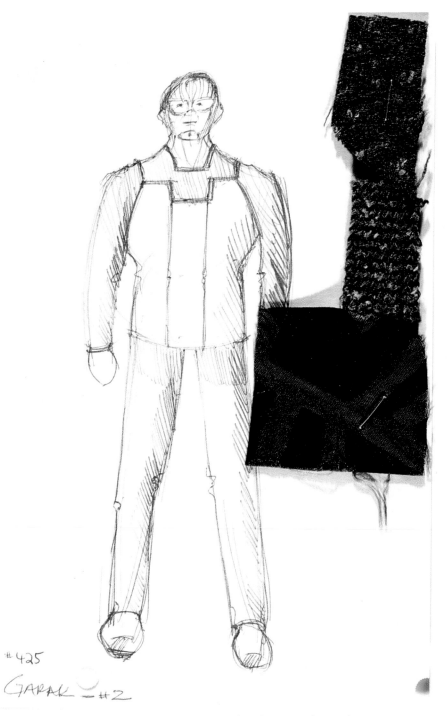

#425

GARAK #2

The first Cardassian civilian costume design, for plain, simple Garak

SKETCHES COURTESY OF ROBERT BLACKMAN

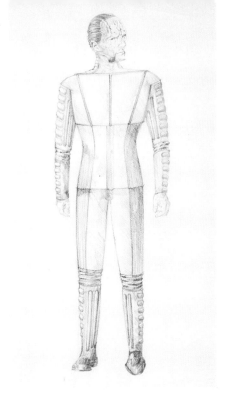

A Cardassian uniform variant

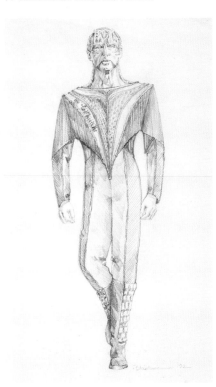

The new, more streamlined Cardassian uniform created for *Deep Space Nine*

distillation of the STAR TREK universe. The crew was united under one flag. There was no ship and there was little physical exploration. More importantly, what remained of STAR TREK was the firmly established background details of the twenty-fourth century, the ever-more-complex consistency of future history and technology, and the determination of Berman and Piller and their production crew to create an arena for adventure and storytelling that would live up to the STAR TREK name.

Which they did.

Deep Space Nine was an instant success, sharing many viewers with *The Next Generation*, adding new viewers of its own, demonstrating once and for all the deeply appealing richness of what Gene Roddenberry had wrought.

It wasn't the characters, it wasn't the ship.

STAR TREK was a state of mind. And millions still wanted to share it.

A NEW STARSHIP

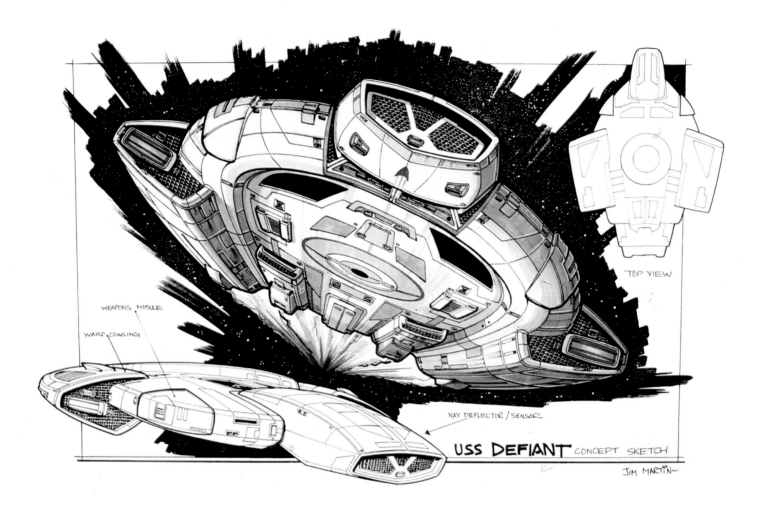

WEAPONS MODULE

WARP COWLING

TOP VIEW

NAV DEFLECTOR / SENSOR

USS **DEFIANT** CONCEPT SKETCH

JIM MARTIN

I dentifying a need to open up the storytelling possibilities for *Deep Space Nine*, the producers gave Sisko and his crew a new starship in the third season—the *U.S.S. Defiant*. According to the series' backstory, the *Valiant*-class ship had been developed to fight the Borg, and is now stationed at DS9 to help guard against the Dominion.

As these design sketches indicate, the *Defiant* was designated a *Valiant*-class vessel because that was the first name it was given.

RAIL CHROME OR STEEL

LIGHT

CARPET TO MATCH

DS9 DEFIANT TRANSPORTER

MARTIN

ALL ARTWORK DRAWN BY JIM MARTIN

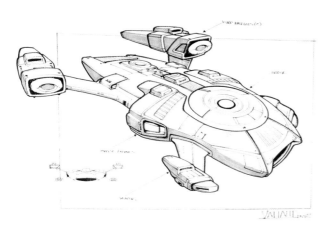

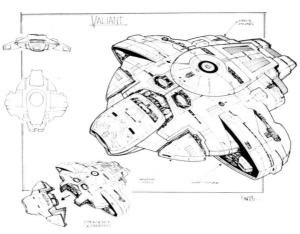

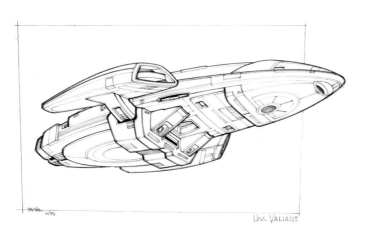

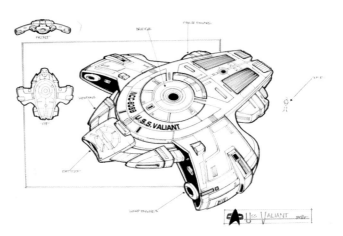

A SAMPLING OF SHIPS

Much has been said about how Gene Roddenberry's vision of humanity's future offers hope to us today. On a more prosaic note, STAR TREK productions offer hope to all who have ever sat in the back of the classroom, doodling spaceships while the teacher drones on. Someday, a lucky few might get paid to draw those spaceships, just like *Deep Space Nine* illustrator Jim Martin.

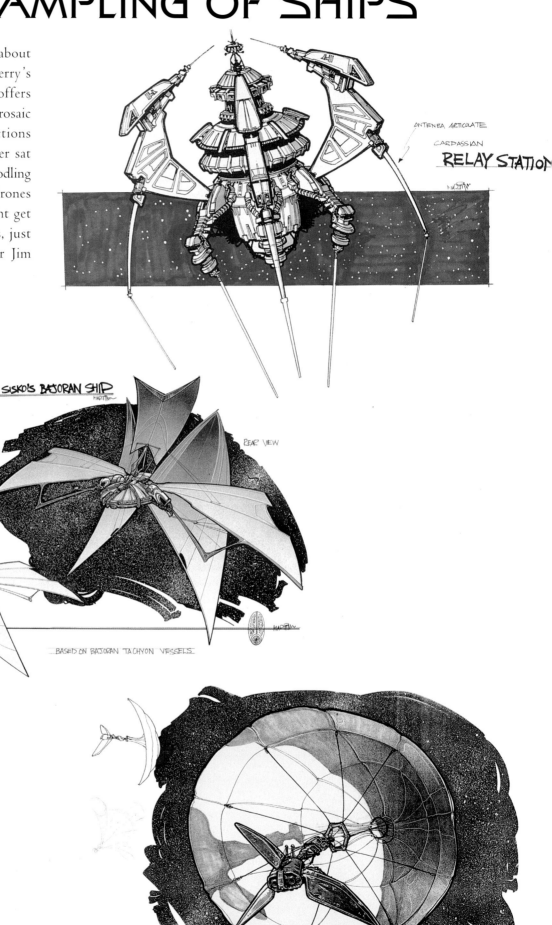

ANTENA ARTICULATE
CARDASSIAN
RELAY STATION

SISKO'S BAJORAN SHIP

REAR VIEW

FRONT

BASED ON BAJORAN TACHYON VESSELS

SISKO'S BAJORAN SHIP
"PARACHUTE-STYLE"

ALL ARTWORK BY JIM MARTIN

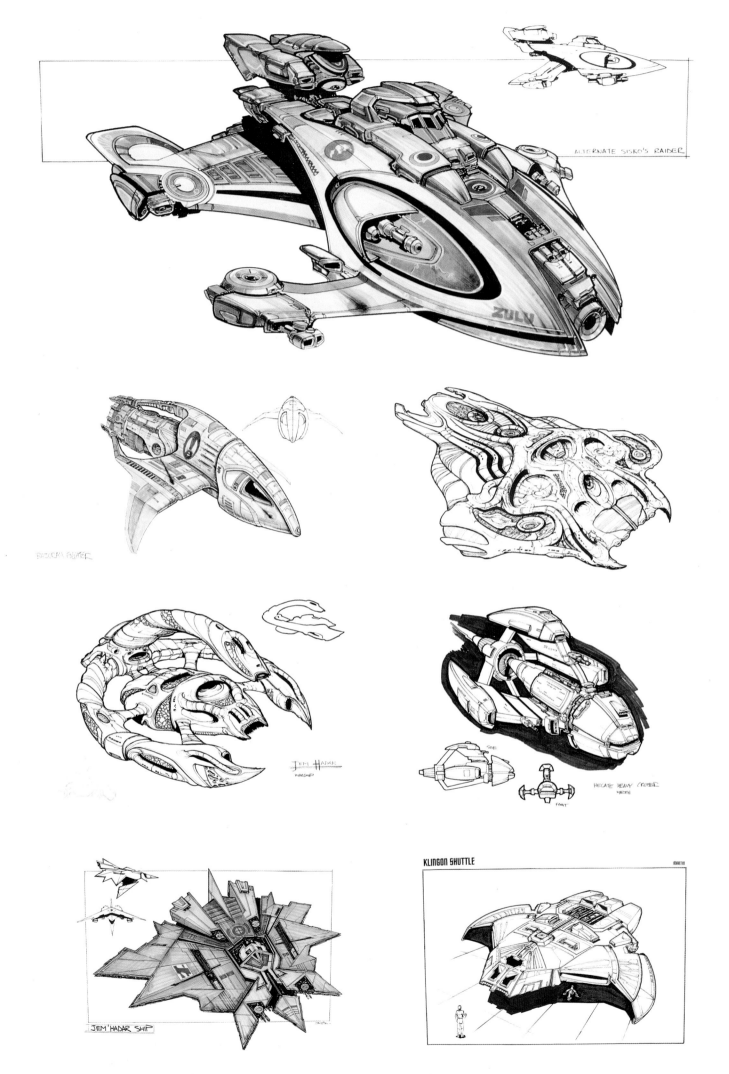

ALTERNATE SISKO'S RAIDER

ZULU

JEM HADAR
WARSHIP

HECATE HEAVY CRUISER

JEM'HADAR SHIP

KLINGON SHUTTLE

NEW SETTING, NEW UNIFORMS

As STAR TREK: DEEP SPACE NINE entered preproduction, once again Robert Blackman was called upon to modify the Starfleet uniforms originally designed by William Ware Theiss.

In keeping with the more informal environment of a Cardassian space station in constant need of repairs, Blackman created a new look that would evoke the feel of a worker's outfit more than a military uniform. Note the pushed-up sleeves and open collars on these sketches.

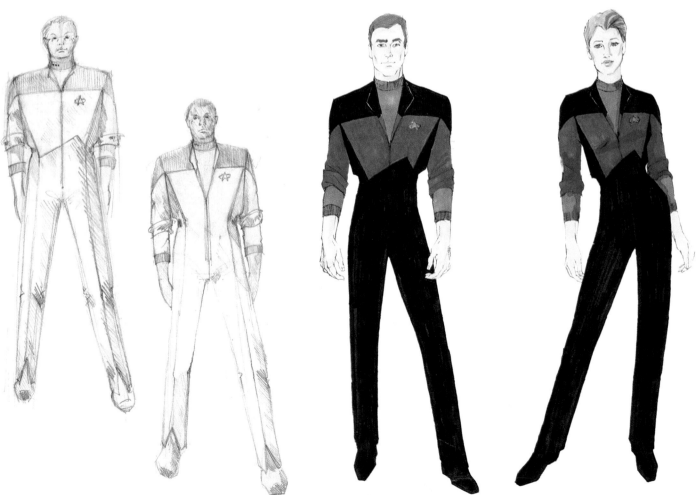

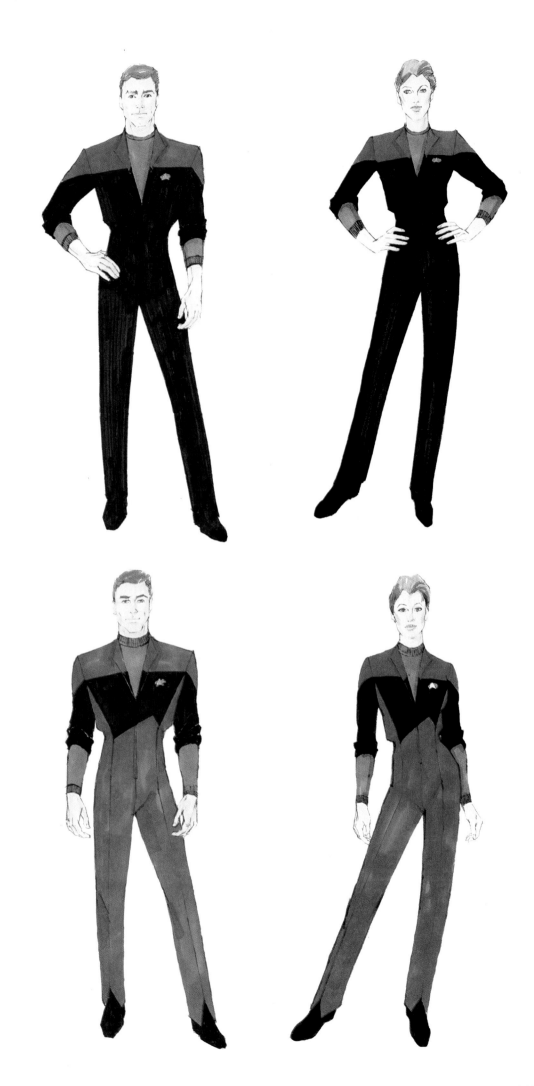

PENCIL SKETCHES BY ROBERT BLACKMAN. COLOR ARTWORK BY LOIS DEARMOND

STRANGE VISITORS FROM OTHER PLANETS

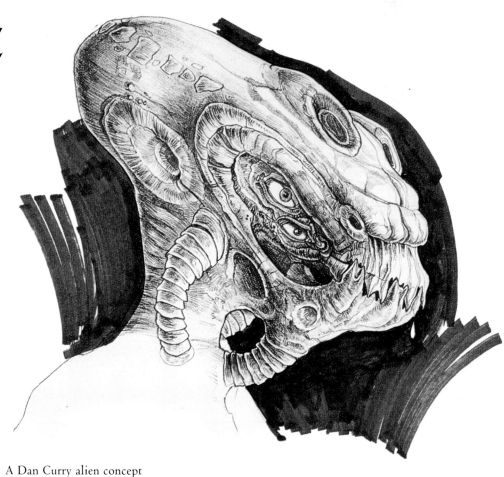

T he *DS9* station plays host to a wide variety of alien life-forms, not all of them humanoid.

A Dan Curry alien concept

While this might look like a weird alien plant to some, devotees of Roger Corman might detect an homage to the star of the 1956 movie *It Conquered the World*.

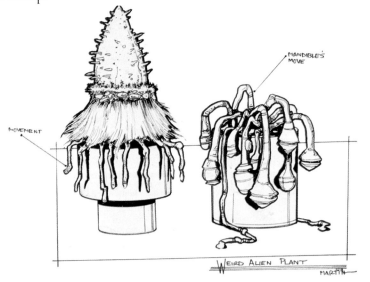

Cardassian voles

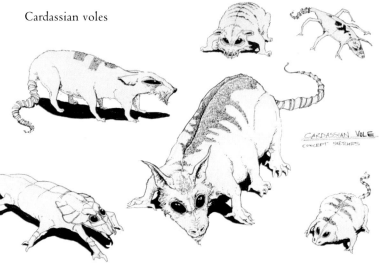

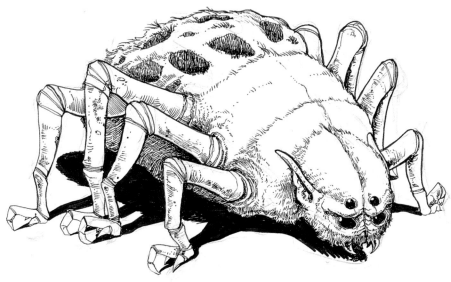

POLUKA SPIDER

This Poluka spider had many parents. With Jim Martin's design sketches as a guide, Property Master Joe Longo bought a battery-powered spider toy at a garage sale, had the motor stepped up, then turned the high-speed arachnid over to—who else?—makeup artist Michael Westmore. Westmore added latex features, extra eyes, and fur and spikes. For once, he had an actor who didn't complain about being buried in makeup.

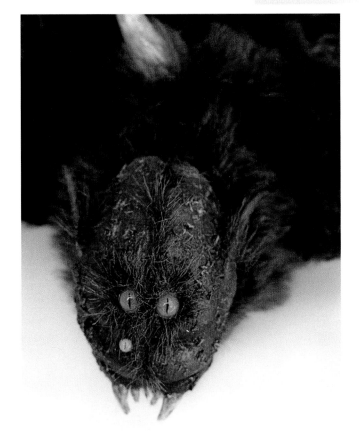

From the beginning, the producers knew there would be more aliens on *DS9* than on the *Enterprise*-D. Thus, in the series' preproduction stage, Michael Westmore had the rare luxury of planning ahead to create a rich set of background aliens, rather than responding to each script as it came along. Here's one of the regulars at Quark's.

NEW FROM STARFLEET R&D

The wear and tear of years of use requires key props on all STAR TREK projects to be replaced from time to time. The designers use these replacements as opportunities to update designs, as seen in these comparisons between the old Mark VI tricorders and the new and improved Mark VIIs.

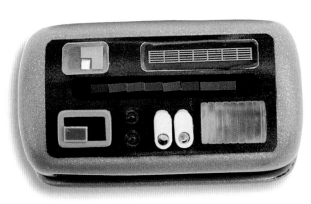

Some of the early Mark VI tricorders had a detachable sensor scanner, as seen in the upper part of this photograph. The new Mark VIIs have built-in sensor scanners.

PHOTOGRAPHY BY ROBBIE ROBINSON

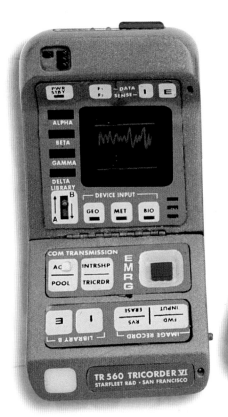

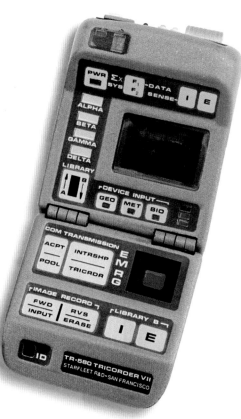

A side-by-side comparison of the two generations of tricorders from Starfleet R&D. Both versions include interior lights and LEDs to make for active displays during filming. Note that this particular Mark VI tricorder has an upside-down control surface. Chances are this fine detail will never show up on the typical television screen.

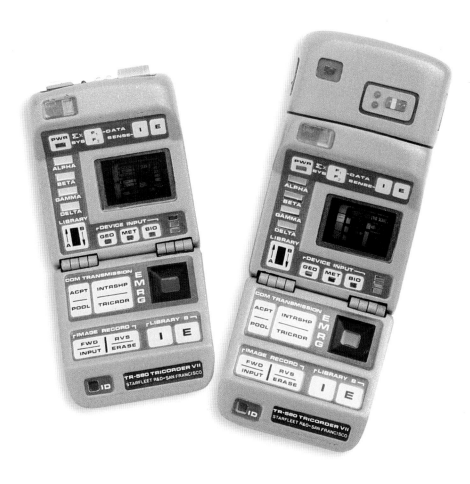

A side-by-side comparison of the Mark VII general tricorder and medical tricorder. The medical tricorder retains a version of the separate scanner originally found in the first Mark VIs.

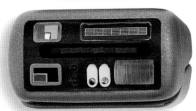

On the far left are two different models of the Mark VII general tricorder. The top tricorder is a "stunt" or "breakaway" model. This is simply a light and inexpensive plastic shell designed for use in the background, or to be worn by actors and stunt people in active situations where there's a chance it might be damaged. The shell does not open, has no electronic parts, and its finishing details consist of a simple sticker.

The working model with functioning lights and LEDs is below. To the right is the top of the medical tricorder with scanner in place.

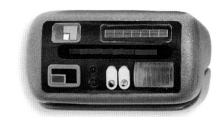

On the far right the scanner has been removed from the medical tricorder. The scanner has a separate battery and working LEDs for use in close-ups.

FUN WITH FERENGI

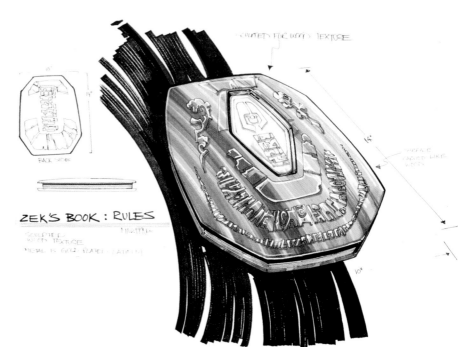

Actors, costumers, and make-up artists aren't the only ones to have fun when a new race and culture is explored on STAR TREK. Here's a sampling of some of the detailed props that have been created on *Deep Space Nine* to bring the Ferengi to life.

ZEK'S BOOK : RULES

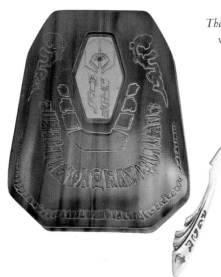

The New Rules of Acquisition, written by the Grand Nagus himself

Just in case you were wondering, when Ferengi die, their ashes are placed in these decorative containers and sold.

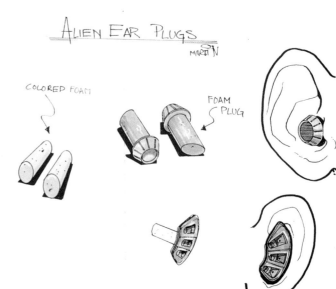

ALIEN EAR PLUGS

COLORED FOAM

FOAM PLUG

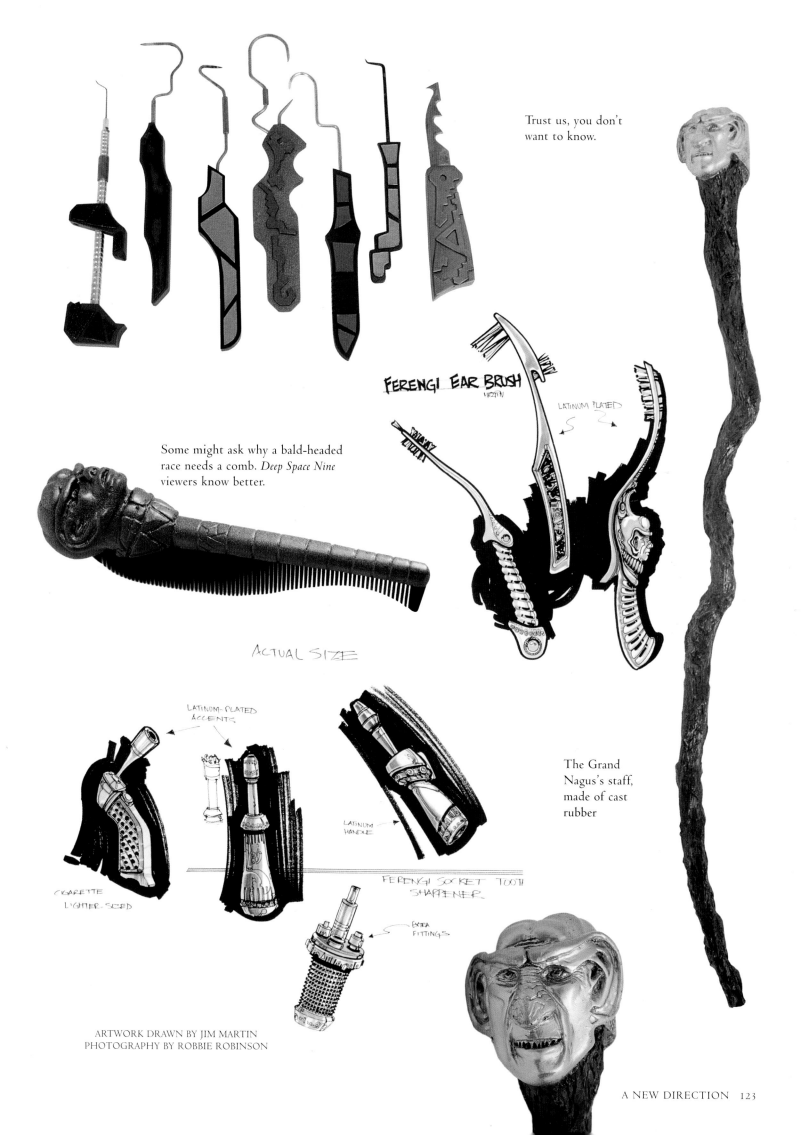

Trust us, you don't want to know.

FERENGI EAR BRUSH

LATINUM PLATED

Some might ask why a bald-headed race needs a comb. *Deep Space Nine* viewers know better.

ACTUAL SIZE

LATINUM-PLATED ACCENTS

LATINUM HANDLE

The Grand Nagus's staff, made of cast rubber

CIGARETTE LIGHTER-SIZED

FERENGI SOCKET TOOTH SHARPENER

EXTRA FITTINGS

ARTWORK DRAWN BY JIM MARTIN
PHOTOGRAPHY BY ROBBIE ROBINSON

A MORE DANGEROUS PLACE

eep *Space Nine*'s production designer, Herman Zimmerman, acknowledges Gene Roddenberry's wish that the weapons of STAR TREK avoid the look of twentieth-century armaments. However, he also acknowledges the requirements of presenting stories to a twentieth-century audience. To help establish threats and the possibility of action, it's often necessary for viewers to recognize weapons as weapons right away, without expository dialogue. Thus on *DS9*, STAR TREK weaponry has, for the most part, returned to recognizable designs.

...A Cardassian hand weapon designed by Rick Sternbach

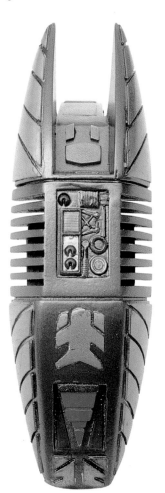

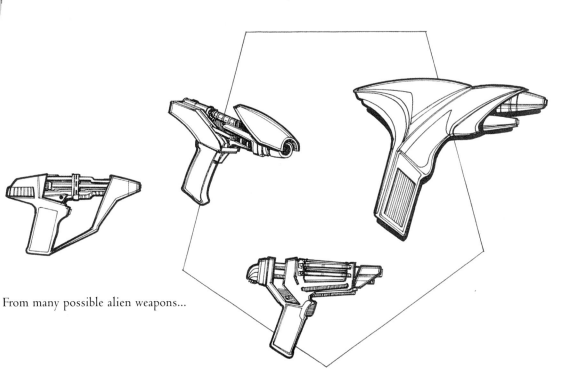

From many possible alien weapons...

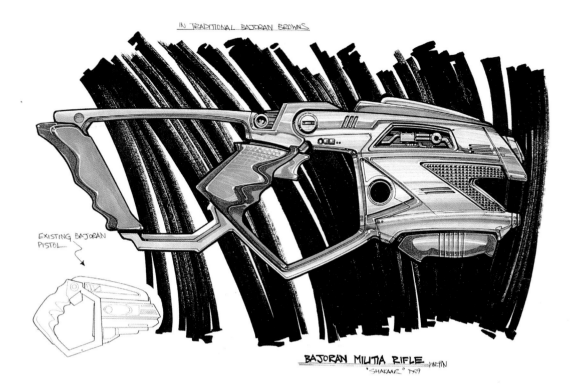

IN TRADITIONAL BAJORAN BROWNS

EXISTING BAJORAN
PISTOL

BAJORAN MILITIA RIFLE MARTIN
"SHAKAAR" DS9

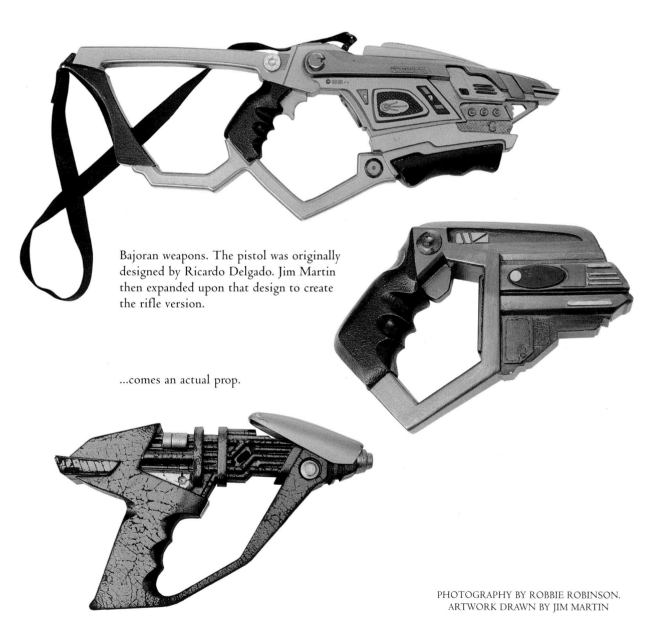

Bajoran weapons. The pistol was originally designed by Ricardo Delgado. Jim Martin then expanded upon that design to create the rifle version.

...comes an actual prop.

PHOTOGRAPHY BY ROBBIE ROBINSON.
ARTWORK DRAWN BY JIM MARTIN

WEAPONS, PART 2

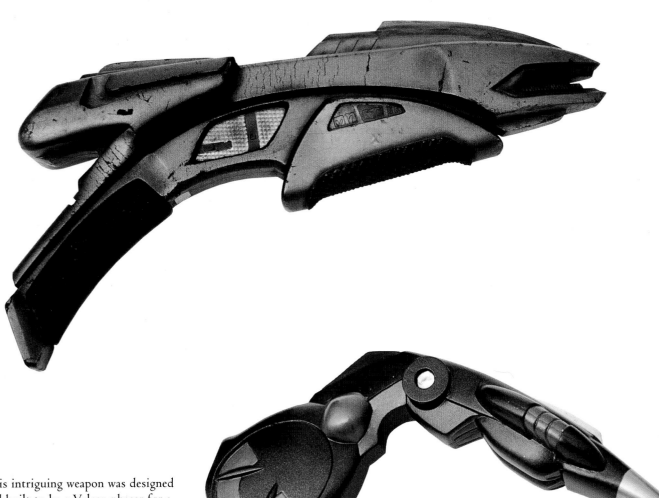

This intriguing weapon was designed and built to be a Vulcan phaser for a specific episode of *Deep Space Nine*. However, it was cut from that episode, and now is used as a generic alien weapon.

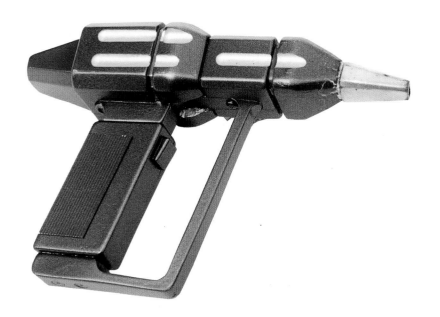

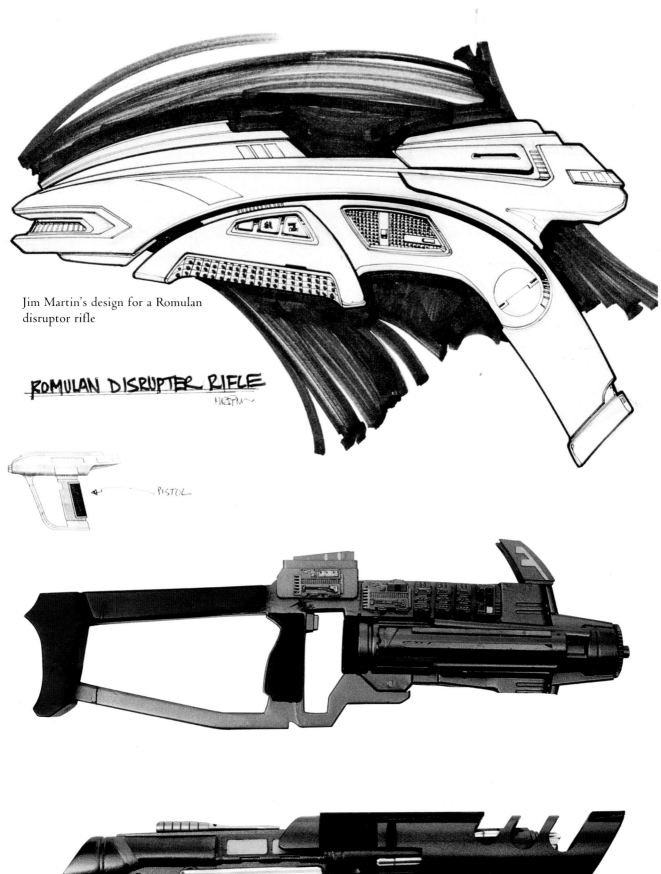

Jim Martin's design for a Romulan
disruptor rifle

ROMULAN DISRUPTER RIFLE
MARTIN~

PISTOL

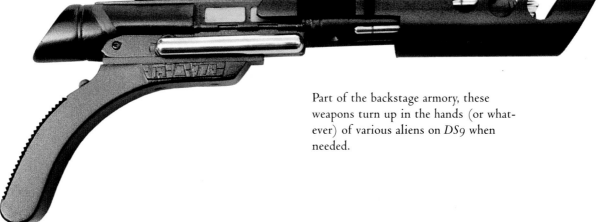

Part of the backstage armory, these
weapons turn up in the hands (or whatever) of various aliens on *DS9* when
needed.

IT'S THE LITTLE THINGS

ALL PHOTOGRAPHY BY ROBBIE ROBINSON

*D*eep Space Nine is no different from any other STAR TREK production in that every prop, no matter how inconsequential or ordinary, has to appear to belong to the twenty-fourth century.

Of course, on *DS9*, the word "ordinary" doesn't quite mean what it does on twentieth-century Earth.

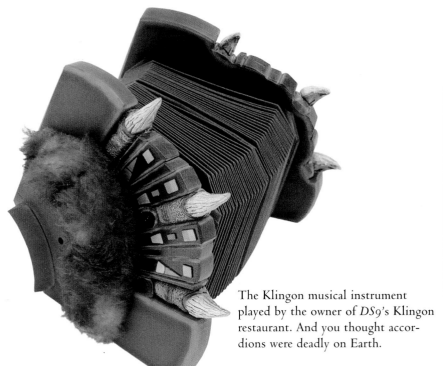

The Klingon musical instrument played by the owner of *DS9*'s Klingon restaurant. And you thought accordions were deadly on Earth.

The box in which the Bajoran Tears of the Prophets are reverentially kept

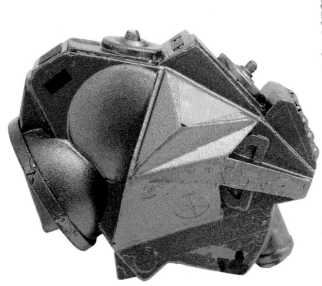

Property Master Joe Longo admits that even he doesn't really know what this tiny Cardassian contraption is, but it's very popular and has appeared in numerous episodes with numerous uses.

A self-sealing stem bolt and its protective cover. Whatever a stem bolt is, 100 gross are worth seven tessipates of Bajoran land.

More small Cardassian devices with diverse uses

One of Dr. Bashir's diagnostic devices

Odo's bucket, to which he used to have to retreat each day in his liquid form

While Gene Roddenberry was firm in his belief that by the twenty-fourth century Earth would have outgrown the need for money, the Ferengi had other ideas. Hence, the coin of the frontier—gold-pressed latinum.

FROM THE SHELVES OF QUARK'S PLACE

This selection of bottles comes from the *Deep Space Nine* prop department and further illustrates the meaningful detail STAR TREK designers enjoy adding to their work.

"Wee Bairns" was Scotty's pet name for the engines on the original *Enterprise*. The bottle with the leather wrappings is a re-creation of the Saurian brandy bottle from *The Original Series*. The original used red leather. The real whiskey bottle from which the Saurian version is made was originally produced as a commemorative design for the Dickel distillery of Tennessee.

The brown bottle with the mountain-and-leaf label design comes from one of Avery Brooks's favorite iced-coffee drinks.

PHOTOGRAPHS BY
ROBBIE ROBINSON

MULTIPLYING PADDS

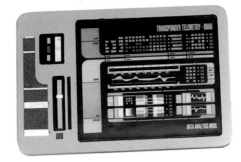

W hat began on the original *Starship Enterprise* as the ubiquitous wedge of black wood with a magic-slate writing surface has given rise to a variety of handheld computer interface devices, now known as padds. The acronym stands for Personal Access Display Device.

Starfleet padds used on *Deep Space Nine*

The fuzzy type on this sticker from the back of a Starfleet padd is acceptable as a finishing detail because the limited resolution of the television screen means that even perfect type could never be read. The phrase "Optical Data Net" is the source of the acronym ODN heard on current STAR TREK episodes and refers to the fiber-optic data transmission conduits used by Federation computer networks.

Further detail can be seen on the backs of the Klingon and Cardassian padds.

Clockwise from the upper left, these are Cardassian, Ferengi, Bajoran, and Klingon versions of padds.

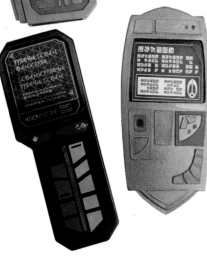

This Bajoran padd displays the face of a notorious Bajoran criminal who bears a striking resemblance to *Deep Space Nine*'s visual effects producer, Dan Curry.

CHAPTER SEVEN

THE NEVERENDING STORY

STAR TREK:
VOYAGER
1995

STAR TREK: VOYAGER

The Next Generation had shown that STAR TREK was not dependent on characters. *Deep Space Nine* had shown that it was not dependent on a ship. What else could be removed from the equation?

How about the known universe?

That was STAR TREK VOYAGER's point of departure.

With the fourth STAR TREK series—and by now there were no adjectives left to describe the

Though *Voyager's* visual-effects producer Dan Curry is as comfortable with a brush as he is with a computer keyboard, computer technology has helped speed up many of the design processes on the new series. These images are video prints showing Curry's electronic sketches of possible matte-painting elements to be added to a sequence in the pilot episode.

unlikely process of spinning off a third series from an original almost thirty years old—a ship was brought back into the mix, but virtually nothing else came with it.

The sector of the galaxy the *Voyager* travels through does not provide the comfort of the Federation, the security of Starfleet, or the familiarity of any of the established STAR TREK aliens and cultures built up over three decades. All the show offered was a small crew, only some of whom were bound by the STAR TREK ideals upon which the Federation was founded.

To no one's surprise, that was enough. This STAR TREK was an overwhelming success as well.

Once again, the threads of continuity behind the scenes served to create a solid new variation on the STAR TREK adventure. Creators

Rick Berman, Michael Piller, and Jeri Taylor, who had joined *The Next Generation* in its fourth season, drew on experienced personnel who had completed the seventh and final season of the second STAR TREK series to serve as the production crew for the fourth. Thus, unlike most fledgling series, the first season of *Voyager* went almost as smoothly on the technical end as an eighth year of *The Next Generation*.

Richard James, a six-year veteran as production designer on *The Next Generation,* directed the *Voyager* design effort to create a new starship, inside and out. Once again, Michael Westmore and Robert Blackman took up the challenge of visually creating and costuming an entire quadrant of never-before-seen alien races.

The lessons learned on *The Next*

The development of Robert Blackman's designs for *Voyager*'s resident alien, Neelix

Ethan Phillips as Neelix. Makeup design by Michael Westmore

Richard James's comprehensive sample book of colors and fabrics used on the *Voyager* set, to help contributing designers maintain consistency

Generation and *Deep Space Nine* resulted in the most visually and technically sophisticated sets ever built for a STAR TREK production, with video displays now joined to backlit Okudagrams. The constant glow and flicker of screens makes the new *Voyager* bridge the center of a vast information-gathering network, just as Matt Jefferies had imagined the bridge of the *Enterprise* to be thirty years earlier, before he discovered how much it would cost to have union projectionists behind each display.

Most significantly, as an indication of what the future of television production will be, the *Voyager* starship exists as a richly detailed miniature *and* as a computer-generated model indistinguishable to all but an expert eye. (Both versions are used in the impressive opening credits sequence. Can you spot the difference between the two?) For STAR TREK, the barrier of computer-

generated models had been broken in the movie STAR TREK GENERATIONS. But, less than a year later, the technology and associated costs of realistic CGI had made the technique practical for the small screen as well.

It seems fitting that STAR TREK has survived long enough to be affected by the same technology that was considered science fiction at its birth. Motorola flip-phones for communications, Newton personal digital assistants for handwritten computer access, magnetic resonance imaging for medical diagnoses at a distance...what was once the realm of writers' and artists' imagination is now part of our daily lives.

But though some of its original technology might be in danger of being eclipsed by science fact, STAR TREK lives on, as fresh and as enticing as it was in the beginning.

Perhaps it's because Gene

Roddenberry took it upon himself to acknowledge the passage of time in his creation, insuring that as STAR TREK's audience changes, so does the future it looks forward to.

Perhaps in *Voyager*, Berman, Piller, and Taylor have finally succeeded in reducing STAR TREK to the elusive single theme that might just unite all its different productions—our drive to journey elsewhere.

And, perhaps in the end, STAR TREK's enduring appeal might just be as simple as Captain Janeway's command at the end of *Voyager*'s pilot episode—"Set a course...for home."

The future will always be the place to which we all are traveling. As long as STAR TREK continues, it will always show us the way.

ALMOST THERE

These photos show a proof-of-concept design maquette constructed by Rick Sternbach of what was believed to be a final direction for the design of the new *Voyager* starship. As the level of finishing shows, it was never intended to be photographed in detail. Instead, this model, which had arisen out of dozens of production meetings, was intended to be a final stage in the approval of the ship's ultimate design. With modifications, it would then normally function as a guide for those model-builders bidding on the construction of the final ship.

However, in this case, the model served to inspire the producers to send Richard James's team back to their drawing boards with a new direction that would result in the final approved configuration for Starfleet's newest vessel.

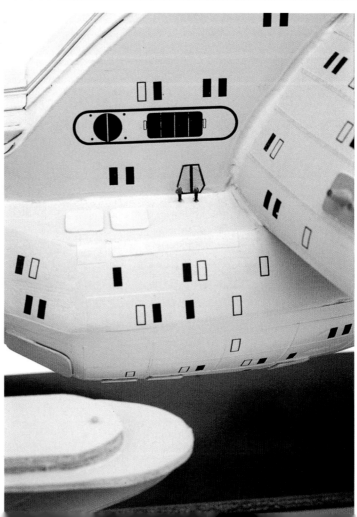

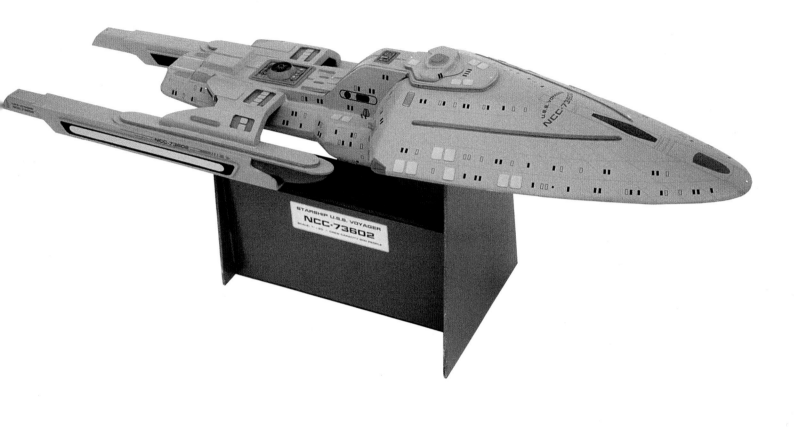

PHOTOGRAPHS BY ROBBIE ROBINSON

ONCE MORE UNTO THE

The heart of STAR TREK for the nineties, and beyond

After six years as production designer on *The Next Generation*, Richard James was no stranger to the legacy of STAR TREK and the production requirements of episodic television. Yet when given the assignment to create a new STAR TREK starship from the inside out, once again he faced the designer's nightmare—a totally blank page.

For his first meeting with *Voyager*'s creators and producers, James decided to push the boundaries of everything that had gone before. Did the bridge have to be dominated by a single large viewscreen? Could command functions be decentralized? Was it time to break the traditional bridge mold?

By exhaustively reexamining the dramatic requirements and technological underpinnings of the STAR

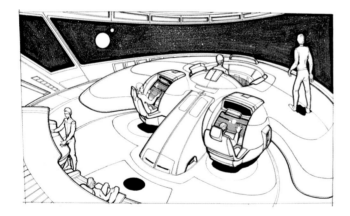

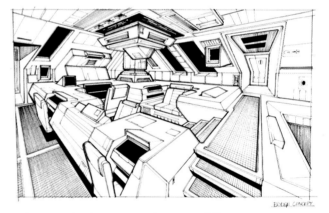

As part of the *Voyager* design team, Jim Martin created these preliminary bridge concept drawings, following Richard James's direction to question everything that had gone before in STAR TREK bridge design.

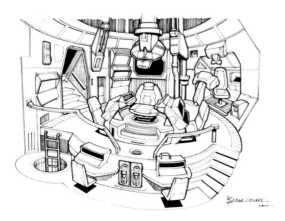

BRIDGE, DEAR FRIENDS

TREK bridge without preconceptions, James rediscovered the strengths of the basic template laid out by Matt Jefferies almost thirty years earlier. For better or worse, the television audience still related to the main bridge viewscreen as a windshield—thus it would be dead center and the point of reference toward which all bridge personnel faced.

But with the broad strokes of the bridge's layout firmly embedded in STAR TREK's past, Richard James and his team went on to bring a fresh new interpretation to the heart of any STAR TREK adventure, investing it with a sleek, efficient, and welcoming appearance that made *Voyager* something all its own—the STAR TREK for the nineties, and beyond.

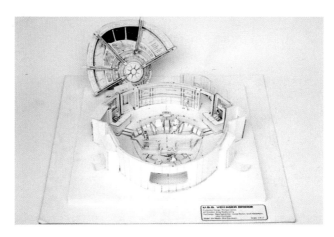

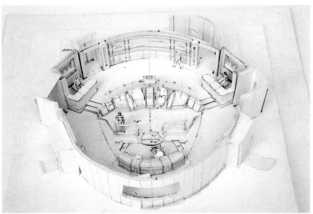

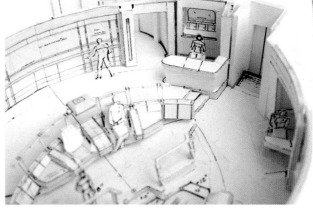

Before construction of the final set, this foamcore mock-up cut from the actual blueprints served as the final proof-of-concept model.

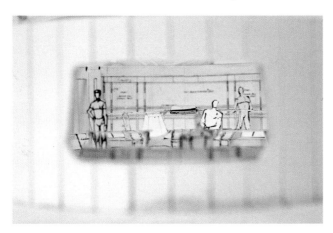

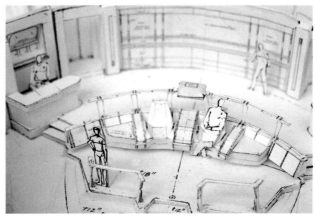

TOUCH-DOWN

In the days of *The Original Series,* it was too expensive to show the *Enterprise* landing on a different planet each week. Thus, the time-honored science-fiction invention of matter transmission was incorporated into the STAR TREK universe as the transporter. Not only was beaming down a landing party less expensive than landing a miniature starship, the procedure kept stories moving quickly. It also kept any STAR TREK spaceship—with the exception of shuttlecraft—from ever landing on a planet for the next thirty years.

However, from the beginning of the *Voyager*'s design process, as shown in the computer-generated images on this page, the idea of making her the first starship built to land on a planet was in the designers' minds.

It took only a few months for the story possibilities to inspire the writing staff, and a *Voyager* landing was originally scheduled to take place by the end of the first season.

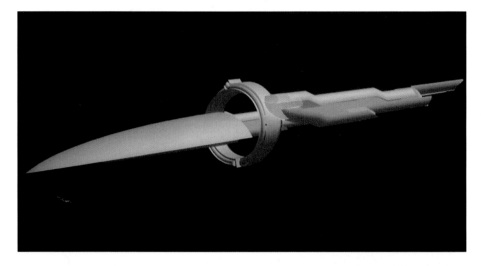

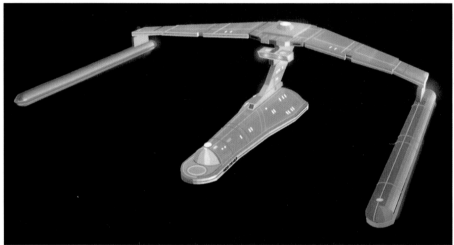

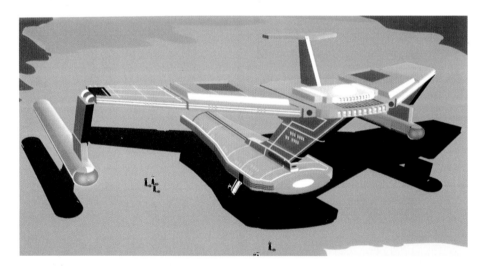

Early design concepts for *Voyager,* rendered through CGI by Rick Sternbach

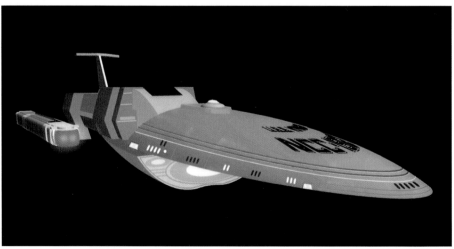

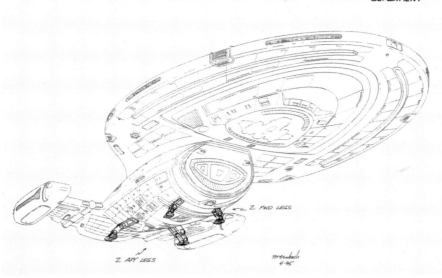

The *Voyager*'s designers cleverly included landing-leg panels on the blueprints of the ship, just in case the writers ever decided to take up the challenge of landing the ship.

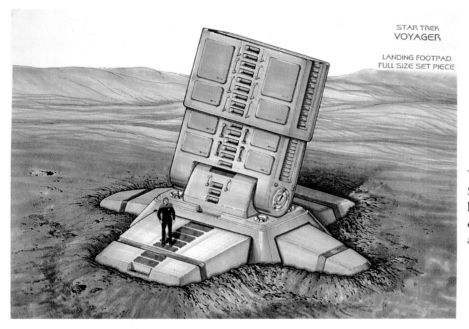

This concept painting by Rick Sternbach depicts a full-scale landing leg prop. However, in the final version of the episode "The 37's," the legs were added as computer-generated elements.

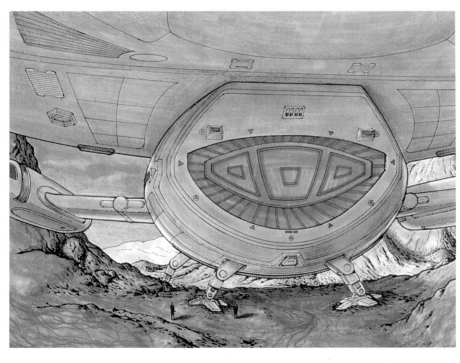

As this concept painting by Rick Sternbach suggests, four relatively small legs could not support the bulk of the *Voyager* without an assist from the starship's artificial gravity systems.

PILOT CONCEPTS

Concept drawings for the Array, which draws the *Voyager* into the Gamma Quadrant

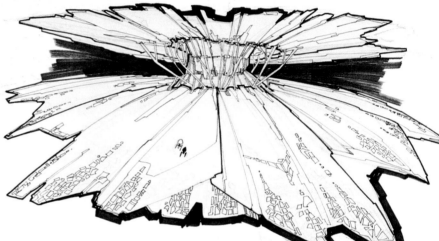

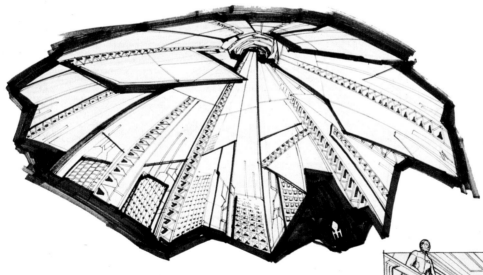

Concept drawing of the *Voyager*'s engine room, continuing the open two-story design originated by Mike Minor for the motion picture *Enterprise* into the workstation area.

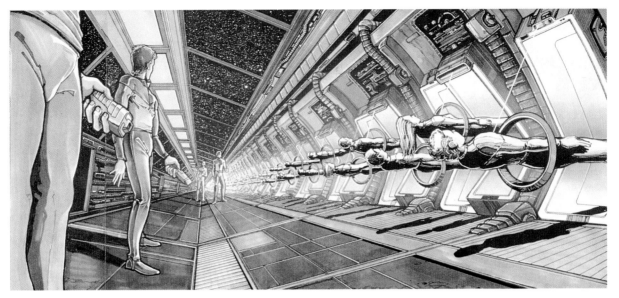

Three versions of a key set for the pilot episode: a concept drawing by Jim
Martin; a foamcore mock-up based on blueprints; and the final set

A DAN CURRY GALLERY

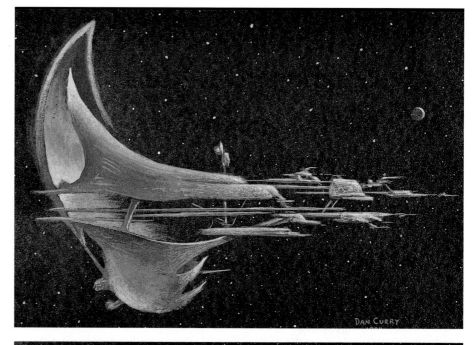

Dan Curry is the consummate Renaissance man of STAR TREK. Now visual-effects producer for both STAR TREK: DEEP SPACE NINE and STAR TREK VOYAGER, he joined *The Next Generation* in its first season as a visual-effects coordinator. Since then he has gone on to become a second-unit director, an episode director, a matte painter, visual-effects artist, production illustrator...and basically deserving of a book of his own.

These are some of Dan Curry's contributions to the design of the show.

Dan Curry's concept drawings for the Array the *Voyager* encounters in the pilot episode

Dan Curry's concept drawing for a large Kazon vessel—the Klingons of the Gamma Quadrant

DAN CURRY
1994

SELLING THE TITLE SEQUENCE

In the heat of production, design sketches can be and often are little more than shorthand pencil markings on napkins, script pages, or whatever other scraps of paper are nearby. However, at the beginning of the production process, when so many elements need to be established, input is required from people not always connected with the day-to-day operation of making a show. Thus, initial design sketches tend to be more detailed, so that little can be left to chance.

These storyboards were drawn by Rick Sternbach, following original sketches by Dan Curry, specifically to present the opening title sequence to the executives watching over the show. The end result based on these storyboards is one of the most visually dramatic sequences ever created for television.

4. We begin to see solar disk.

5. Major solar prominence bursts from surface; see more solar disk.

6. *Voyager* flies under arch of solar prominence.

7. Giant flare explodes from beneath camera; wipe to:

8. Title card against drifting starfield.

9. Title dissolves out; starfield continues drift.

10. *Voyager* cruises majestically into frame.

11. More details of the new Starfleet vessel are revealed.

12. The starship glides out of frame.

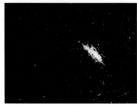

FADE IN:

1. Camera pans right as solar flare erupts.

2. Flare shoots past camera.

3. Flare dissipates; continue panning right.

DISSOLVE TO:

13. *Voyager* skims through thin layers of colored gas, leaving a wake. *Voyager* is at first obscured, but becomes more apparent as it nears the surface.

14. Camera pivots and pulls back as *Voyager* continues through the gas layers.

15. *Voyager* continues pushing through gas clouds.

16. *Voyager* leaves swirling eddies as it leaves the gas cloud.

DISSOLVE TO:

17. Camera moves down over soft nebular clouds; a small rocky moon drifts through background.

18. Continue moving down to reveal more fragmentary moons in orbit of a gas-giant world.

19. Camera reveals foreground moon orbiting gas giant.

20. *Voyager* swoops over strange landscape; moon is possibly only a few miles across.

PAN UP AND DISSOLVE TO:

21. Drifting starfield; camera moves up and left.

22. Camera begins passing through icy ring plane.

23. Camera continues pass through rings.

24. Reveal *Voyager,* pan with ship from left to right.

24A. *Voyager* heads farther into distant space.

DISSOLVE TO:

25. Moon pans left, creating eclipse and flare. Reveal *Voyager* out of light. Ship passes background planet.

26. *Voyager* turns and heads toward distant nebula.

27. *Voyager* bends wings to prepare for warp speed.

28. *Voyager* jumps to warp speed.

PART TWO

THE BIG PICTURE

STAR TREK ON FILM

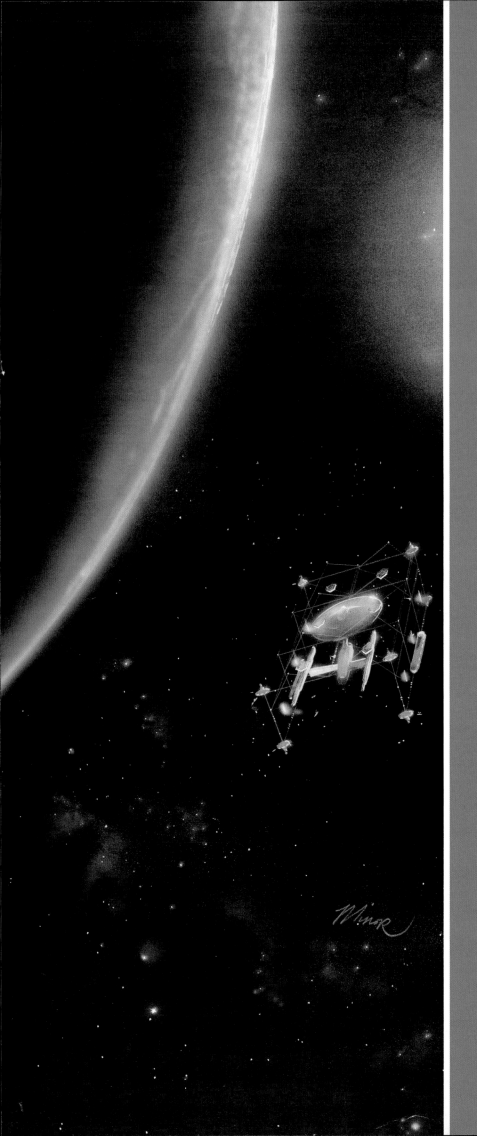

CHAPTER ONE

THE DREAM FULFILLED

STAR TREK: THE MOTION PICTURE 1979

OVERLEAF An early Mike Minor painting showing the space office complex, a travel pad, and the *Enterprise* in spacedock

Uncertainty over the final script during production led to this carefully story-boarded and filmed "Memory Wall" sequence being cut from STAR TREK: THE MOTION PICTURE. As time and money pressures continued to build, other elaborately planned sequences were dropped even before they could be filmed.

STAR TREK:
THE MOTION PICTURE

As early as *The Original Series'* third season, Gene Roddenberry had spoken of making a STAR TREK motion picture. At the 1968 World Science Fiction Convention held over the Labor Day weekend in Oakland, California, he drew enthusiastic applause when he told a rapt audience his plans for filming a prequel to the series, telling the story of how Kirk and his crew had met at Starfleet Academy. For that weekend at least, STAR TREK was on a roll. But the Tuesday after Labor Day, the real world intruded and kept the opening of the first STAR TREK movie at bay for more than a decade.

Yet the *idea* of a STAR TREK movie continued as Roddenberry's—and Paramount's—dream throughout that decade, sometimes coming tantalizingly close to becoming reality, only to be snatched away by the capriciousness of Hollywood deal making.

In the spring of 1975, Paramount entered into a deal with Gene Roddenberry in which he would write the script for a low-budget STAR TREK feature, tentatively to cost between two to three million dollars.

When Roddenberry delivered his script—*The God Thing*—in August of that year, Barry Diller, the president of Paramount, rejected it, but asked Roddenberry to write another. At the same time, the studio also invited other writers, including Harlan Ellison, Robert Silverberg, and STAR TREK veteran John D. F. Black, to try their hand at pitching a suitable story.

In the meantime, Gene Roddenberry went back to work on a second script, this time with cowriter Jon Povill. Once again, Paramount passed. But despite the trouble they were having finding a script, the studio's interest in making a STAR TREK movie continued to grow.

By the time the first space shuttle had been christened *Enterprise* in September 1976, Paramount officially green-lighted a STAR TREK movie with a budget of $10 million.

Jerry Eisenberg was hired to produce and Phil Kaufman to direct, with Ken Adam as production designer and Ralph McQuarrie as production illustrator. (Some of their preliminary design work for the new *Enterprise* can be seen in Chapter Four: The STAR TREK That Never Was.) The writers for this new film venture were Chris Bryant and Allan Scott, who had also written *Don't Look Now*. Their script was titled *Planet of the Titans,* and ultimately it, too, was rejected by Paramount.

About this time, the first *Star Wars* film was released and became an instant blockbuster. Paramount executives, believing that the motion-picture audience could support only one major science-fiction franchise, decided that the tremendous impact of *Star Wars* doomed any chance of STAR TREK's succeeding at the box office.

But they also believed there was still value in the franchise, so on June 10, 1977, STAR TREK:

PHASE II was announced—a brand-new syndicated STAR TREK television series (see Chapter Four) to be produced by Roddenberry and Harold Livingston.

Of the thirteen episodes initially ordered for the series, one began as a revision of a story that Roddenberry had developed for another science-fiction series he had created, *Genesis II*. Though the pilot for the series had been made, *Genesis II* had not been picked up, and the story, "Robot's Return," had gone nowhere.

But Roddenberry asked novelist Alan Dean Foster to revise the story to make it suitable for the new STAR TREK series. Foster's revised story, now called "In Thy Image," was greeted so enthusiastically by Roddenberry and Livingston that the decision was made to develop Foster's treatment as the new series' two-hour pilot episode.

But at the same time the creative development of the new series was building, the business structure behind it was unraveling.

Paramount had planned to make STAR TREK: PHASE II the cornerstone of a new, fourth television network (as, in fact, STAR TREK VOYAGER would become the cornerstone of a fifth network, UPN, eighteen years later). But the proposed new network was not coming together as securely as Paramount had hoped, and plans for it were canceled, leaving *Phase II* a series without a home. At the same time, 1977's other science-fiction blockbuster, *Close Encounters of the Third Kind*, opened to box-office numbers rivaling those of *Star Wars*.

All at once, Paramount executives saw the error of their ways. *Star Wars* had not been a one-time wonder. *Close Encounters* proved that the audience for science-fiction films

was ongoing. Determined to tap into that market with a STAR TREK feature, Paramount executives quickly made the decision to green-light *Phase II*'s pilot episode, "In Thy Image," as a theatrical release, eventually bumping its television budget up to $15 million, of which almost two-thirds would go to special effects.

What the executives didn't know was that they now had the proverbial tiger by the tail. And by the time the tiger was unleashed on the public, that $15 million budget would have ballooned to $44 million. (To be fair, the movie itself cost only about $25 million to make. The extra $20 million or so represented all the costs Paramount had incurred over the years on all the other STAR TREK projects that were not made.) In contrast, that first *Star Wars* film had cost only $9 million.

Looking back over sixteen years, it's easy to see where the first STAR TREK film went wrong. At the same time, since it launched the industry's most successful science-fiction-film franchise and paved the way for STAR TREK's triumphant and multifaceted return to television, it's easy to be forgiving of those mistakes. Generally, reviewers panned STAR TREK: THE MOTION PICTURE. The *Washington Post* called it "a passive adventure." *New York* magazine headlined its review "Voyage to the Bottom of the Barrel." And Gene Siskel proclaimed that when Persis Khambatta was not on the screen, "the film teeters toward being a crashing bore."

Yet the film set an all-time record with an opening weekend gross of $11.8 million, grossed a spectacular $17 million at 850 theaters in its first week, and ended up as the second top-grossing film of

1979, beaten only by *Kramer vs. Kramer*. True, its total domestic box-office take of $80 million was not enough to offset its cost, but once foreign and television earnings had been added, to say nothing of the ongoing video sales, there is no question that the movie was a resounding success by the only definition that really matters in Hollywood—it had found its audience.

So how did it happen that a movie trounced by reviewers and "serious" filmgoers scored so well with its fans? For the same reason so much of STAR TREK succeeds—for all its shortcomings, *The Motion Picture*'s heart was unquestionably in the right place. If the film was slow, at least it was respectful. If it was too reminiscent of *The Original Series* episode "The Changeling," at least it let fans revisit the *Enterprise* in wide-screen 70mm. And if the mad rush to meet the release date resulted in edits and cuts that made the story line hard to follow, at least the entire crew had been reassembled and sent out on a continuing mission.

In this case, "the entire crew" doesn't just refer to the actors, either. For many of the behind-the-scenes talents who worked on *The Original Series* had also been brought back for this new outing. Many, such as production illustrator Mike Minor, had returned to Paramount to work on STAR TREK: PHASE II, only to see their new television sets torn apart and rebuilt to withstand the more intense scrutiny of the motion-picture camera. Fred Phillips, the makeup artist who had created Mr. Spock's appearance in the first pilot, was also back casting pointed ears. And though the *Enterprise* herself, also remade for *Phase II*, was ultimately scrapped and redesigned

and rebuilt by a new group of designers, updated features such as her new, flattened nacelles and tapered struts echoed the sketches of her original designer, Matt Jefferies.

To re-create the magic of *The Original Series,* Gene Roddenberry had gathered together those who had made that magic in the first place.

And they did it again.

When STAR TREK: THE MOTION PICTURE premiered, on December 7, 1979, Roddenberry's creation finally transcended the medium of its creation, ceasing to be a mere television series, at last becoming a true phenomenon.

A NEW ENTERPRISE TAKES FLIGHT

The level of detail that can appear on a movie model is far greater than that which can appear on a model for television. Thus, the *Enterprise* built for the unproduced second television series was set aside and a new model was constructed.

The movie *Enterprise* still followed the basic updating initially developed by Matt Jefferies and Joe Jennings, but new and more detailed modifications were added by a variety of designers from Abel & Associates and Magicam. The illustrations on these pages show some of the contributions made by Andrew Probert.

ARTWORK COURTESY OF ANDREW PROBERT

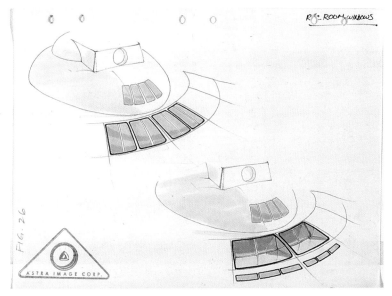

FIG. 26

ASTRA IMAGE CORP.

REC-ROOM WINDOWS

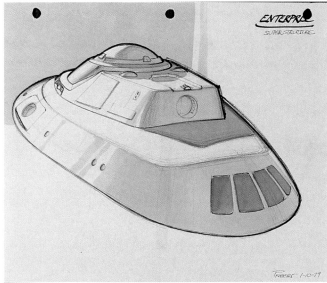

ENTERPRISE
SUPER-STRUCTURE

PROBERT 1-10-79

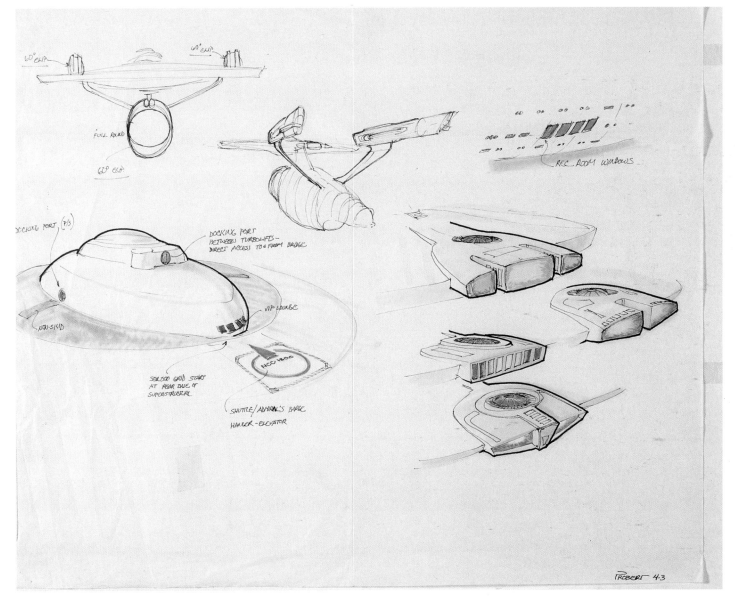

60" ENT.

60" ENT.

FULL ROUND

60" ELA.

DOCKING PORT (P/S)

DOCKING PORT
BETWEEN TURBOLIFTS—
DIRECT ACCESS TO & FROM BRIDGE

REC. ROOM WINDOWS

NON-SKID

VIP LOUNGE

SENSOR GRID START
AT REAR EDGE OF
SUPERSTRUCTURE

NCC-1800

SHUTTLE/ADMIRAL'S BARGE
HANGER-ELEVATOR

PROBERT 4-3

SELF-ILLUMINATION

As a special photographic effects director, Douglas Trumbull asked himself what kind of light source would be illuminating the *Enterprise* in deep space. The answer was—none. Thus, he came up with the movie *Enterprise*'s system of self-illumination, similar to the tail-fin floodlights used on commercial airliners today. Without it, the *Enterprise* would be only a dark silhouette among the stars.

ARTWORK BY ANDREW PROBERT
COURTESY OF THE ARTIST

NEW DIRECTIONS

One month after Paramount announced that STAR TREK would return as a motion picture, these concept drawings were completed, showing detailed reworkings of the bridge and engine room sets already built for the television series.

While the Mike Minor control stations have been retained on the bridge, note the addition of the realistic detail of safety lights on the bridge stairs, and the proposed new chair supports.

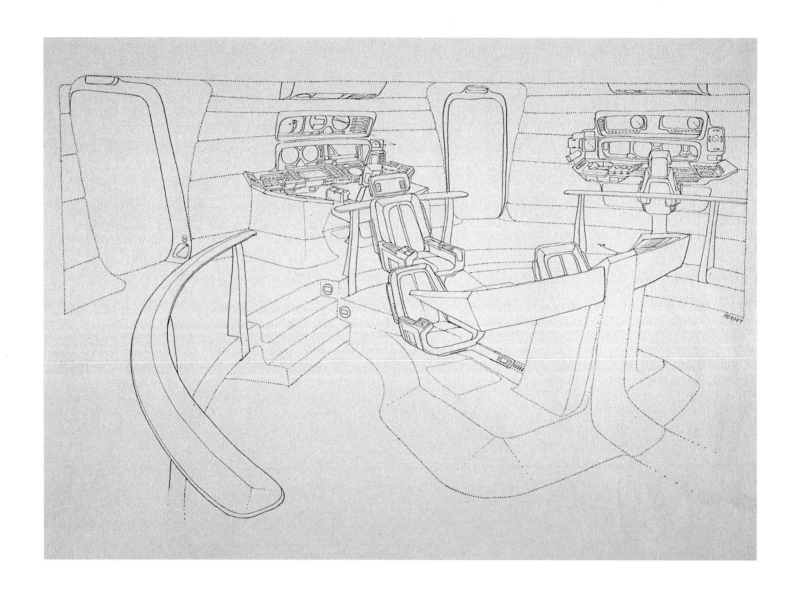

INSIDE THE NEW ENTERPRISE

The final appearance of the new *Enterprise* interiors combines the design input of original designer Matt Jefferies, as well as Mike Minor, Joe Jennings, movie production designer Harold Michaelson, and director Robert Wise. Control details were developed by Lee Cole,

and control screen readouts by Cole, along with Minor, Rick Sternbach, and Jon Povill.

The attitude dome on the bridge ceiling was created by Harold Michaelson and designed by Mike Minor. The redesigned chairs contain Michaelson's automatic restraint system—the first and only time any type of bridge seat restraint has appeared in a STAR TREK production—as well as a unique, vertebrae-like structure designed with set decorator Linda DeScenna. (Supposedly they provide massage functions.)

Michaelson was also responsible for redesigning the *Enterprise* corri-

dors, which had been built for the second series. Ironically, Gene Roddenberry had been unhappy with the new corridors, because he felt they made the *Enterprise* look too much like a hotel. Michaelson's redesigns ended up being used in *The Next Generation*'s *Enterprise*-D, which was criticized as looking even more like a hotel.

Michaelson was also responsible for the revamped look of the transporter room. He placed the operators in a shielded control area to help convey the idea of the fantastic energies being employed by the technology.

MAKING IT ALL FIT

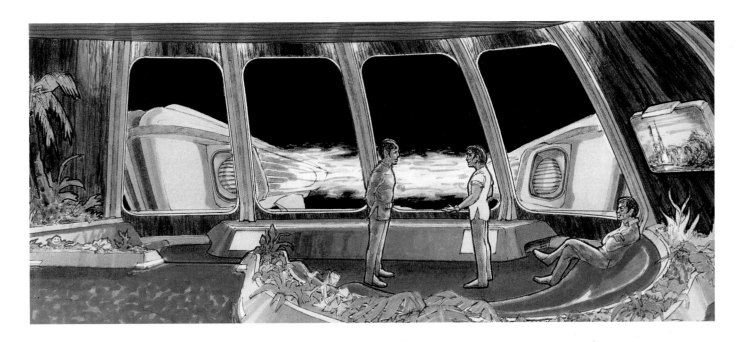

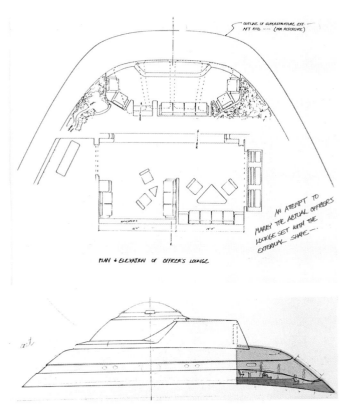

PLAN + ELEVATION OF OFFICER'S LOUNGE

AN ATTEMPT TO MARRY THE ACTUAL OFFICER'S LOUNGE SET WITH THE EXTERIOR SHAPE.

A key concern for all STAR TREK set designers is that the sets they build somehow conform to the structure of the starship they are supposed to exist within. Here we see Andrew Probert's development sketches for an officers' lounge in the saucer section's upper dome. The production photograph shows how the room was finally—and less expensively—constructed.

ALL ARTWORK BY ANDREW PROBERT
COURTESY OF THE ARTIST

CARGO BAY
SKETCH TESTS

Even after the set had been designed and built, the production staff experimented with different cargo-bay configurations, as shown on these pages.

The actual set, bare walls and all

One possible configuration

ARTWORK BY ANDREW PROBERT. COURTESY OF THE ARTIST

OVERLEAF Another Mike Minor concept painting of a travel pod leaving the space office complex

Probert at work on the painting on the previous page

An unused configuration, hindered by the fact that no such window had been built into the movie model

Another view of Probert's design

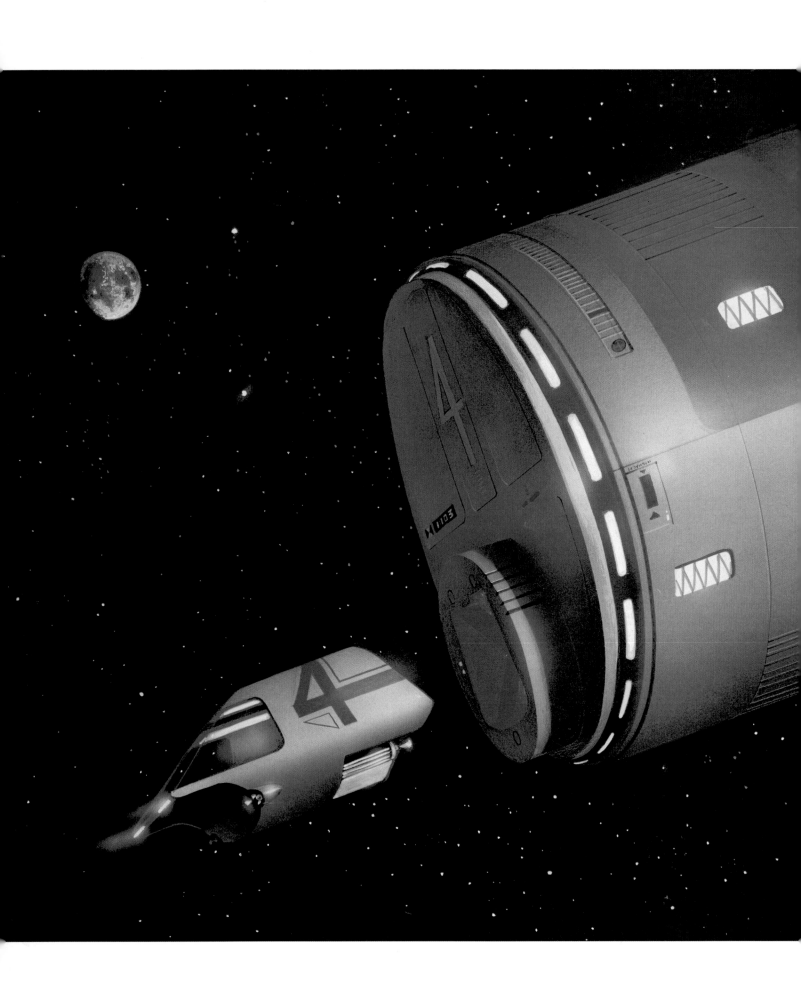

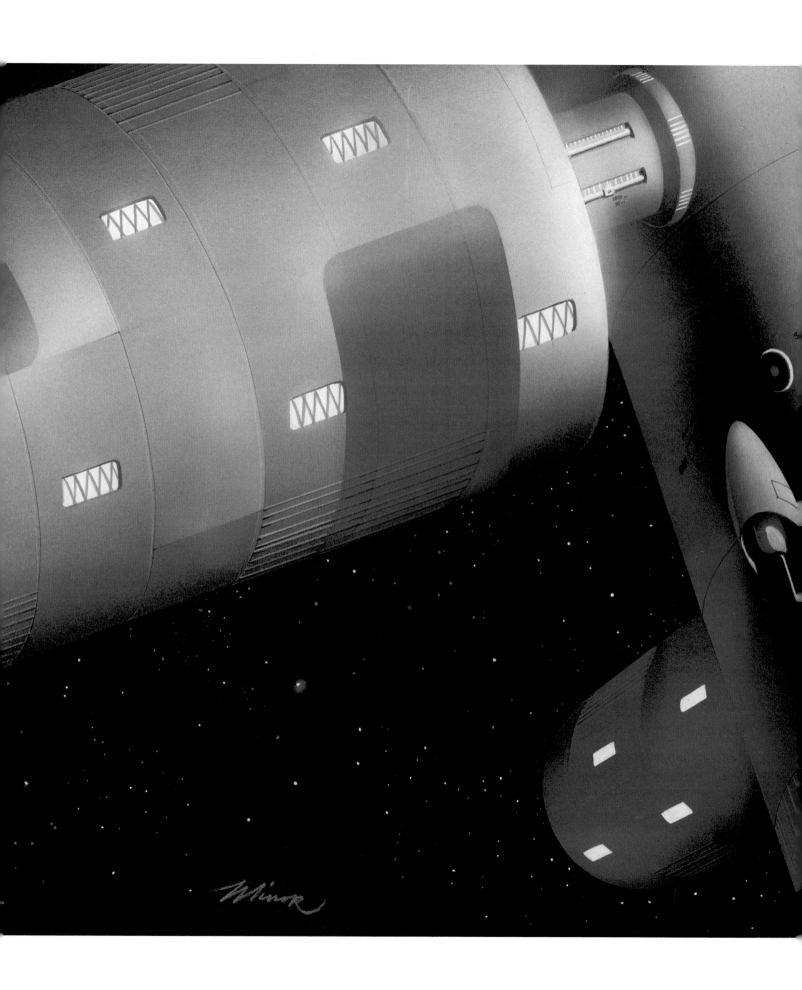

COMMUTING IN SPACE

STAR TREK's transporters are a wonderful invention for speeding a story along, but sometimes a story should move at a more leisurely pace. Admiral Kirk's —and the audience's—first look at the refitted *Enterprise* is one of those moments. Thus, with the *Enterprise's* transporters not working, Scotty takes Kirk to the *Enterprise* in a travel pod, setting the stage for a detailed tour of the starship's exterior.

For some close-up shots of the travel pod sequence, live footage of William Shatner and James Doohan was matted into the travel pod's viewport. For other, long-distance shots, detailed puppets filled in for the actors.

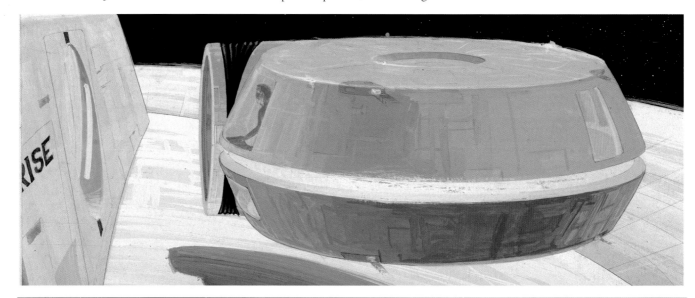

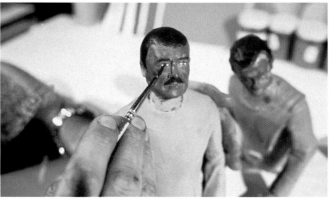

ARTWORK COURTESY OF ANDREW PROBERT

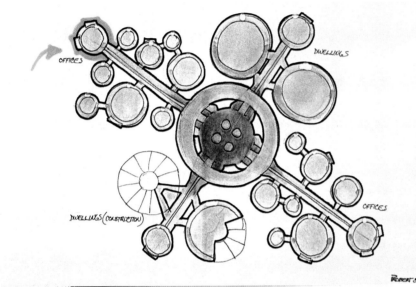

THE ORBITAL OFFICE

Like Spacedock and the *Enterprise,* an orbital office complex was also built for the second television series. But the demands of motion-picture quality once again required a new model.

The final model as constructed by Magicam…

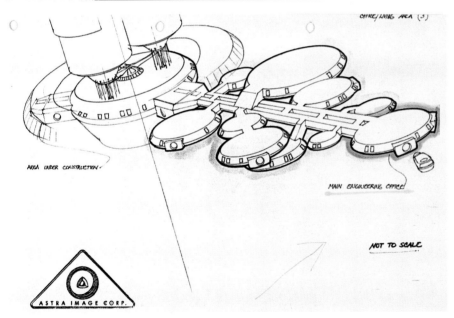

Preliminary office complex designs by Andrew Probert

…and as it appears in the movie

SPACEDOCK—THE $200,000 STORY DEVICE

To provide an explanation for the differences between the original *Enterprise* and the new version, which was to appear in the second series, the writers of the television movie, "In Thy Image," came up with the idea of the *Enterprise* having been refitted in an orbital drydock—Spacedock. A Spacedock was built for use in the television production, but was set aside when the latest STAR TREK project became a feature film, and a new version was built by Magicam.

An early Andrew Probert concept painting for the movie Spacedock, dated April 1978. Note that the finishing details of the new movie *Enterprise* have yet to be finalized, specifically around the navigation dome and the main sensor dish.

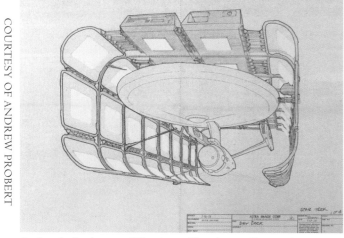

Probert's further modification of his design, from July 1978

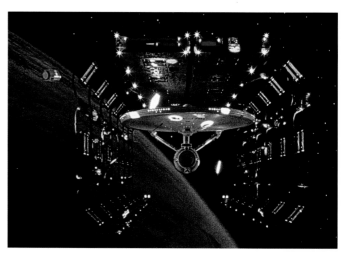

Spacedock—the final version

In the words of *The Motion Picture's* special photographic effects director, Douglas Trumbull, a Klingon battle cruiser should look like "an enemy submarine in World War II that's been out at sea for too long."

Andrew Probert's conceptualization of what lurked beneath the battle cruiser's oddly shaped bridge helped set the Klingon style for all the STAR TREK productions to follow.

INSIDE A KLINGON BATTLE CRUISER

KLINGON BRIDGE

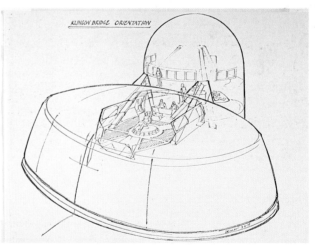

KLINGON BRIDGE ORIENTATION

A FIRST GLIMPSE INSIDE V'GER

Mike Minor also contributed these spectacular concept illustrations suggesting one possible look for the cavernous interior of the returning V'Ger space probe.

ARTWORK BY MIKE MINOR. COURTESY OF PARAMOUNT PICTURES

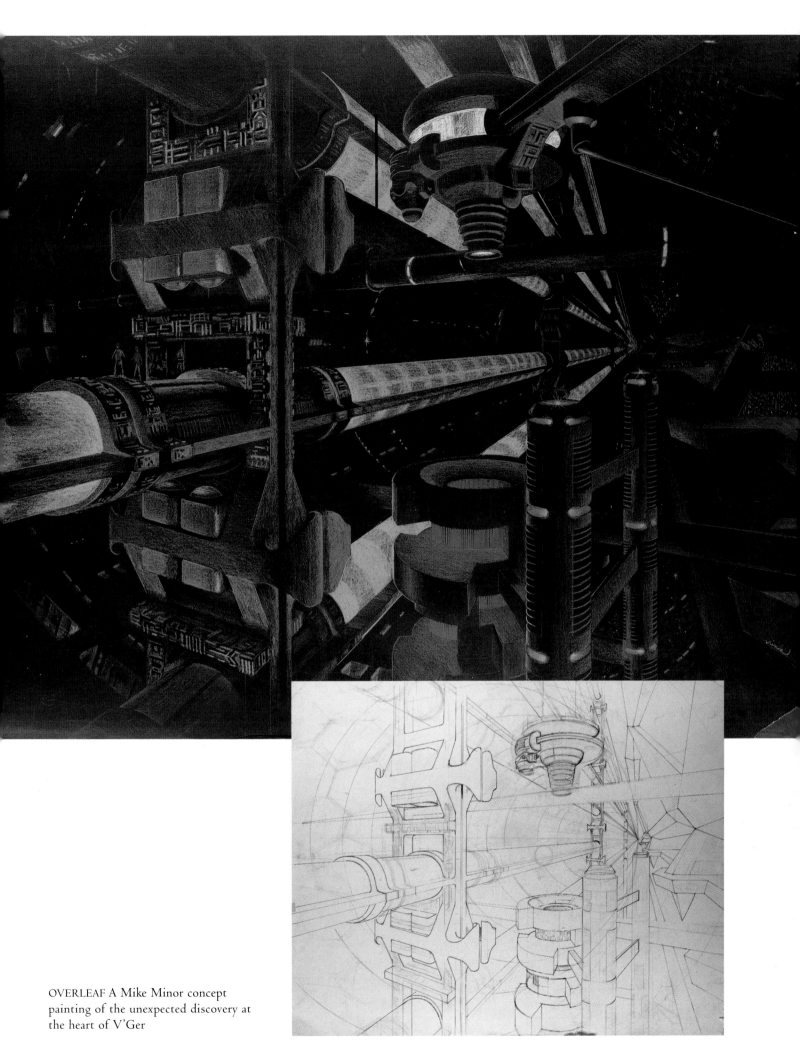

OVERLEAF A Mike Minor concept
painting of the unexpected discovery at
the heart of V'Ger

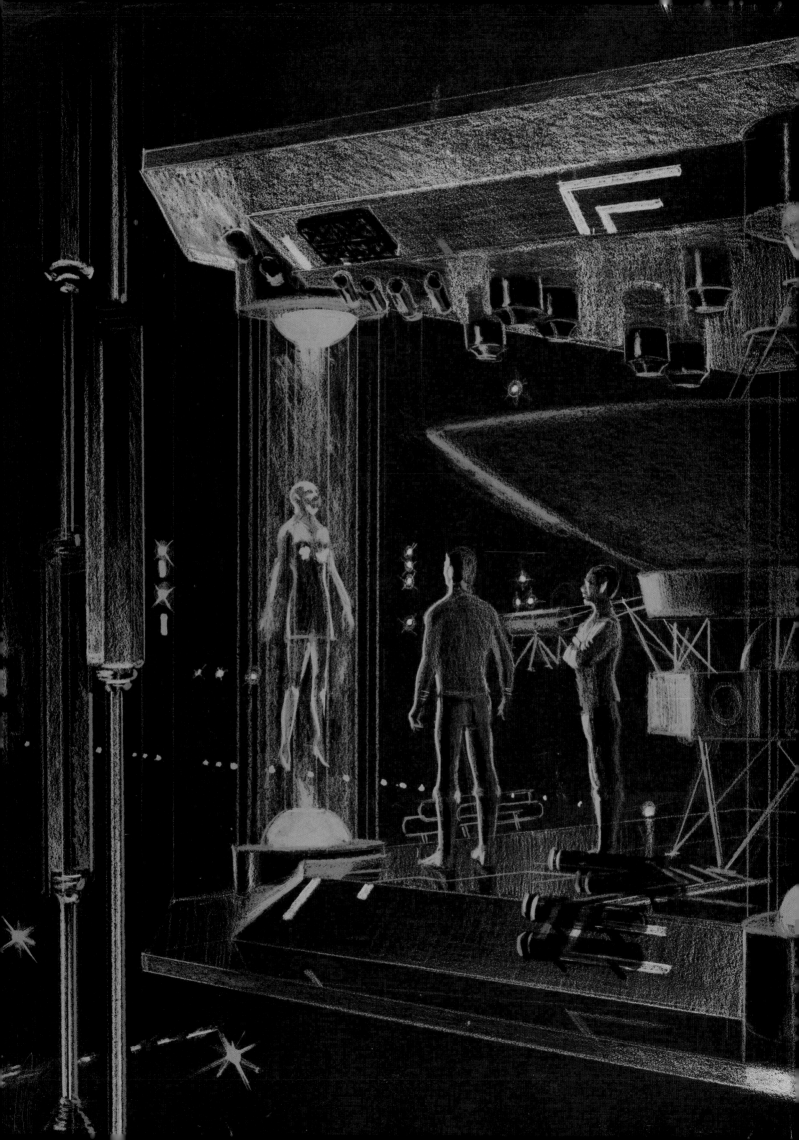

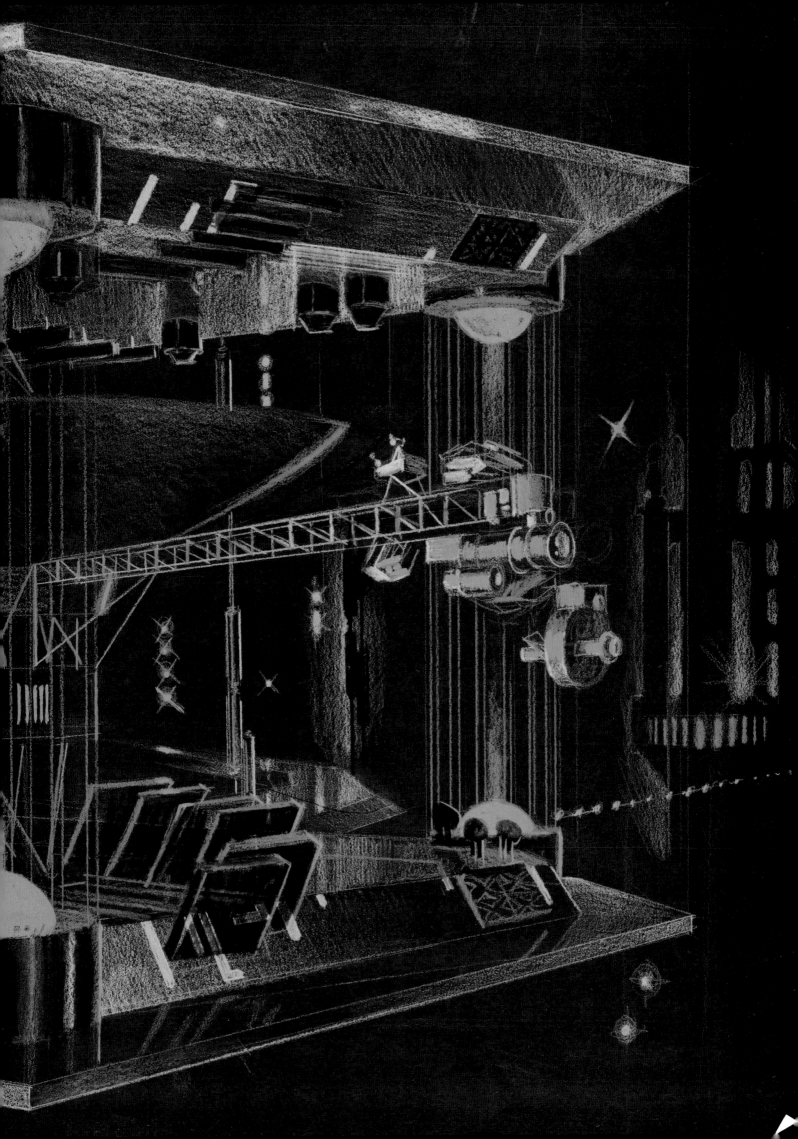

An ambassador from Betelgeuse. The ambassador's robes are made from a fabric personally selected by Cecil B. DeMille in 1939, and then lost in storage on the Paramount lot until found by costume designer, Robert Fletcher.

The Betelgeusean ambassador's attendant

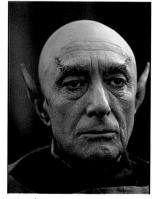

A Vulcan master

A FRED PHILLIPS GALLERY

Fred Phillips had designed Spock's famous pointed ears for the original pilot episode, "The Cage." Fourteen years later, during the production of *The Motion Picture*, Phillips cast his 2000th Spock ear! (Television ears could be used three to four times, because the small screen wouldn't show their deterioration. But for *The Motion Picture*, Leonard Nimoy averaged three new sets of ears each day.)

In addition to Vulcans, Phillips also designed—and redesigned—a large cast of aliens for STAR TREK's first screen outing.

A male Andorian

A Zaranite. The Zaranites' costumes were made from old suedes left over from *The Ten Commandments*.

A female Andorian

An Arcturian clone prepares for duty.

A Megarite

A Saurian

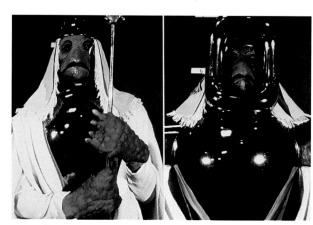

According to Gene Roddenberry and Susan Sackett, co-authors of *The Making of Star Trek: The Motion Picture*, the *Motion Picture* Rigellians differed from the Rigelians mentioned in "Journey to Babel." The former were said to be descended from a race of saber-toothed turtles. Seriously.

A ROBERT FLETCHER GALLERY

After more than 30 years' experience designing costumes for ballet, opera, stage, and television, Robert Fletcher had his first movie assignment, STAR TREK: THE MOTION PICTURE. In addition to garbing the many aliens in the production, Fletcher was also given the challenge of coming up with a new design for Starfleet uniforms. The original, brightly colored tunic approach, created by William Ware Theiss, was considered by director Robert Wise to be too garish when seen on the large screen. Thus Fletcher developed a series of uniforms in muted fabrics.

A new engineering safety suit

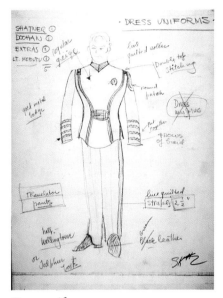

Dress uniform

An early test of the less formal, Class B uniform

Spock's Vulcan masters

Ambassadorial wear

Earth civilian styles

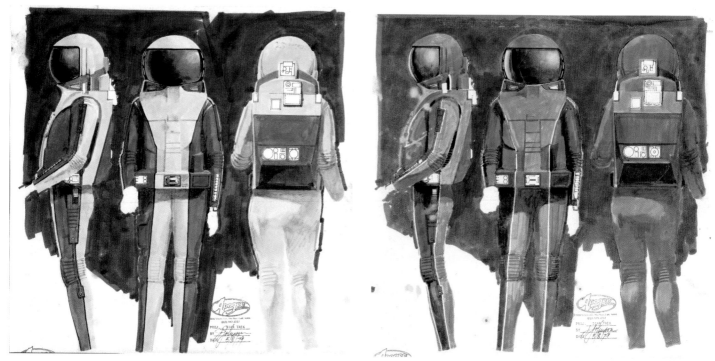

SPACESUIT COLOR CONCEPTS BY J. JOHNSON. COURTESY OF STARLAND

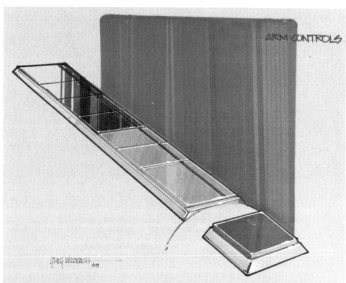

SPACESUIT DETAIL ILLUSTRATIONS BY GREG WILZBACH. COURTESY OF STARLAND

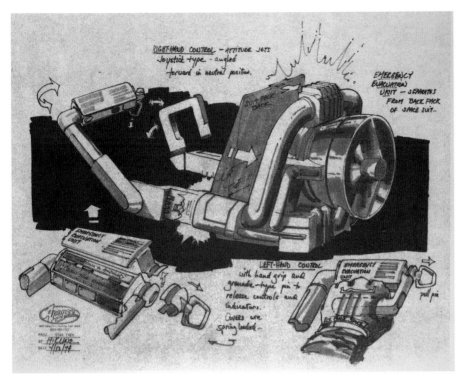

A NEW SPACE-SUIT FOR A NEW VOYAGE

Despite the fact that STAR TREK adventures revolve around the exploration of space, spacesuits are seldom seen. With its pivotal V'Ger spacewalk by Kirk and Spock, STAR TREK: THE MOTION PICTURE attempted to add a bit of outer-space drama to the STAR TREK mix.

Final suits were manufactured close to these designs, then reused with modifications in the second STAR TREK feature. After that, a Paramount contractor recalls seeing Kirk's space helmet in a dumpster on the Paramount lot. There are few things more important than STAR TREK at Paramount, but one of them appears to be storage space.

EMERGENCY EVACUATION UNIT DRAWINGS BY M. KLINE.
COURTESY OF STARLAND

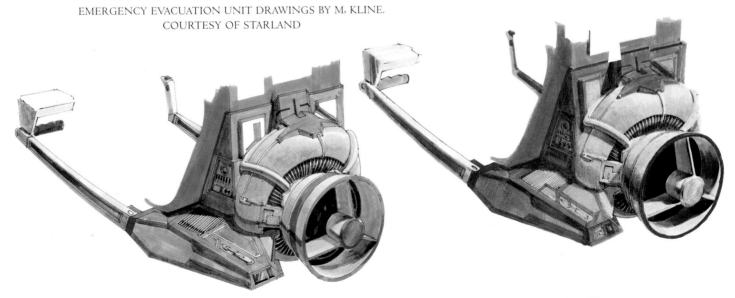

EMERGENCY EVACUATION UNIT COLOR CONCEPTS BY J. JOHNSON. COURTESY OF STARLAND

REINVENTING THE FUTURE

S TAR TREK's longevity has resulted in the phenomenon of a second-generation of behind-the-scene workers whose first involvement with STAR TREK was as fans. Andrew Probert, one of the key designers for both STAR TREK: THE MOTION PICTURE and, later, the *Next Generation* series, was one of these fans. When he was first hired as a designer for *The Motion Picture,* he said he was sent "into spasms of euphoria!"

This personal connection and dedication to STAR TREK appears in these prop designs by Probert. The tricorder and Klingon disruptors clearly echo the original series' designs, while updating them in terms of sleekness and finishing detail.

The electronic clipboard, on its way to becoming the *Next Generation's* ubiquitous padd, is a flattened rendition of the wedge-shaped electronic memo pads used on *The Original Series,* and the medikit owes its layout to Dr. McCoy's hypospray "holster." This intentional repetition and enhancement of key design elements over the years has added to the sense of STAR TREK's inhabiting a unified and evolving universe of its own.

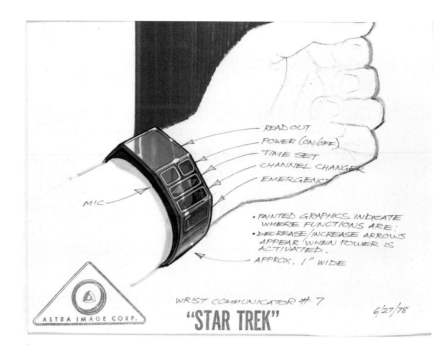

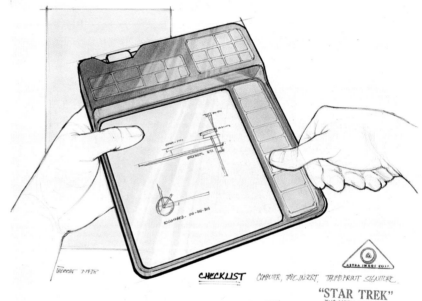

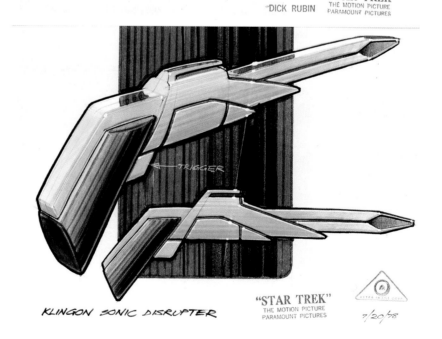

POP-OUT SCANNER —

"STAR TREK"   TRICORDER   6/26/78

TRICORDER

MAIN SCANNER

HAND SCANNER

DISC TAPE COMPART-MENT

NOTE:
• TOP READOUT & CONTROLS ARE FOR THE MAIN SCANNER.
• FLIP-OUT CONTROLS (LOWER) ARE TO READ THROUGH SMALL SCANNER (HAND)

"STAR TREK"   6.28.7

ALL ARTWORK BY ANDREW PROBERT
COURTESY OF MARTIN NUETZEL

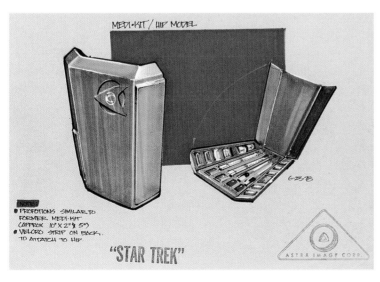

MEDI-KIT/HIP MODEL

NOTE:
• PROPOTIONS SIMILAR TO FORMER MEDI-KIT (APPROX. 10" X 2" & 5")
• VELCRO STRIP ON BACK TO ATTATCH TO HIP.

"STAR TREK"   6.23.78

MEDI-KIT

VELCRO BACK

"STAR TREK"   6.23.78

THE DEVIL IN THE DETAILS

As always, everything in a STAR TREK production from background devices to table decorations must be created from scratch to maintain the illusion that we are seeing the future.

These designs by Andrew Probert show the inventiveness that fills every frame of STAR TREK: THE MOTION PICTURE, whether the camera dwelled on the item or not. Indeed, except for simpler versions of the cargo containers, few of these designs actually were ever constructed.

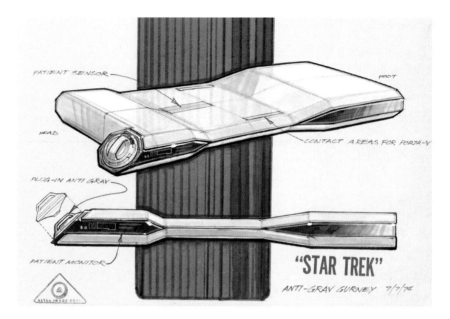

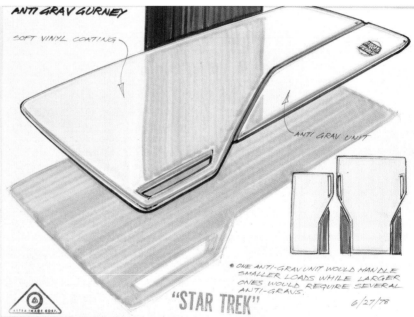

Plug-in antigrav units for the contoured antigrav gurney pictured to the right

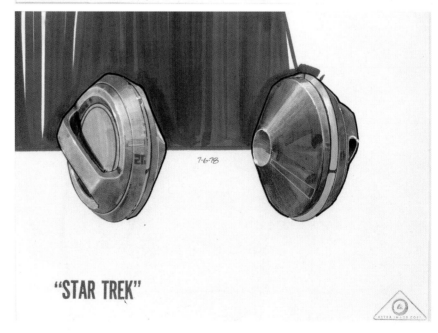

ALL ARTWORK BY ANDREW PROBERT
COURTESY OF MARTIN NUETZEL

"STAR TREK" TRICORDER 6/26/78

POP-OUT SCANNER

TRICORDER

MAIN SCANNER

HAND SCANNER

DISC TAPE COMPART-MENT

Notes:
• TOP READOUT & CONTROLS ARE FOR THE MAIN SCANNER.
• FLIP-OUT CONTROLS (LOWER) ARE TO READ THROUGH SMALL SCANNER (HAND)

"STAR TREK" 6-28-7

ALL ARTWORK BY ANDREW PROBERT
COURTESY OF MARTIN NUETZEL

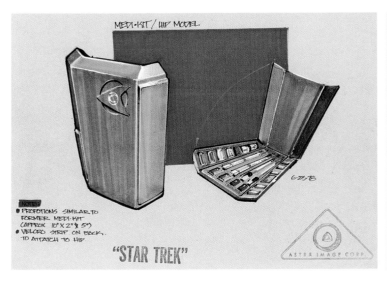

MEDI-KIT / HIP MODEL

Notes:
• PROPORTIONS SIMILAR TO FORMER MEDI-KIT (APPROX 10"X 2"& 5")
• VELCRO STRIP ON BACK TO ATTATCH TO HIP

"STAR TREK"

MEDI-KIT

VELCRO BACK

"STAR TREK"

THE DEVIL IN THE DETAILS

As always, everything in a STAR TREK production from background devices to table decorations must be created from scratch to maintain the illusion that we are seeing the future.

These designs by Andrew Probert show the inventiveness that fills every frame of STAR TREK: THE MOTION PICTURE, whether the camera dwelled on the item or not. Indeed, except for simpler versions of the cargo containers, few of these designs actually were ever constructed.

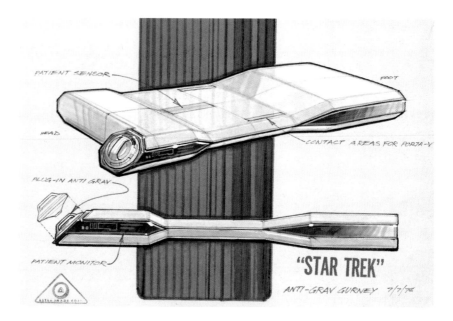

Plug-in antigrav units
for the contoured antigrav gurney
pictured to the right

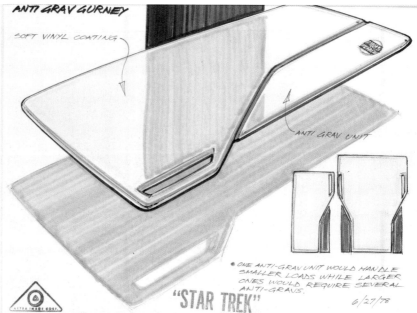

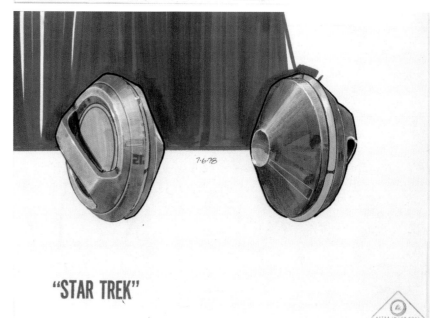

ALL ARTWORK BY ANDREW PROBERT
COURTESY OF MARTIN NUETZEL

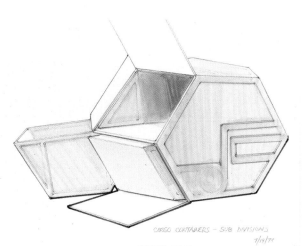

CARGO CONTAINERS - SUB DIVISIONS
7/19/78

"STAR TREK"
THE MOTION PICTURE
PARAMOUNT PICTURES   DICK RUBIN

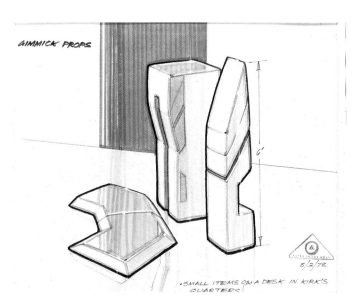

8/3/78

• SMALL ITEMS ON A DESK IN KIRK'S QUARTERS

PROPS & ALIENS

RA IMAGE CORP.

"STAR TREK"

"STAR TREK"

TOP SECRET

CARGO AREA
7/12/78

RECREATION ROOM GAME

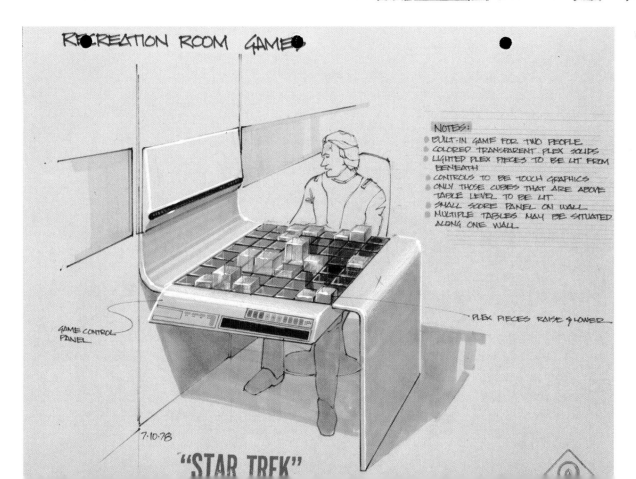

GAME CONTROL PANEL

NOTES:
• BUILT-IN GAME FOR TWO PEOPLE
• COLORED TRANSPARENT PLEX SOLIDS
• LIGHTED PLEX PIECES TO BE LIT FROM BENEATH
• CONTROLS TO BE TOUCH GRAPHICS
• ONLY THOSE CUBES THAT ARE ABOVE TABLE LEVEL TO BE LIT
• SMALL SCORE PANEL ON WALL
• MULTIPLE TABLES MAY BE SITUATED ALONG ONE WALL

PLEX PIECES RAISE & LOWER

7·10·78

"STAR TREK"

THE ART OF STORYBOARDING, 1

A motion picture crew on a major production can cost $50,000 *an hour,* not including the salaries of the stars. That means each second the director slows things down by thinking about what to do next can cost more than $13.

That's one of the key reasons for using storyboards—they enable directors to do their expensive thinking beforehand: choosing camera angles, blocking actors, deciding pacing.

In the production of STAR TREK films, which involves the complex combining of live-action footage with visual effects such as miniature photography and computer animation, and special effects such as sparking bridge consoles and phaser explosions, storyboards are even more important to the planning process. Indeed, they are crucial to the process by which visual effects companies prepare their bids for undertaking the work.

After the fact, storyboards provide a fascinating look at the evolution of a final film. Some storyboard sequences depict entire scenes never shot, or once shot, deleted from the final film. Other sequences reveal intermediate design stages, as in these storyboards featuring the unusual Starfleet symbols on the uniforms of the characters, and the "old" elements on the *Enterprise,* such as the round navigation dome.

The storyboards on the following pages depict V'Ger's "whiplash" attack on the *Enterprise* in *The Motion Picture.* The name ASTRA stands for "A STAR TREK, Robert Abel" production. The final effects for this sequence in the completed film were created under the direction of Douglas Trumbull.

SEQ. 5.0   SC. 162   PAGE 3   DATE 9-8-78

DESCRIPTION

SEQ. 5.0   SC. 163   PAGE 4   DATE 9-6-78

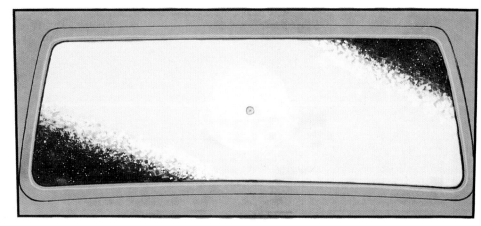

DESCRIPTION

SEQ.   SC. 161   PAGE 3   DATE 9-6-78

DESCRIPTION

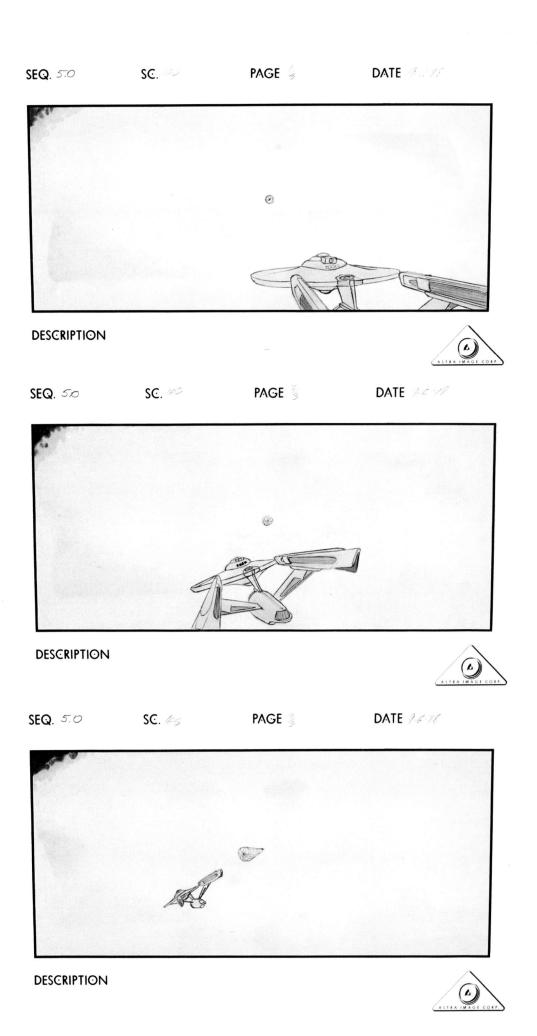

SEQ. 5.0　　　SC. 160　　　PAGE ⅓　　　DATE 2.6.78

DESCRIPTION

SEQ. 5.0　　　SC. 160　　　PAGE ⅔　　　DATE 2.6.78

DESCRIPTION

SEQ. 5.0　　　SC. 165　　　PAGE ⅔　　　DATE 2.6.78

DESCRIPTION

THE ART OF STORYBOARDING, 2

SEQ. 5.0   SC. 166   PAGE   DATE

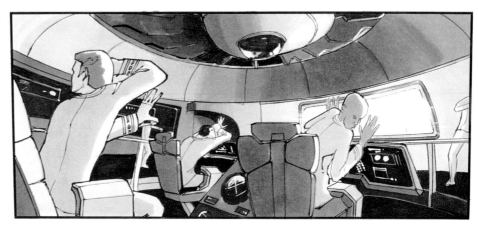

DESCRIPTION

SEQ. 5.0   SC. 167   PAGE 3   DATE

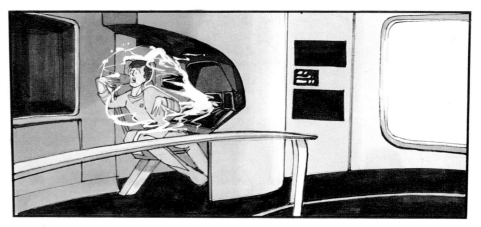

DESCRIPTION

SEQ. 5.0   SC. 167   PAGE   DATE

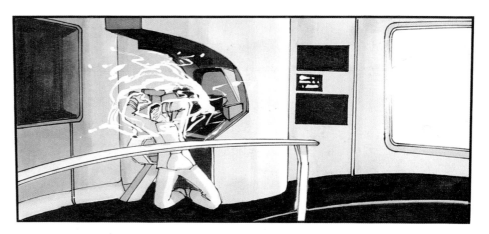

DESCRIPTION

SEQ. 5.0   SC. 157-3   PAGE 3   DATE 9.9.77

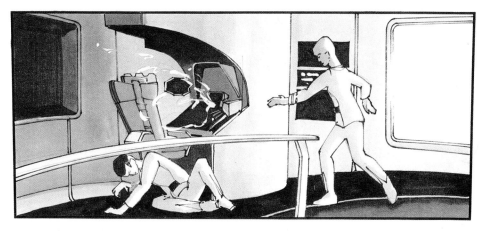

DESCRIPTION

SEQ. 5.0   SC. 157   PAGE 4   DATE 9.9.77

DESCRIPTION

SEQ. 5.0   SC. 30   PAGE 3   DATE

DESCRIPTION

THE ART OF STORYBOARDING, 3

SEQ. 5.0   SC. 173   PAGE 4   DATE 9.8.78

DESCRIPTION

SEQ.   SC. 172   PAGE 4   DATE 9.8.78

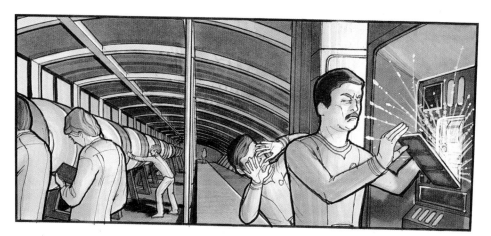

DESCRIPTION   ENGINE ROOM. A JUNIOR MAN IS USING WHAT A PANEL. IT SPARKS AS SPOCK AND HIS MEN WORK FEVERISHLY TO REPAIR THE PANELS. (CUT TO 173.)

SEQ.   SC. 173A   PAGE 4   DATE 9.8.78

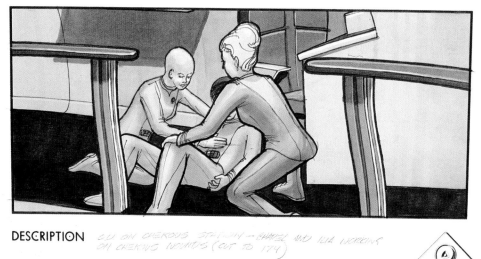

DESCRIPTION   C.U. ON OVEROUS STATION — CHAPEL AND ILIA WORKING ON OVEROUS INCIDENT. (CUT TO 174)

SEQ. *5.0*   SC. *174*   PAGE *4*   DATE *7-2-78*

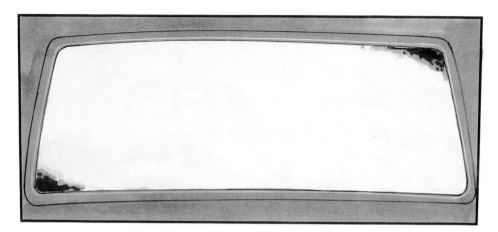

DESCRIPTION

SEQ.   SC. *175A*   PAGE *5*   DATE *7-8-78*

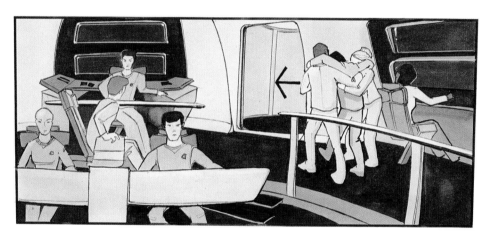

DESCRIPTION *AS KIRK REMAINS VESS STANDS WALKING HER SOME SPACE - CHEKL AND ORMOLU MEET THE SPOCK ... (CUT ON 175)*

SEQ.   SC. *176*   PAGE *6*   DATE *9-8-78*

DESCRIPTION *...*

THE ART OF STORYBOARDING, 4

SEQ. *5.0* SC. *177* PAGE *7* DATE *7.8.78*

DESCRIPTION

SEQ. *5.0* SC. *178* PAGE *7* DATE *7.8.78*

DESCRIPTION

SEQ. SC. *181* PAGE *4* DATE *7.8.78*

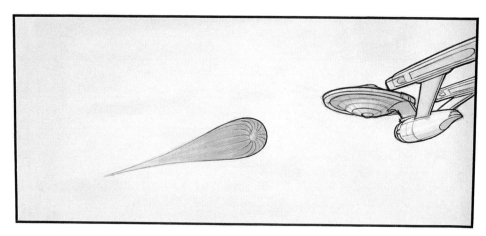

DESCRIPTION *WARPLASH SHERRY SHOT BLASTING POWER THE ENTERPRISE.*
(CUT TO 182)

SEQ.   SC. 82   PAGE   DATE 1.8.78

DESCRIPTION

SEQ.   SC. 83   PAGE   DATE 1.8.78

DESCRIPTION

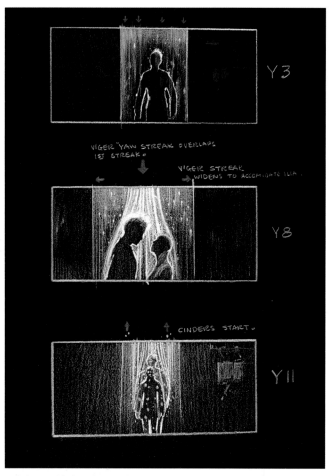

VIGER "YAW STREAK OVERLAPS 1ST STREAK.

VIGER STREAK WIDENS TO ACCOMIDATE ILIA.

CINDERS START.

Decker and the Ilia probe unite.

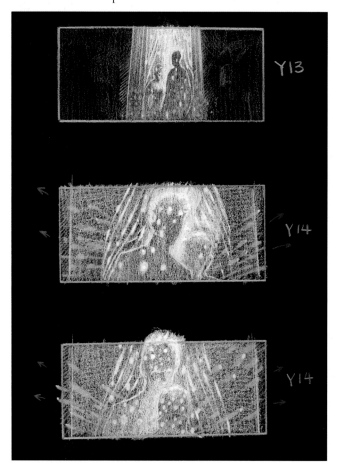

SHOT OF SUN AGAINST A GRAY SKY—

"GRAY" VIGER (ALMOST CLOUD LIKE) STARTS TO ECLIPSE

THE SUN — THE COLOR OF THE SUN AGAINST VIGER

CHANGES TO BRIGHT REDS — CORONA EFFECT.

Rough storyboards of V'Ger's appearance from Earth

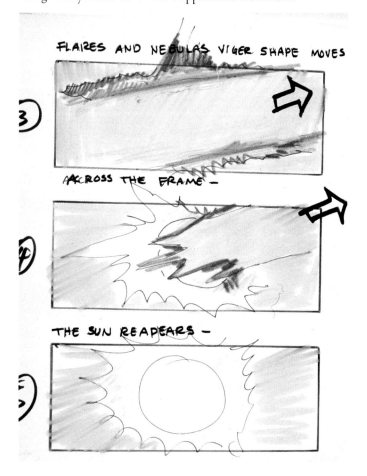

FLAIRES AND NEBULAS VIGER SHAPE MOVES

ACROSS THE FRAME—

THE SUN REAPEARS—

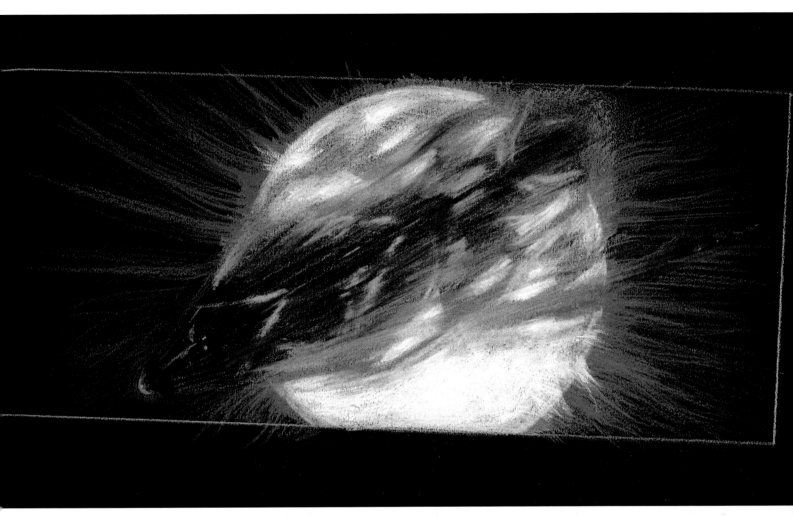

A more finished presentation of V'Ger eclipsing the sun

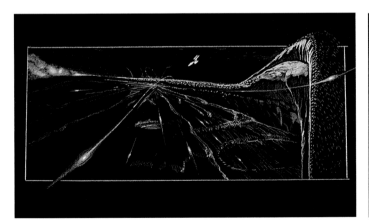

The *Enterprise* inside the V'Ger cloud

STORYBOARDS COURTESY OF PARAMOUNT PICTURES

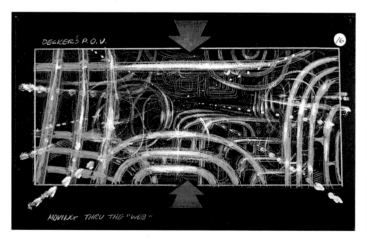

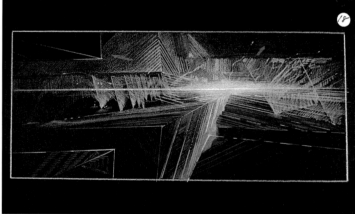

The *Enterprise* continues her voyage through V'Ger.

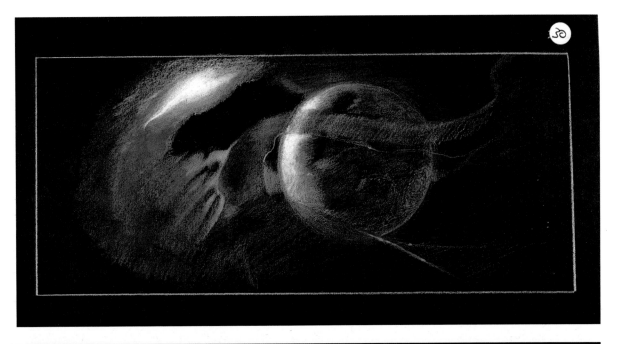

V'Ger's manifestation near Earth. Note the "face" below the light in the final panel.

A SAUCER SEPARATION THAT NEVER WAS

Throughout most of the filming of *The Motion Picture*, a final ending for the story had yet to be developed. Designer Andrew Probert provided the producers with his own script suggestions for a visually dramatic conclusion, and storyboarded the key event.

For the record, the possibility of the original *Enterprise*'s undergoing a saucer separation was first mentioned in *The Original Series* episode "The Apple." But it was not until the pilot episode of *The Next Generation* that the maneuver was finally depicted.

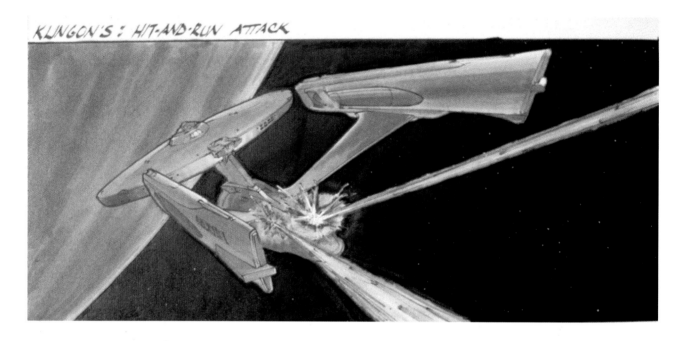

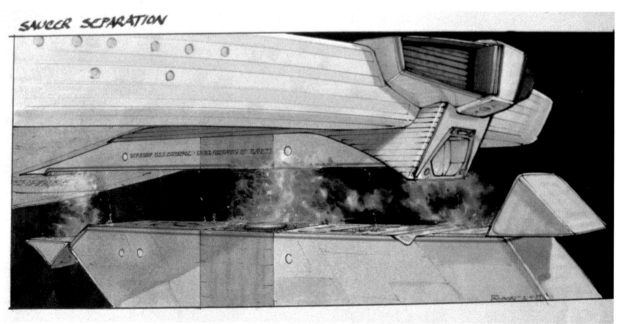

ARTWORK COURTESY OF ANDREW PROBERT

ENGINEERING SECTION — VIEWED FROM SEPARATED SAUCER

SAUCER LIFTOFF

ENTERPRISE SAUCER — IN PURSUIT OF KLINGONS.

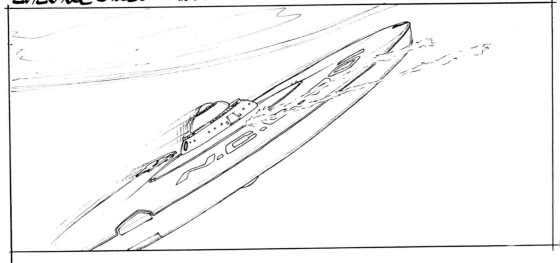

CHAPTER TWO

ONE BIG HAPPY FLEET

STAR TREK II: THE WRATH OF KHAN 1982

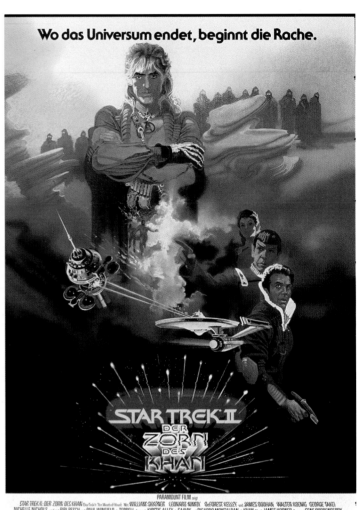

The Wrath of Khan in Japan

The Wrath of Khan in Germany

STAR TREK II:
THE WRATH OF KHAN

arly in 1980, one week into his new job as a producer for Paramount's television division, Harve Bennett was asked to meet with Barry Diller, Michael Eisner, and Charles Bludhorn, the head of Paramount's parent company, Gulf + Western. Wasting no time, Bludhorn immediately asked Bennett if he had seen STAR TREK: THE MOTION PICTURE and, if so, what he had thought of it.

Bennett recalls that in situations such as that, he has one rule—rigorous honesty. He *had* seen *The Motion Picture.* What he remembered most about it was that his children, who usually sat quietly through most films, had pestered him throughout for snack-bar treats and visits to the bathroom. There was nothing Bennett could do but to tell Bludhorn that he thought the movie had been "really boring."

"Can you make a better picture?" Bludhorn asked.

Not quite certain what was going on, Bennett replied that he could at least make a movie that was less boring.

Then Bludhorn asked, "Could you make it for less than forty-five million dollars?"

Bennett, with his television production background, answered, "Where I come from, I could make five movies for that."

To which Bludhorn responded, "Do it."

Thus the second STAR TREK film began its journey to the screen.

Once again, the project was not script-driven. Instead, it was the overall idea of STAR TREK that propelled the project. *The Motion Picture,* in spite of its shaky reviews, had set box-office records. The enormous science-fiction audience that had made *Star Wars* and *Close Encounters* into hits had translated into success for STAR TREK as well. Even with a $45 million price tag, *The Motion Picture* would end up earning money for the studio, even if it never reached the Hollywood definition of "profitable."

Putting everything together, it was apparent to Paramount executives that if a second STAR TREK film could do almost as well, without being burdened by the excess development costs and special-effects overruns that had inflated *The Motion Picture*'s bottom line, then Paramount could be looking at a movie-franchise gold mine.

The hard questions to be answered now were, which elements had contributed to *The Motion Picture*'s success, and which could be eliminated from future productions? The answers to those questions would serve to define STAR TREK for its next three outings, until the next stage in its evolution, STAR TREK: THE NEXT GENERATION.

Rightly or wrongly, one element that Paramount felt could be dropped from the development of a new STAR TREK film was Gene Roddenberry, who was perceived to share some of the responsibility for the special-effects management that had gone awry, and for the slow story. Though Roddenberry would continue to have input at every stage of the filmmaking process, and though his thoughts and philosophy would continue to influence the underpinnings for STAR TREK's unique vision of humanity's future, he would no longer exercise control over his creation. Paramount executives were gambling on the notion that STAR TREK had grown beyond the ability of any one person to dominate it. Time would prove them right.

The first defining "filter" for STAR TREK: THE MOVIE II, as it was then known, was its budget—$8.5 million. Even allowing for the extra development costs attached to *The Motion Picture,* that amount was just about a third of what the first film had cost to make. (The studio's favorable reaction to the first two weeks of footage prompted the executives to add an extra $2.5 million to the budget.)

Paramount tried to soften the financial limitations by pointing out that Bennett could use all the sets from the first film, along with the $50,000 model of the *Enterprise* and any of the unused special-effects sequences. Unfortunately, as Bennett quickly learned, the sets had been vandalized, the model stolen, and there were no unused special effects that were usable.

Being a newcomer to STAR TREK, Bennett recruited many of the behind-the-scenes production crew who had served on *The Motion Picture* in order to insure continuity of effort. Designer Mike Minor—now art director and working under Production Designer Joe Jennings—relished the challenge of returning

For the second film outing, the wrist communicators of *The Motion Picture* were replaced with an updating of *The Original Series'* design.

to the sets he had helped design for *Phase II,* then seen revamped for the first film. "The first movie was pretty washed out," he said. "Visually, it had no heart. It was stiff." The changes he helped bring to those same sets for STAR TREK II: THE WRATH OF KHAN made them, he felt, "a lot brighter looking, snappier." Minor attributed a great deal of the improved look of the bridge, especially, to graphic designer Lee Cole, who helped add much of the sets' new detailing.

Redecorating the sets instead of building new ones was not the only form of television penny-pinching that Bennett brought to the production. Some sets from the first film were simply rechristened and used as completely different locations. For example, the *Motion Picture*'s striking, Andrew Probert–designed Klingon bridge was split into two new sets—the space station transporter facility and the *Enterprise*'s torpedo room. Even the *Enterprise*'s bridge did triple duty as itself, the Starfleet bridge simulator, and the bridge of the *Reliant.*

Because the talents and expertise of a talented crew helped hide many of the cost-cutting strategies of this leaner STAR TREK production, the most noticeable contribution to the look of the second film came from its director, Nicholas Meyer.

Like Bennett, Meyer had not been familiar with STAR TREK before he was offered his assignment. Thus, like Bennett, Meyer brought his own, independent analysis of what he thought STAR TREK should be, rather than relying on what had gone on in the past. To this day, fans still debate whether Meyer's contributions (in *The Wrath of Khan* and in STAR TREK VI: THE UNDISCOVERED COUNTRY, which he also directed) were strictly in keeping with Roddenberry's vision for STAR TREK. But the fact that STAR TREK movies have continued to prosper while this debate continues seems to indicate that Meyer's impact on the look of the STAR TREK universe has been accepted by the movie audience.

Meyer, like Mike Minor, reacted

negatively to the cool, stripped-down appearance of the twenty-third century as depicted in *The Motion Picture.* Under his direction, the sleek, austere Starfleet uniforms were completely redesigned by Robert Fletcher to evoke a more military feel. In one walk through the bridge, Meyer joked that he had cost the production $60 thousand, simply by having the set builders add more blinking lights and signage.

One contentious addition Meyer made to the bridge was a NO SMOKING sign. An unrepentant cigar-smoker himself, Meyer recalls, "Everyone had a fit over that. 'How can you say that? It's the future.' And I said, 'Why have they stopped smoking in the future? They've been smoking for four hundred years. You think it's going to stop in the next two?'" Meyer would go on to face a similar debate over his decision to include a galley complete with pots and pans in the *Enterprise* of STAR TREK VI, when established Trek lore dictated a more futuristic food synthesizer system.

The other major contributor to the look of STAR TREK II was producer Robert Sallin. Again, like Bennett, Sallin brought a different production mentality to the film. His background included directing and producing hundreds of commercials, which typically are notorious for their breakneck schedules and tight budgets.

With Mike Minor producing detailed storyboards for each draft of the script, Sallin created an elaborate chart system for tracking and describing each special-effects shot that would be required, literally down to a frame-by-frame accounting. As the film's preproduction stage progressed, Sallin's meticulous planning led him to an inevitable conclusion—there was only one company that could deliver the high-quality special effects the movie required: Industrial Light & Magic, the company formed by George Lucas to create the visual effects for *Star Wars,* and which has gone on to become one of the leading effects facilities in the movie industry.

In keeping with the tight budget requirements for the film, ILM also worked with material from the first film. The new *Enterprise* built for *The Motion Picture* was recovered, touched up, and reused. (Several smaller versions were also constructed.) The space office complex last seen orbiting Earth was turned upside down, redressed with additional detail, and became the Regula I space lab. But ILM also built the completely new *Reliant* (from designs by Joseph Jennings and Mike Minor), and created the most spectacular use of computer-generated imagery yet to appear in a

movie—the Genesis Tape, showing how the Genesis device can turn a lifeless planet into a living one in only minutes.

The STAR TREK tradition of many different workers contributing in many different ways is ably demonstrated by the story of the Genesis device. An early draft of the story was titled *The Omega Device*. The device was to be one of awesome destructive power—in other words, a bomb. Not the most original of threats. But during a preproduction meeting, Mike Minor suggested that the device could be part of a terraforming project—that is, a device of creation, not destruction. Harve Bennett immediately jumped up, hugged Minor, and told him, "You saved STAR TREK!"

Minor went on to create the matte painting tests for the Genesis cave, basing them in part on the underground caverns produced by Martian heat rays in the classic 1953 movie *Invaders from Mars*. As for the Genesis Tape demonstrating the device's ability to bring forth life from nonlife, that slightly-more-than-one-minute sequence took ten ILM artists six months to create. It was designed by visual-effects supervisor Jim Veilleux, and produced by a team headed by Alvy Ray Smith and Loren Carpenter.

At first, the end result of this new approach to STAR TREK was much the same as that which had greeted the first film. Critics were less than overwhelmed. David Denby, writing in *New York* magazine, didn't even consider STAR TREK II to be a movie because of the constraints placed upon the director by what

had already been established about the STAR TREK universe. He reports that the film has "the same tacky sets, the contrived situations, the Boy Scout speeches about democracy, honor, and feeling versus logic" that the series had, only with a bigger budget. *People* magazine called the pacing in the writing and directing of the film "leaden." The *Washington Post* stated that STAR TREK II couldn't compare visually with *Star Wars*—despite the fact that ILM was responsible for the visual effects in both films— and that "the *Enterprise* still looks like a toy boat in a lava lamp." Only one reviewer, Peter Schickel of *Time* magazine, seemed to have sensed the true appeal of a STAR TREK film, when he said audiences will leave the theaters "with a pleasant sense of having caught up with old friends and found them to be just fine."

But in the end, and once again, it mattered little what the reviewers said. STAR TREK II: THE WRATH OF KHAN continued in the tradition of the first film by setting an all-new box-office record for opening weekend gross—$14.4 million. The movie would go on to be the fifth-highest-grossing film of 1982, with a total domestic take of $85 million. And fifteen years and five more movies later, many fans still pick *The Wrath of Khan* as the best one of the motion picture series.

Thus, the outcome of the executives' gamble was definite and unassailable. Without question, STAR TREK had taken on a life of its own.

THE RELIANT

For the climactic space battle between Kirk and Khan, a new Starfleet starship was needed—one that would appear distinctively different from the *Enterprise*, yet still fit comfortably within the STAR TREK universe.

By using components similar to the saucer and engine nacelles of the *Enterprise*, Mike Minor and Joe Jennings designed the *U.S.S. Reliant* and accomplished both goals.

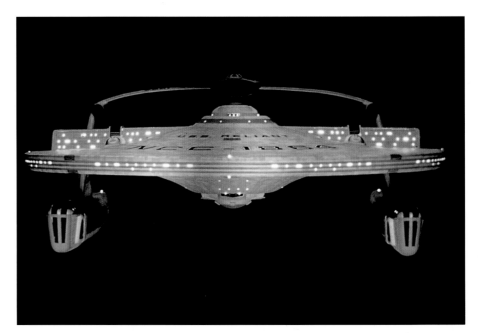

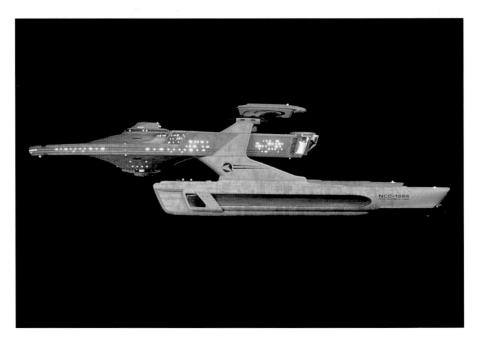

A NEW LOOK

I n *The Wrath of Khan,* the muted pastel *Enterprise* of *The Motion Picture* acquired a darker, more hard-edged military atmosphere, in keeping with director Nicholas Meyer's vision of STAR TREK as a Horatio Hornblower adventure.

Art director Mike Minor's concept paintings for the spectacular Genesis Cave

PAINTINGS COURTESY OF BOB BURNS

GENESIS

Perhaps it's fitting that the most memorable visual images from *The Wrath of Khan* center on the Genesis Device—a story element created by art director Mike Minor during a preliminary story conference for the film.

At the time, the Industrial Light & Magic computer-animation sequence showing the Genesis effect was state of the art, though within the film it was presented as a simulation to allow the audience to accept its unconvincing look, scan lines and all. Today, of course, Industrial Light & Magic has advanced computer animation to such an incredible degree that the company created entire starships for STAR TREK GENERATIONS that are impossible for all but an expert to distinguish from a real model. By the time the eighth STAR TREK feature is released, even the experts will be hard pressed to tell what's real and what exists only within the computer.

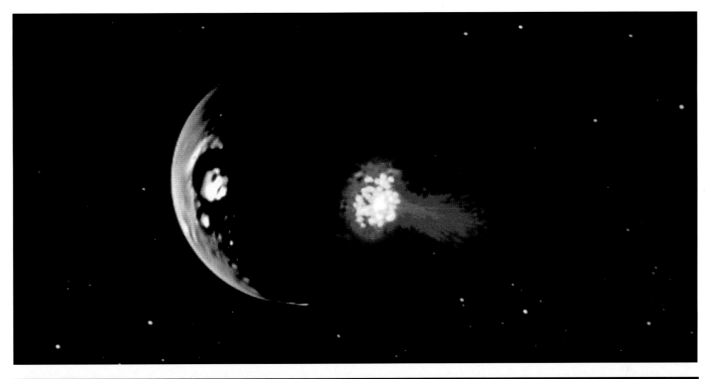

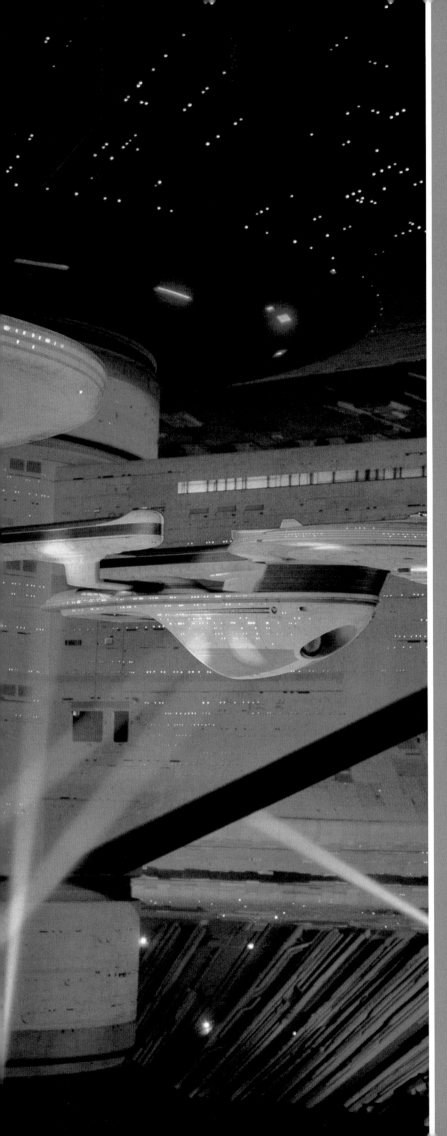

CHAPTER THREE

A REAL COMEBACK

STAR TREK III: THE SEARCH FOR SPOCK
1984

STAR TREK III:
THE SEARCH FOR SPOCK

The Search for Spock in Germany

Though Spock died in *The Wrath of Khan,* the ending of that movie clearly set up the possibility that he would be back. Scotty had been killed and brought back in "The Changeling," McCoy in "Shore Leave," so why couldn't that be the case with a Vulcan? Especially when that Vulcan wanted to direct.

As a direct sequel to *The Wrath of Khan, The Search for Spock* was able to draw directly on what had been built for the earlier movie. This gave the production the equivalent of two movies' worth of sets, costumes, and props, making the film much more visually interesting.

Robert Fletcher's Starfleet cos-

tumes remained the same. New Klingon costumes were required, but they followed the design he had established in *The Motion Picture.* At first, the script had called for Romulans to be involved in trying to track down the secrets of the Genesis Planet, but director Leonard Nimoy convinced producer Harve

Once again, the movie *Enterprise* bridge was reused with minor changes to finishing details and lighting design.

The impressive Spacedock model, designed by David Carson and Nilo Rodis, made its first appearance.

Inside Spacedock

Bennett that Klingons were more theatrical. However, as the script was subsequently changed, the name of the villains' spaceship wasn't. Thus, what was originally and logically a Romulan Bird-of-Prey became a Klingon Bird-of-Prey. Fortunately, STAR TREK consistency is resilient enough to absorb some of these departures from what has gone before.

Industrial Light & Magic, which had done such a noteworthy job on visual effects for *The Wrath of Khan,* was once again asked to participate in this film. Not only did the company provide four new ships, it also became involved in the creation of props, including all the Klingon gear, and the ferocious "dog" kept by the Klingon commander.

The climactic destruction of the *Enterprise* near the movie's end was seen as an opportunity by some designers to move ahead with the development of a more sophisticated starship. But though the actual bridge set was blown up, the producers saved the large *Enterprise* model, destroying a smaller one instead.

For the first time, critical response to a STAR TREK film improved significantly. Not all the reviews were raves, but many critics were finally taking the time to ignore their automatic reaction to the premise of a space movie based on a canceled television series, and to try to understand what gave STAR TREK its appeal to so many dedicated followers. The *Washington Post* went so far as to say that the cast "are such agreeable, familiar old fix- tures that you feel absurdly protec- tive and tender about them." *USA Today* said the film "strikes the best balance between story and effects, between characters and action, and between humor and melodrama." And *Time* magazine's Richard Schickel said the movie "is the first space opera to deserve that term in its grandest sense."

The third STAR TREK film's opening weekend gross broke the record that had been set only a week before by *Indiana Jones and the Temple of Doom,* which itself had just broken the previous record set by *The Wrath of Khan.*

There was no doubt about it. A fourth STAR TREK film was inevitable.

A DESIGN EXPLOSION

*T*he *Search for Spock* brought a number of new STAR TREK designs to the screen—from the smallest props to one of the most impressive and durable starships yet, as well as one of the smallest and most easily made. All designs on these pages are from Industrial Light & Magic.

A Klingon communicator

A Klingon knife with spring-loaded secondary blades

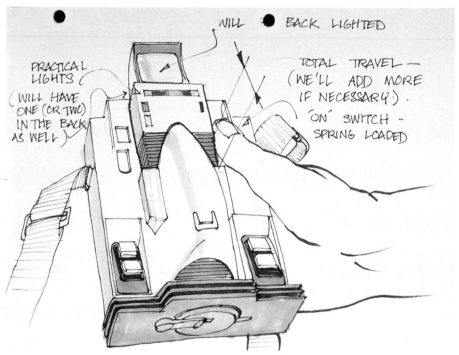

WILL ● BACK LIGHTED

PRACTICAL LIGHTS ((WILL HAVE ONE (OR TWO) IN THE BACK AS WELL)

TOTAL TRAVEL — (WE'LL ADD MORE IF NECESSARY). 'ON' SWITCH — SPRING LOADED

A preliminary sketch of the Klingon tricorder

A Klingon tricorder

A Starfleet tricorder

Merritt Butrick as Kirk's son, David Marcus, using a Starfleet tricorder

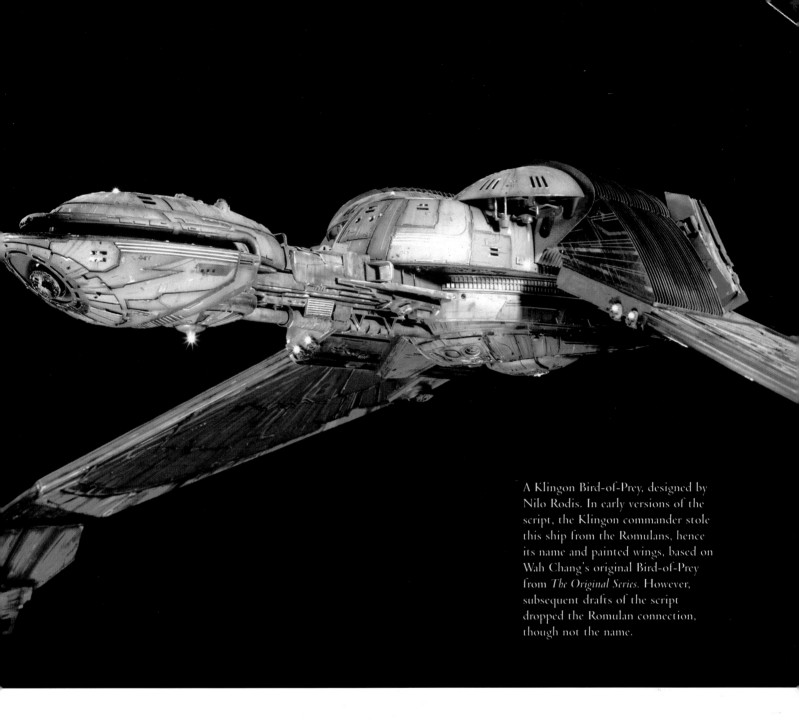

A Klingon Bird-of-Prey, designed by Nilo Rodis. In early versions of the script, the Klingon commander stole this ship from the Romulans, hence its name and painted wings, based on Wah Chang's original Bird-of-Prey from *The Original Series*. However, subsequent drafts of the script dropped the Romulan connection, though not the name.

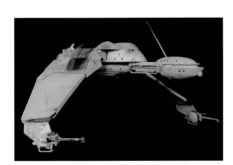

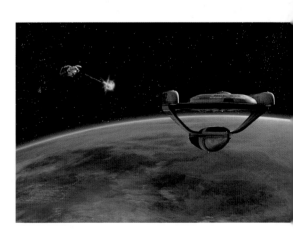

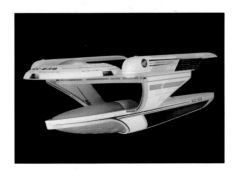

SPACEDOCK CONCEPTS

The Starfleet Spacedock facility was designed by David Carson and Nilo Rodis.

Note the tiny *Enterprise* model used in the concept model photographs to indicate scale. The final Spacedock

model went on to appear in several *Next Generation* episodes.

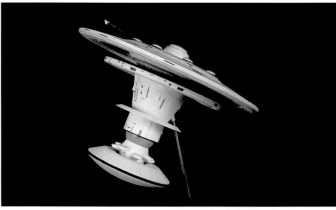

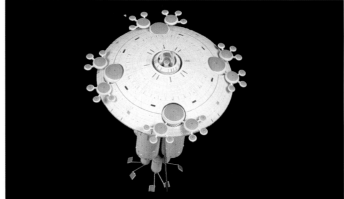

EXCELSIOR CONCEPTS

The *U.S.S. Excelsior* was designed by Bill George and made its first appearance in *The Search for Spock* as a state-of-the-art starship, which turned out to be no match for Kirk's *Enterprise*. The *Excelsior* went on to become Captain Sulu's ship in *The Undiscovered Country* and, with modifications, the ill-fated *Enterprise*-B in *Generations*. The model also appeared as various other starships in *The Next Generation*.

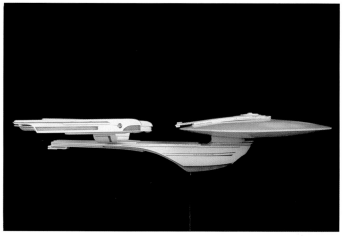

With refinements to the saucer and the nacelles, this concept model is close to the final *Excelsior* design.

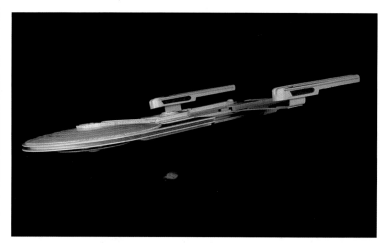

One possible *Excelsior*

PAINTING AND PHOTOGRAPHS COURTESY OF INDUSTRIAL LIGHT & MAGIC

Excelsior bridge concept

GENESIS PLANET CONCEPTS

The death of the *Starship Enterprise*

Kirk and Kruge battle as the planet tears itself apart.

Kirk beams up at the last moment.

The Klingon landing party encounters Rock Eels.

The Bird-of-Prey escapes.

PAINTING BY DAVID CARSON

VULCAN CONCEPTS

Planet Vulcan had previously been seen briefly in *The Original Series* episode, "Amok Time," and in *The Motion Picture*. In both productions, Vulcan was depicted as a red, sere planet, though all that was shown of its civilization were two ancient and remote religious sites.

In keeping with what had gone before, *The Search for Spock* called for another such location—Mount Seleya, site of the *fal-tor-pan* ceremony which reunited Spock's *katra* with his regenerated body.

In the landing concept paintings, note the design development from a simple shuttle, to an early variant of the Bird-of-Prey, to a more final version.

Mount Seleya concepts

Bird-of-Prey landing concepts

Shuttle holding Kirk and McCoy lands on Vulcan in a dropped sequence from an early version of the script

OLD
FRIENDS
AND NEW

Surprisingly, in STAR TREK: THE SEARCH FOR SPOCK it was costume designer Robert Fletcher who brought the Klingons back to the STAR TREK universe, specifically at the request of director Leonard Nimoy.

Fletcher, whose first movie assignment had been *The Motion Picture,* and who had been brought back for *The Wrath of Khan,* now found his duties encompassing the redesign of Fred Phillips's redesign of STAR TREK's favorite bad guys.

Working with Tom Burman of the Burman Studio, who fabricated Fletcher's designs, the third-generation Klingons in this film sported bony foreheads that were less pronounced than those seen in *The Motion Picture.*

As far as Klingon costumes were concerned, everyone liked the costumes Fletcher had created for the opening sequence of *The Motion Picture.* Unfortunately, of the twelve costumes produced for that film, six had since been destroyed or had disappeared on publicity tours. The remaining six had been loaned out to an episode of *Mork and Mindy* to appear as a pile of space junk, and had been modified beyond repair.

Fletcher had new, slightly modified Klingon outfits made, retaining an air of feudal Japanese design, which he felt was part of the Klingon authoritarian attitude. These designs are still in use on STAR TREK productions today.

An early makeup *and* costume test for Christopher Lloyd, as Commander Kruge. Costume and makeup design by Robert Fletcher

Cathie Shirriff as Valkris, in a Robert Fletcher costume harkening back to the less-is-more days of William Ware Theiss

Robert Fletcher was given responsibility for the makeup designs for the third film's cast of more than 250 Vulcans. All told, the production required almost 500 pairs of Vulcan ears, and 350 costumes.

Dame Judith Anderson as the Vulcan high priestess, T'Lar

Lloyd as Kruge in the final film

ALIENS DESIGNED BY TOM BURMAN OF THE BURMAN STUDIO

LIFE NOT AS WE KNOW IT

As the preliminary concept drawings show, the Klingon landing party was originally intended to meet with ferocious carnivorous creatures on the Genesis Planet. However, as the character of the Klingons developed, it was apparent that *they* should be the most ferocious creatures present. Thus, the Klingon commander is the one who vanquishes the monster... until Kirk vanquishes the Klingon commander.

ROCK EEL FINISHING A KLINGON

ROCK EELS

CONCEPT DRAWINGS COURTESY OF
INDUSTRIAL LIGHT & MAGIC

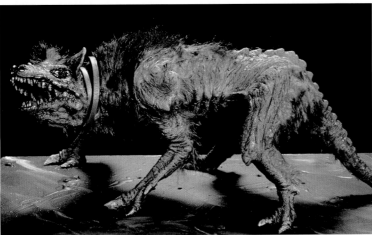

The Klingon commander's pet was not in the script, but was created as a piece of "atmosphere" by the Industrial Light and Magic effects chief, Ken Ralston. The full-size puppet was built by David Sosalia and was brought to life by three offscreen puppeteers, including Ralston, hidden beneath the commander's chair.

To no one's surprise, tribbles survived the transition from television to the big screen.

CHAPTER FOUR

A WHALE OF A STORY

STAR TREK IV: THE VOYAGE HOME
1986

STAR TREK IV: THE VOYAGE HOME

Released in 1986 for STAR TREK's twentieth anniversary, STAR TREK IV: THE VOYAGE HOME remains the most successful of the seven STAR TREK movies. It is also the most light-hearted of the series, despite its lofty themes. Director Leonard Nimoy was responsible for both attributes.

Early in the planning stage with producer Harve Bennett, Nimoy had decided, "no dying, no fist-fighting, no shooting, no photon torpedoes, no phaser blasts, no stereotypical 'bad guy.' I wanted people to really have a great time watching this film, to really sit back, lose themselves, and enjoy it. That was the main goal. And if somewhere in the mix we lobbed a couple of bigger ideas at them, well, then that would be even better."

Another unique element of *The Voyage Home* was its use of time travel as a key plot device. In terms of story, it set the stage for humor as the twenty-third-century crew of the *Enterprise* collided with contemporary twentieth-century life. In terms of production costs, though, it freed the production to shoot on location without the need to create an expensive illusion of the future in every frame.

With half the movie set in the present, *The Voyage Home* contained the least amount of science-fiction design of any of the films, which, ironically enough, is thought to account for its wide general appeal.

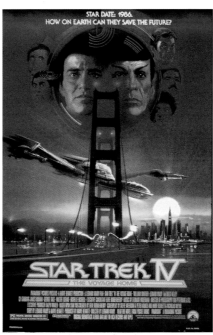

An alternate poster concept used on the video box

For the half of the film that was set in the future, Nimoy and Bennett wisely retained the winning team that had contributed to the success of the previous two films. Once again, Industrial Light & Magic provided spectacular visual effects. Interestingly enough, one of the most convincing effects in the film was so realistic that few people noticed that in most shots the humpback whales were either miniatures shot at ILM or life-size robotic replicas shot in the Paramount parking lot.

This time out, the critics' response to the movie mirrored its fortunes at the box office. Understanding its appeal, *USA Today* said the film would "delight those who don't know a tribble from a Romulan," and that the truly funny script "turns Kirk and his followers into the most uproarious out-of-towners to hit the Bay area since the Democrats in 1984." Referring to the movie's reduced use of visual effects, the review went on to note that without "the usual special-effects camouflage, the performers prove themselves more capable actors than ever before."

But Janet Maslin of the *New York Times* summed up the movie's impact best when she noted that *The Voyage Home* "has done a great deal to ensure the series' longevity."

STAR TREK V was already waiting in the wings.

STAR TREK THE VOYAGE HOME

The Voyage Home in France

"WE'VE COME HOME"

ILM's Ken Ralston was the person most responsible for the destruction of the *Enterprise* in *The Search for Spock*. Part of his desire to blow up the starship model built for the first movie was to free the moviemakers to "put together a more state-of-the-art spaceship for the next film."

However, by the time that next film—*The Voyage Home*—began production, the decision had been made to end the story with the crew returning to duty on a duplicate of their original ship. Though that decision saved the production tens of thousands of dollars by not requiring the design and construction of a new version of the *Enterprise,* it took ILM more than six weeks to repair and repaint the original model to make it look new after all it had been through in the preceding three movies.

The new control panels on the *Enterprise*-A's bridge marked a significant turning point in the evolution of STAR TREK's visual appearance. For the first time the large, jeweled buttons and controls that had been a staple of the ship's design since *The Original Series* were replaced with sleek, smooth panels detailed with backlit displays. These displays would eventually be incorporated into every other STAR TREK production and eventually became known as Okudagrams—a tip of the hat to their creator, STAR TREK's scenic art supervisor and technical consultant, Michael Okuda, who first joined the STAR TREK production team on *The Voyage Home*.

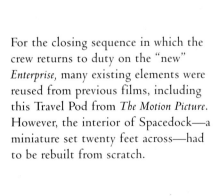

For the closing sequence in which the crew returns to duty on the "new" *Enterprise,* many existing elements were reused from previous films, including this Travel Pod from *The Motion Picture*. However, the interior of Spacedock—a miniature set twenty feet across—had to be rebuilt from scratch.

Starfleet Headquarters, convincingly though inexpensively dressed with large-scale back-projection panels

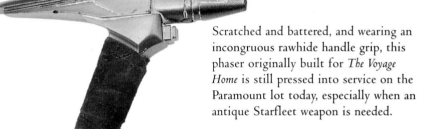

Primitive physical buttons remained on the bridge of the Klingon Bird-of-Prey, though Okudagrams were used for visual displays.

Scratched and battered, and wearing an incongruous rawhide handle grip, this phaser originally built for *The Voyage Home* is still pressed into service on the Paramount lot today, especially when an antique Starfleet weapon is needed.

MORE OLD FRIENDS AND NEW

Though most of STAR TREK IV: THE VOYAGE HOME took place in 1986 San Francisco, STAR TREK's trademark collection of aliens was not forgotten in the movie's opening and closing sequences. The creatures of *The Voyage Home* were created by Richard Snell Designs, with Dale Brady, Shannon Shea, Craig Caton, Brian Wade, Allen Feurstein, and Nancy Nimoy.

With costumes once again by Robert Fletcher, Mark Lenard made his fifth appearance in a STAR TREK production, his third as Spock's father, Sarek…

…while Jane Wyatt reprised her role as Spock's mother, Amanda.

An Andorian, whose receding hairline shows how his antennae are attached—a detail that would have been too expensive in the days of *The Original Series,* when Andorians first appeared

A distinguished member of the Federation Council

More distinguished ladies and gentlemen
and what-have-yous

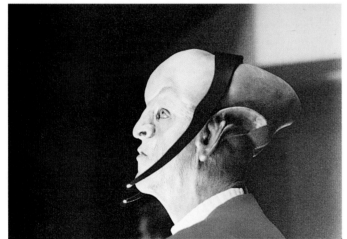

239

PUTTING IT ALL TOGETHER

Like every STAR TREK production before and after, *The Voyage Home* was a result of all the tricks and techniques of modern moviemaking—from elaborate, life-size mechanical creatures and miniature models, to computer-generated images, to the seamless blending of film and paintings to create landscapes that don't exist, except in the artists' imaginations.

The only part of Starfleet Headquarters that is real is the strip of Oakland airport on which the actors were filmed. Matte painting elements were painted by Chris Evans.

After viewing the first shots of the alien probe, ILM's Ken Ralston devised a new and more mysterious look for the vehicle by having it painted black, so it would be defined only by reflections.

The Bird-of-Prey departs Vulcan in a scene composed of miniature foreground rocks, live-action photography of Amanda and Saavik, the Bird-of-Prey model, and a motion-controlled model of the Vulcan sun.

The crew's trip through time, computer-generated by ILM Computer Graphics

Matte painting studies by ILM's Chris Evans—the first step in the process of making imaginary landscapes real

The old and the new mix on the parking lot of Industrial Light & Magic as a furniture-foam model of the Bird-of-Prey is flown past a sixteen-foot-tall miniature of the Golden Gate Bridge. The modelmakers used forced perspective to fool the eye by tapering the width of the bridge from sixteen inches in the foreground to two inches in the background.

The Paramount studio parking lot became San Francisco Harbor for the scene in which the whales are released from the crashed Bird-of-Prey.

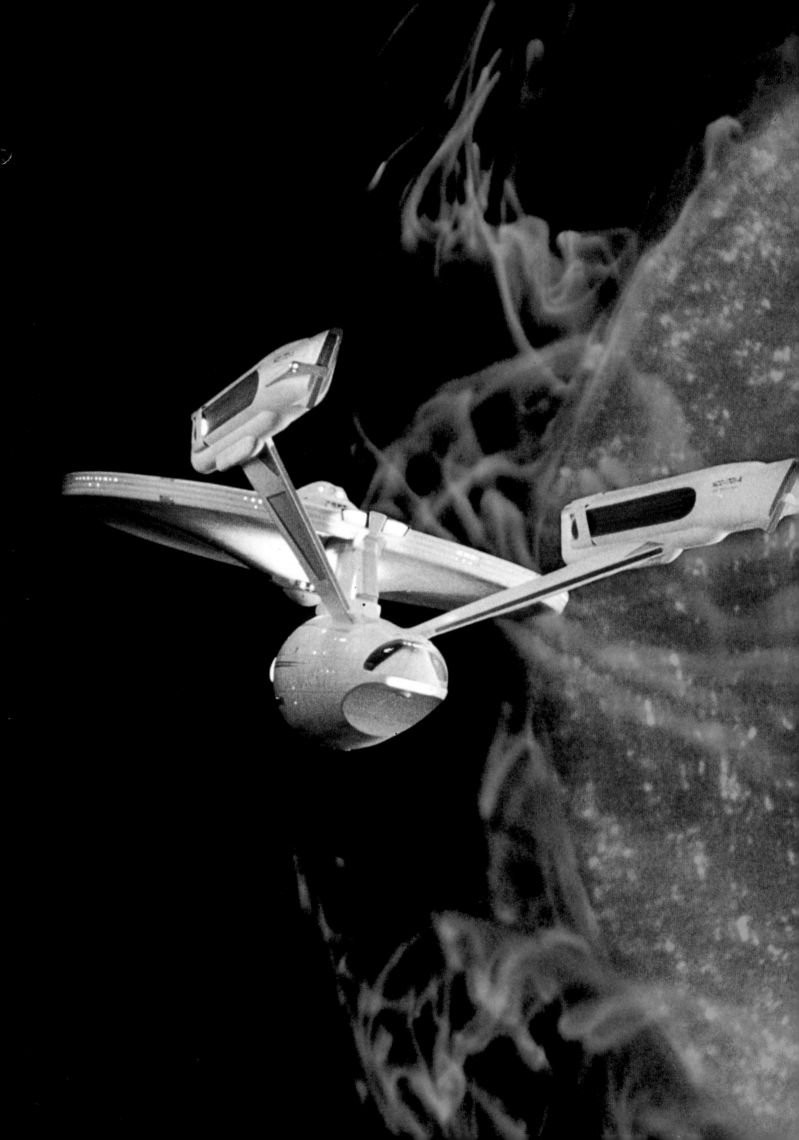

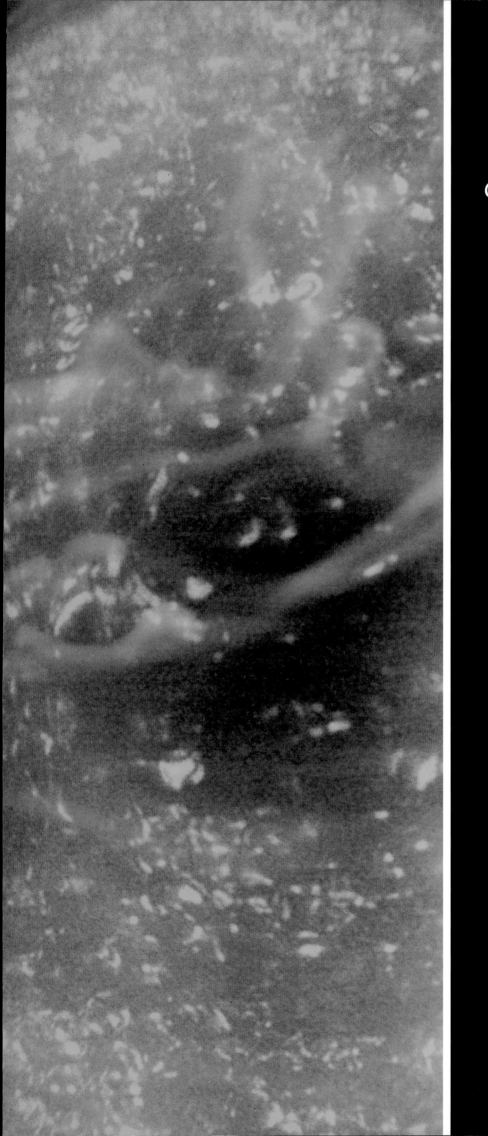

CHAPTER FIVE

THE ULTIMATE TRIP

STAR TREK V: THE FINAL FRONTIER 1988

STAR TREK V: THE FINAL FRONTIER

The fifth STAR TREK film remains the series' "disappointing success." By any ordinary standards, it was a winning and profitable film, yet because it didn't match the still never-equaled $100-million-plus gross of *The Voyage Home,* it is considered not as winning as it should have been. Frustratingly, for first-time movie director William Shatner, many of the conditions that led to the film's reception by the audience were not under his control.

As a story, STAR TREK V: THE FINAL FRONTIER was one of STAR TREK's most ambitious, conceptually and visually. However, because of a series of events that could not have been foreseen, most notably the Writers' Guild strike, which severely cut into the preproduction stage of the movie, STAR TREK's longtime partner, Industrial Light & Magic, was not available to create and produce the movie's visual effects. The resulting pressures of time, unexpected budget cuts, and the necessary learning curve of dealing with the unique demands of a STAR TREK film overwhelmed the replacement visual-effects company, and resulted in a film that was not as visually exciting as the four that had gone before.

A bright spot in the burdened production was the return of Herman Zimmerman to STAR TREK. His redesign of the *Enterprise*-A was a logical transition between the industrial austerity of the original ship and the hotel-like comfort of the *Enterprise*-D.

While some critics responded to the film's failure to match the grandness of its vision, David Ansen of *Newsweek* responded like a true fan, by writing that the movie was "endearing and enduring precisely because it is utterly free of cynicism." Referring to the movie's real strength—the exploration of the characters and their relationships to each other—Ansen added that the cast "know each other's moves so well they've found a shorthand that gets more laughs out of the lines than they deserve....It ain't art, but it's peculiarly satisfying."

As much as the look of STAR TREK is an important part of its success, it is not the only part. In terms of engaging and thoughtful themes and true character interactions, *The Final Frontier* remains a strong addition to the STAR TREK saga.

This combination of photography and painting was used as the "teaser" campaign for *The Final Frontier,* before any other art from the film was released.

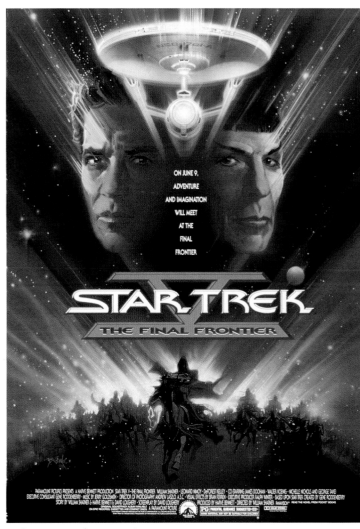

The Final Frontier in Japan, where a minor character took on new importance

A LITTLE BIT OF EVERYTHING

After studying industrial design in school, Nilo Rodis first started work as a car designer. When he decided that "gasoline was not in my blood," he moved on to the military, where he began designing tanks. It was then that Lucasfilm invited him to work on *The Return of the Jedi*. And even though Rodis had never seen either of the first two *Star Wars* films, he spent the next ten years at ILM, drawing storyboards and designing costumes, models, and props. For *The Final Frontier*, his comprehensive approach to design was not wasted, as these sketches show.

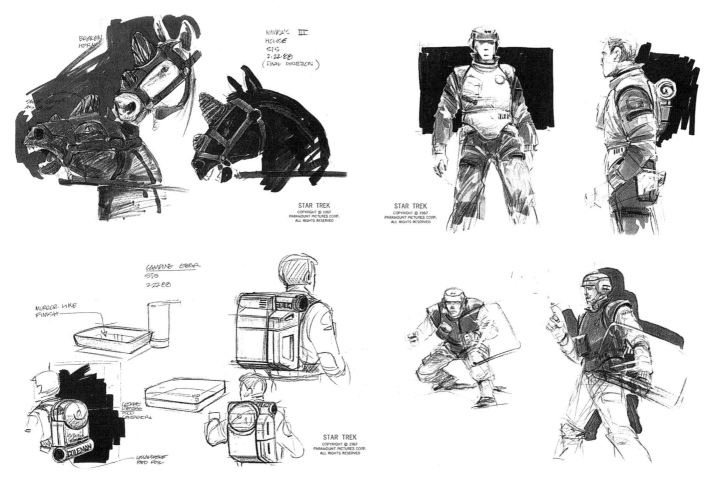

Director William Shatner was so impressed with the sets he had seen for *The Next Generation* that Herman Zimmerman became his first choice as production designer for *The Final Frontier*. Under Zimmerman's direction, the *Enterprise*-A took on a cleaner, brighter appearance, as a logical transition between the past of *The Original Series* and the future of *The Next Generation*.

THE SAME BUT DIFFERENT

For *The Final Frontier*, a new Bird-of-Prey bridge was built under Herman Zimmerman's direction, based on previous designs, but modified to give Klaa a more direct connection with the control of the ship's weapons.

The physical Klingon control buttons, last seen in *The Voyage Home*, have now been completely replaced by backlit Okudagrams, adding many more light sources and thus more visual interest to the set.

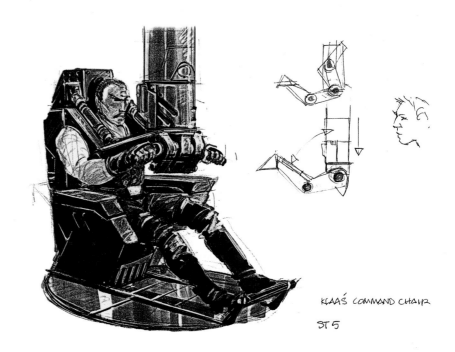

KLAA'S COMMAND CHAIR
ST 5

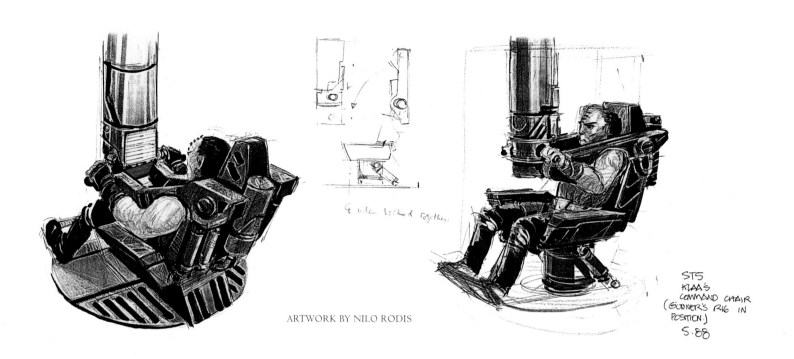

ARTWORK BY NILO RODIS

ST5
KLAA'S
COMMAND CHAIR
(GUNNER'S RIG IN
POSITION.)
5.88

A DIFFERENT LOOK

From the beginning, director William Shatner wanted to make his STAR TREK movie look different from the others—grittier and more realistic. While the overall clean and precise appearance of Starfleet and Federation environments could not be altered without diverging from STAR TREK's past, new locations were fair game for a new look.

Paradise—the "futuristic ghost town" on the planet Nimbus III—became the visual centerpiece for Shatner's vision of a different type of future, as these sketches by Nilos Rodis and props by Greg Jein show.

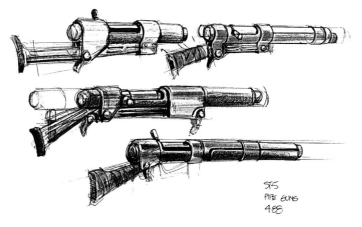

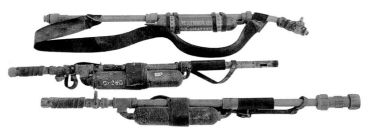

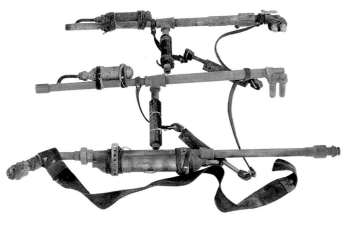

Weapons made from scavenged material, built by model-maker Greg Jein

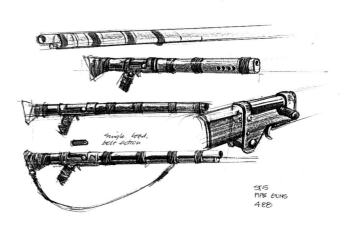

STS
PIPE GUNS
4.88

single feed.
bolt action

STS
PIPE GUNS
4.88

THEY'RE BAAACK

Nilo Rodis had worked on STAR TREK III: THE SEARCH FOR SPOCK and STAR TREK IV: THE VOYAGE HOME as an art director for Industrial Light & Magic, where he had begun working as a designer for *The Return of the Jedi*. By the time STAR TREK V: THE FINAL FRONTIER began production, Rodis had become independent, and was hired as the film's art director under production designer Herman Zimmerman. In addition to his art-directing duties, Rodis also became the film's costume designer when director William Shatner was impressed with the outfits Rodis included in his storyboards. Rodis shared costuming duties with Dodie Shepard, who would go on to work on STAR TREK VI: THE UNDISCOVERED COUNTRY.

Once again, Richard Snell returned as makeup supervisor. For *The Voyage Home*, director Leonard Nimoy had selected a single forehead design to be used for all the Klingons in the film. But for *The Final Frontier*, Snell credits Shatner for allowing him to make each of the Klingon forehead designs as distinctive as fingerprints. "That opened the door and now the sky's the limit."

Charles Cooper as General Koord

Todd Bryant as Captain Klaa

Spice Williams as Vixis

CAST FOAM

ST 5
VIXIS
5.88

KLAA
ST5
5.88

PRE-FORMED
PLATES
(FRONT/REAR)

(FORMED)
CAST FOAM
SHELL
FRONT/REAR

ST5
VIXIS
5.88

ST5
VIXIS
5.88

SKETCHES BY NILO RODIS

WHAT MIGHT HAVE BEEN

As originally imagined, *The Final Frontier* was to be the most visually exciting STAR TREK movie yet made. But the unexpected confluence of the Writer's Guild strike, a new visual-effects house, an immutable opening date, and a shrinking budget left many of the most complex images of the film unrealized.

As Nilo Rodis's sketches show, the rock creatures were conceived as formidable threats to Captain Kirk. When the final cost of the rockman costumes was calculated, the production was limited to a single creature, and when the single creature did not look convincing on film, it was cut from the film completely.

A production still providing a glimpse of the cumbersome rockman costume, which did not look convincing enough for inclusion in the final version of the film

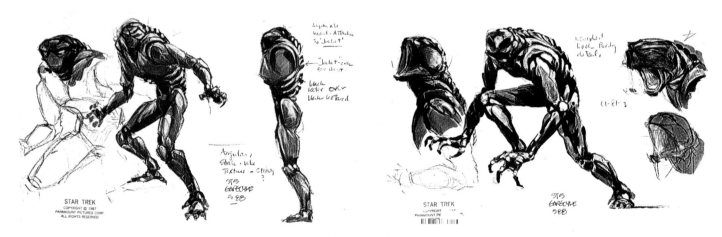

Nilo Rodis's unrealized designs

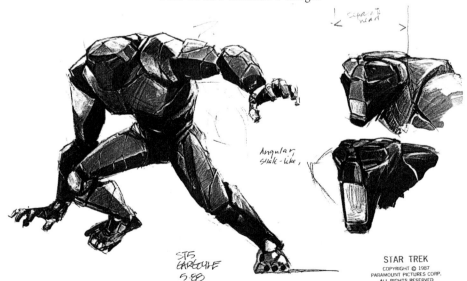

STS 488
GOD ALTAR

Though the "God Altar" set was constructed as planned, the visual effects that were to take place within it to electrify the film's climax and pay off much of what had been set up in the script remained unrealized.

CHAPTER SIX

SIGNATURE PIECE

STAR TREK VI:
THE UNDISCOVERED
COUNTRY
1991

STAR TREK VI: THE UNDISCOVERED COUNTRY

The sixth STAR TREK feature, and the last to include all the regulars from *The Original Series,* marked Nicholas Meyer's return to the director's chair and his grittier take on the STAR TREK universe.

At first, it was intended that the sixth film would be a prequel to *The Original Series,* taking place at Starfleet Academy while Kirk and company were still students. This would have required recasting the familiar roles with younger—and less expensive—actors. The original actors would appear only in a wraparound prologue and epilogue sequence.

This new approach to STAR TREK was eventually discarded by Paramount, and with the twenty-fifth anniversary only a year away, the studio turned to Leonard Nimoy and Nicholas Meyer to speedily come up with an appropriate adventure, using all the original cast members throughout the film.

Nimoy and Meyer developed the concept of having relations between the Klingon Empire and the Federation mirror those between the Soviet Union and the United States, with the Klingon Empire facing collapse and forced to sue for peace.

Within eleven months—a breathtaking pace for Hollywood—one of the strongest of STAR TREK's movie adventures was released in time to celebrate the saga's twenty-fifth anniversary.

The evocative ending, with the *Enterprise* disappearing against "the second star on the right, and straight on till morning," as Captain Kirk read his final log entry, followed by the dramatic flourishes of the key actors' signatures was clearly intended to say farewell to STAR TREK's first and most famous crew.

But like most farewells in the STAR TREK universe, it wasn't really the end.

There would be a STAR TREK VII, and some of the original crew would be around to make that voyage as well.

THE FINAL VOYAGE

For its sixth and final movie outing in STAR TREK VI: THE UNDISCOVERED COUNTRY, the *Enterprise* once again reflected the harsher and more militaristic design sensibility of director Nicholas Meyer. Though Meyer had pushed for and succeeded in giving STAR TREK a visual overhaul when he directed *The Wrath of Khan,* this time even he felt constrained by what had become established. "There are certain things about STAR TREK that are immutable. You don't change them, or you can only change them in very limited, cosmetic ways."

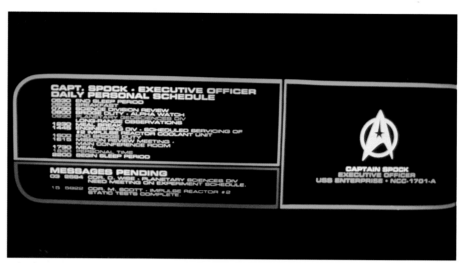

Okudagrams rule

Budget realities dictated that many of the *Enterprise* sets, such as the transporter room, be redressed versions of those built for *The Next Generation.*

Many fans objected to the idea of a twentieth-century-style kitchen on a starship, even though a galley was mentioned in *The Original Series* episode "Charlie X."

SOME OLD, FAMILIAR FACES...

*T*he *Undiscovered Country* featured more aliens than any other STAR TREK movie, many inspired by what had gone before.

Christopher Plummer as General Chang, in a more opulent Klingon uniform by costume designer Dodie Shepard. Plummer wanted to look unlike any other Klingon in STAR TREK, and specifically asked that he be given more subdued forehead bumps in order to humanize the character. Though a wig had been made for the character, Plummer preferred his bald appearance. This caused some restrictions on how he could be photographed during the first few days of production, until the makeup department was able to complete appliances to cover the back of his head.

Michael Dorn as the Klingon defender, an ancestor of his character, Worf, on *The Next Generation*

Rosana DeSoto as Chancellor Gorkon's daughter, Azetbur

David Warner as Chancellor Gorkon, in a makeup design addressing director Nicholas Meyer's desire to have him resemble Abraham Lincoln

...AND SOME NOT-SO-FAMILIAR ONES

Some days of filming required almost eighty makeup artists to create the required number of aliens needed for *The Undiscovered Country*. The artists responsible for the movie's impressive achievement include makeup supervisor Michael Mills and makeup department head Ken Myers. In addition, Richard Snell returned to design and fabricate the Klingon, Romulan, and Vulcan makeup, and Ed French created many of the exotic aliens in key scenes on Rura Penthe and for the Khitomer Peace Conference.

KLINGON SECRETS

Though Klingons had been featured in four of the five previous films and were an ongoing presence in *The Next Generation*, there were still some details of their culture to be visualized in *The Undiscovered Country*.

A matte-painting study of the Klingon courtroom, by Mark Moore of ILM

A Klingon camera used to record the trial of Kirk and McCoy. The control panel surface is part of an ATM model that was used in a street miniature constructed for the remake of *The Blob*.

PHOTOGRAPHY BY ROBBIE ROBINSON

A Nilo Rodis concept drawing of the
Klingon judge's gavel

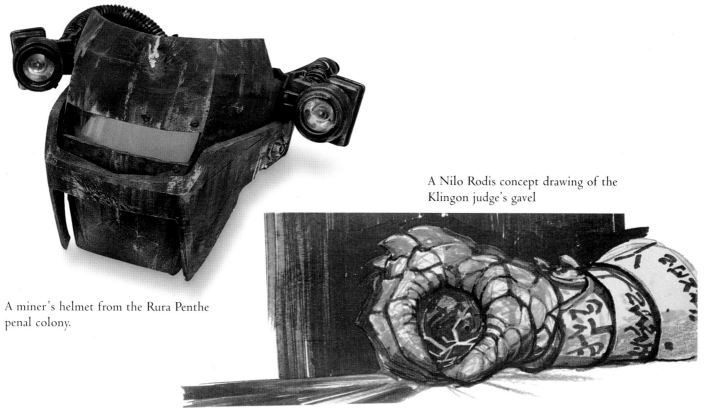

A miner's helmet from the Rura Penthe
penal colony.

BITS AND PIECES

The final helmet, constructed by Greg Jein

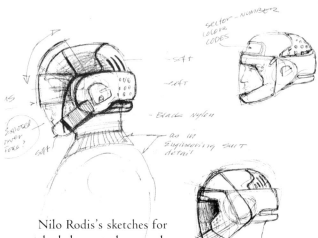

Nilo Rodis's sketches for the helmets to be worn by the assassins beamed onto Chang's ship from the *Enterprise*

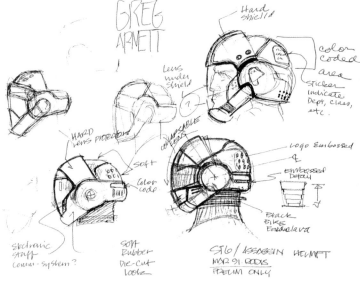

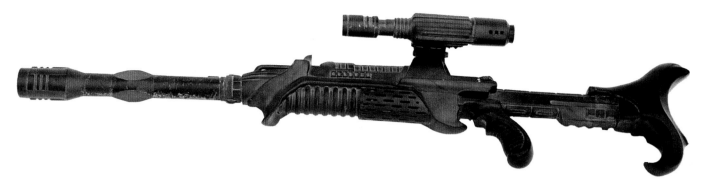

The final Klingon weapon

A "quick-and-dirty" mock-up of the assassin's modular weapon that Greg Jein roughly assembled to help in his design discussions with director Nicholas Meyer. Note the Starfleet phaser as the central component. When viewing this mock-up, everyone suddenly realized that even though the assassin was part of a Starfleet conspiracy, since he was going to be disguised as a Klingon, his weapon should be Klingon as well.

The phasers of *The Undiscovered Country*. The identification tags were intended to help keep track of the props, especially in the event of thefts.

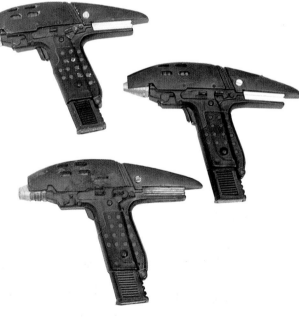

PROP PHOTOGRAPHY BY ROBBIE ROBINSON
COURTESY OF GREG JEIN

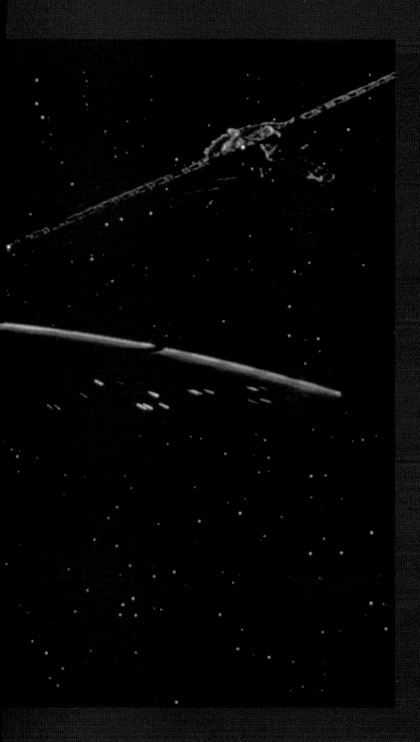

CHAPTER SEVEN

THE
NEXT
STEP

STAR TREK
GENERATIONS
1994

STAR TREK GENERATIONS

As early as *The Next Generation*'s fifth season, Paramount considered the seventh STAR TREK film to be a logical progression in the development of the franchise. The first series had led to six successful films. Eventually the second series would face its final season. What could make more sense than to follow in the footsteps of *The Original Series,* and move the crew of the *Enterprise*-D to the big screen?

But once again, the nature of STAR TREK's appeal to its audience came under scrutiny. At the time, STAR TREK thrived in two different versions on television. Yet how could Paramount be certain that it would do the same in movies?

Rick Berman's answer was to make the seventh STAR TREK film a transitional story, offering audiences both crews in a story that spanned the generations. As he termed it, STAR TREK GENERATIONS would be "the passing of the torch."

With two series in production, STAR TREK had become a major operation on the Paramount lot, staffed by a proven crew with years of experience in the special technical requirements and high quality demanded of a STAR TREK production. As producer of the seventh film, Berman wisely selected many of his key personnel from among that crew's ranks.

Once again, Herman Zimmerman returned to the sets of the *Enterprise*-D, whose creation he had overseen seven years earlier. Michael Westmore and Robert Blackman again weighed in with their expertise in STAR TREK makeup and costume design. And also, after an absence of seven years, Industrial Light & Magic took on the task of filming the *Enterprise*-D, for the first time since "Encounter at Farpoint."

In one sense, the production of *Generations* proceeded as if it were just another episode of the series, filming on the same lot and the same sets. However, everyone involved in the project recognized the difference that would exist in the expectations of the audience.

For seven years, millions of television viewers had followed the adventures of the *Enterprise*-D. Somehow, what turned up on the movie screen had to be bigger and better than anything that had gone before on the small screen.

Herman Zimmerman's approach to that challenge was characteristically simple and profound. He wanted the audience to recognize the sets of the starship, and then, as they noticed the extra details and design flourishes added for the movie, think to themselves, "Oh—this is what it must have looked like all along."

Thus the sets of the *Enterprise*-D, some of which had first been designed and built as the sets for the refitted original *Enterprise* in *The Motion Picture,* were prepared for their final performance. Colors were changed, proportions altered, new details added, all to heighten the illusion of reality that STAR TREK had so painstakingly created. And then, as the cameras rolled for the final time, the sets were dramatically destroyed in the climactic saucer-crash sequence.

In keeping with what had almost become STAR TREK tradition, portions of the demolished sets were salvaged for reuse on *Voyager.* So it is that the transporter disks from *The Original Series* still work to beam up Captain Janeway's crew. The elegant windows of Ten-Forward still function as windows on the stars, albeit in a slightly altered configuration. But there is still no denying that with *Generations,* the first great age of STAR TREK really did come to an end. The next *Enterprise,* to take to the stars in the eighth movie, officially announced in March 1995, will be the first to set off without the guidance, knowledge, or involvement of her creator, Gene Roddenberry.

As someone who always looked to the future, Roddenberry knew this day would come, and had already faced it with the secure and serene acceptance that came from watching his creation flourish in others' hands for more than twenty-five years.

"There's a good chance that when I'm gone," Roddenberry once said, "others will come along and do so well that people will say, 'Oh, that Roddenberry. He was never

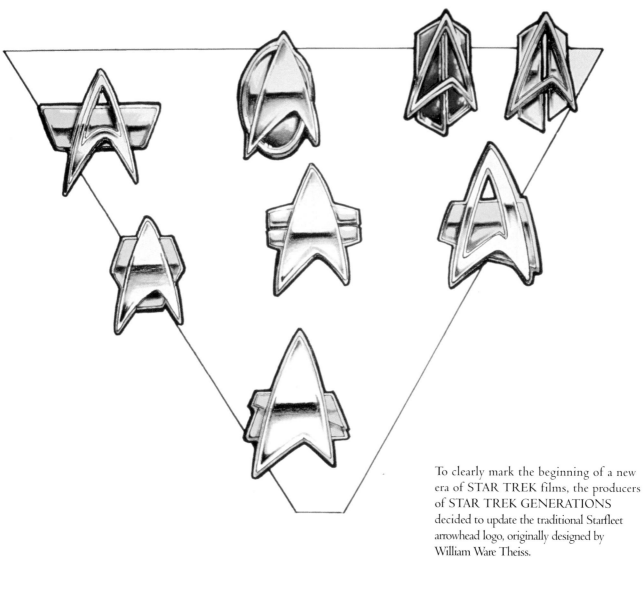

To clearly mark the beginning of a new era of STAR TREK films, the producers of STAR TREK GENERATIONS decided to update the traditional Starfleet arrowhead logo, originally designed by William Ware Theiss.

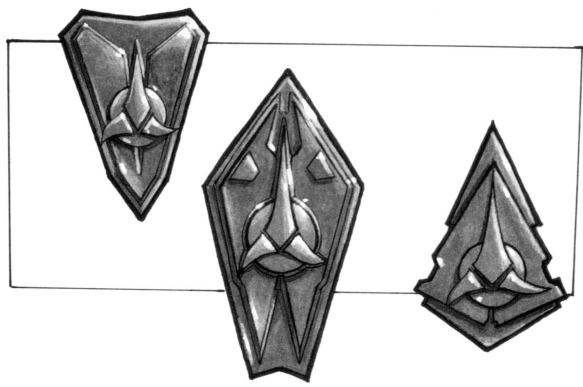

this good.' But I will be pleased with that statement."

There is no doubt that under Rick Berman's direction, STAR TREK will continue to flourish for years to come. And as the progression of images in this collection so clearly illustrates, its presentation will continue to capture us, even as it continues to evolve, no doubt in the hands of people who have yet to graduate from school or perhaps have not yet been born.

But no matter what changes lie ahead, there will always be at the core of each STAR TREK story, each designer's sketch and artist's drawing, the guiding spirit of Gene Roddenberry, still looking to the future with eyes full of wonder and a heart full of hope.

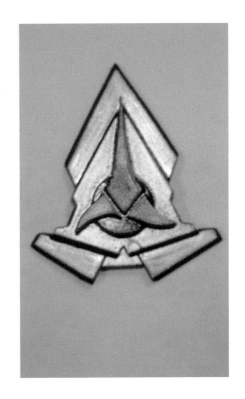

A NEW ENTERPRISE

Though an *Excelsior*-class *Enterprise*-B had been on display on the *Enterprise*-D's ready-room wall for seven years, it was not until *Generations* that the ship was made an official part of the STAR TREK timeline.

The original *Excelsior* model designed by Bill George of ILM was modified and repainted to become the B, with a built-out section added to the engineering hull. Portions of this section could then be broken away to illustrate the damage caused by the Nexus, without harming the actual ship, thus preserving it for other potential appearances in STAR TREK productions to come.

The bridge of the *Enterprise*-B is a modified version of the bridge built for *The Undiscovered Country*. Note that the conn and ops stations are flipped versions of those on the *Enterprise*-D. Also, because of the lag time between shooting the live-action scenes and the visual-effects sequences, this set was finished before the design of the *Enterprise*-B had been finalized. Thus the large schematic at the back of the bridge does not include the enlarged engineering hull.

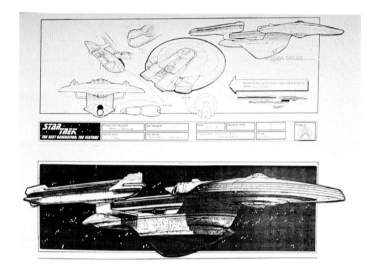

Comparison drawings showing the differences between the *Excelsior* and the new *Enterprise*-B

A completely computer-generated model of the *Enterprise*-B, which was used for all the sequences in which the Nexus light flashed and flickered nearby

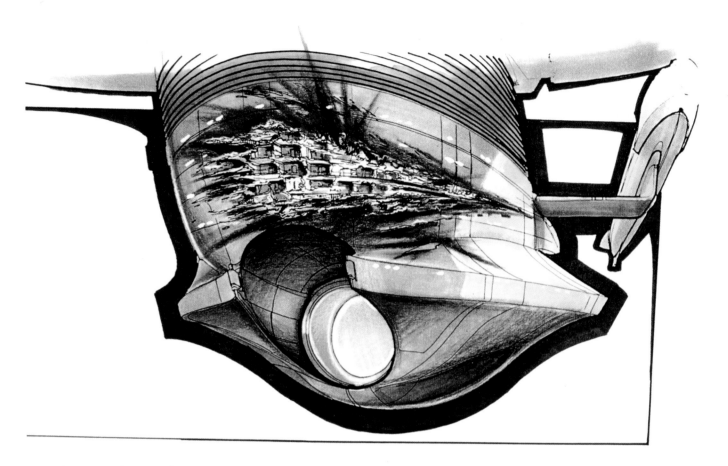

An early concept drawing of Nexus
damage

The new *Enterprise* in a spacedock
harkening back to the open structure
from which the first movie *Enterprise* was
launched in *The Motion Picture*

A TALE OF TWO ENTERPRISES

A motion-picture budget allowed production designer Herman Zimmerman to make some long-awaited modifications to the made-for-television sets he had designed seven years earlier, as well as to add some striking new sets of never-before-seen areas.

The new interior lighting scheme for the *Enterprise*-D included putting amber gels behind some of the transporter lenses from the *Original Series* set.

A concept drawing by John Eaves, showing the addition of side stations to the bridge of the *Enterprise*-D. Side stations were not made a part of the set for *The Next Generation* series because of the added expense of keeping them staffed with extras in each bridge scene.

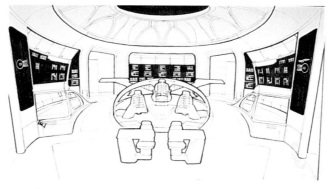

The final movie version of the bridge of the *Enterprise*-D, including more dramatic lighting, richer carpet colors, enlarged ceiling struts, and side stations. Though most of the set was destroyed during the filming of the climactic crash sequence, the wishbone railing is safely stored against the day a new *Enterprise* might be launched from spacedock, carrying the crew of *The Next Generation* to further adventures.

A captain's-eye view of the bridge of the *Enterprise*-B, which retained the Nicholas Meyer color scheme from *The Undiscovered Country*

Note that in these shots of the bridge of the *Enterprise*-B and the deflector room that Michael Okuda and the STAR TREK staff of artists and designers have maintained a distinctive system of signage for Starfleet of the Kirk era, different from the signage of the Picard era, even down to the numbers on the metal railing.

FIVE HUNDRED YEARS OF COSTUMES

Because of the holodeck sequence in which the crew of The *Next Generation* appear in *Generations*, costume designer Robert Blackman's work had to span centuries, as well as take a few detours to other worlds.

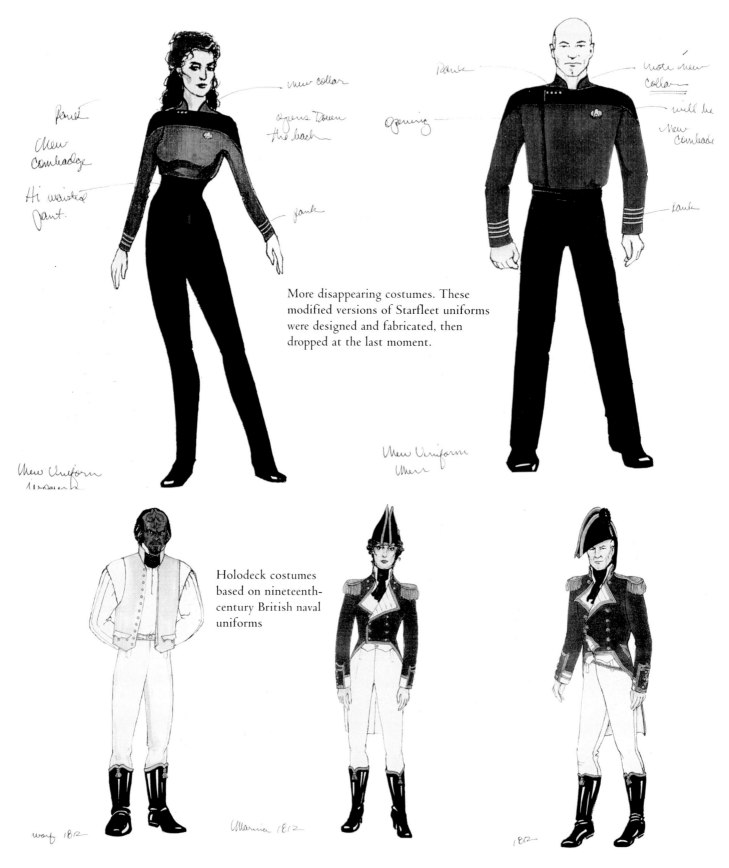

More disappearing costumes. These modified versions of Starfleet uniforms were designed and fabricated, then dropped at the last moment.

Holodeck costumes based on nineteenth-century British naval uniforms

The Duras sisters, Lursa and B'Etor. Robert Blackman's costume designs preserve the flow of STAR TREK history by retaining elements of Robert Fletcher's first movie designs.

Kirk's orbital skydiving outfit was constructed and filmed, though the sequence in which he wore it was deleted from the movie's theatrical release.

FROM THE PAGE TO REALITY...SOMETIMES

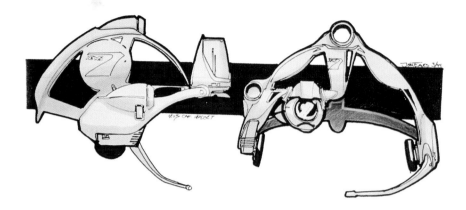

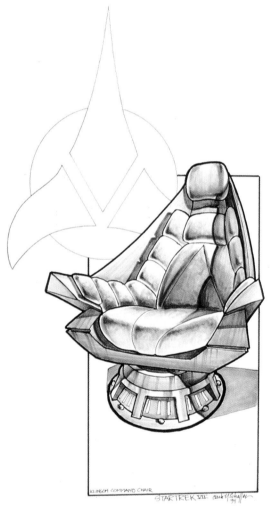

Clark Schaffer imagined a new, impressive command chair for the Bird-of-Prey bridge. But, in this case, the artist's imagination proved too stylish for anything a Klingon might own. The final chair was much more mundane, in keeping with the battered look of the old ship.

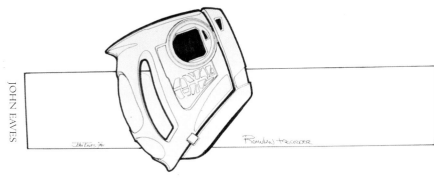

JOHN EAVES

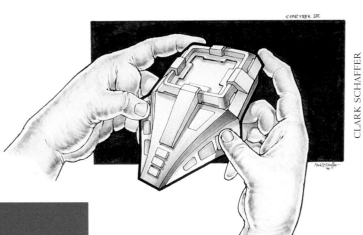

CLARK SCHAFFER

Some of the smaller props
required for *Generations*

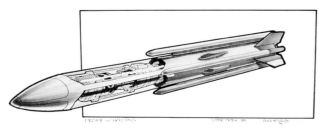

Of these two concepts for Soran's
probe, one clearly set the direction for
the final prop.

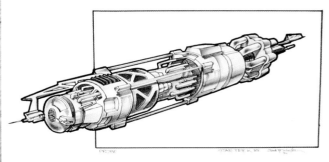

CONCEPT DRAWINGS BY CLARK SCHAFFER

HIGH- AND LOW-TECH STORYBOARDS

It should come as no surprise that Industrial Light & Magic, an industry leader in the field of visual effects, uses the latest computer imaging technology to produce their storyboards, as shown on the next page.

Yet, as the storyboards below demonstrate, the greatest images put on film by the most sophisticated technology still begin as an artist's imaginings, rendered by nothing more than a simple, time-honored pencil.

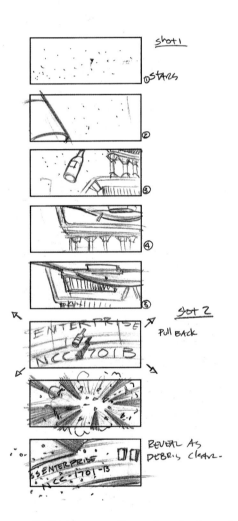

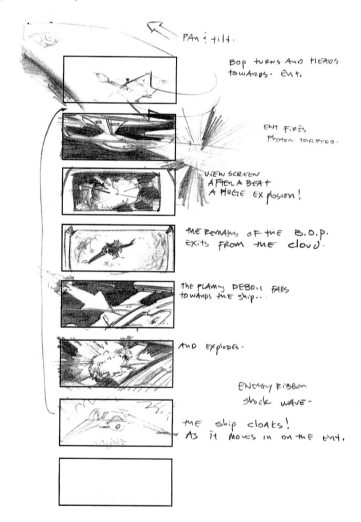

Preliminary pencil storyboards, drawn by Bill George during planning discussion with John Knoll

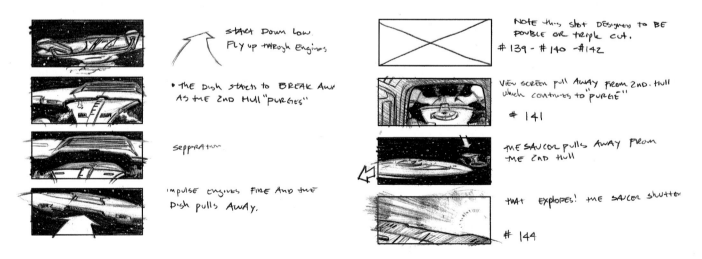

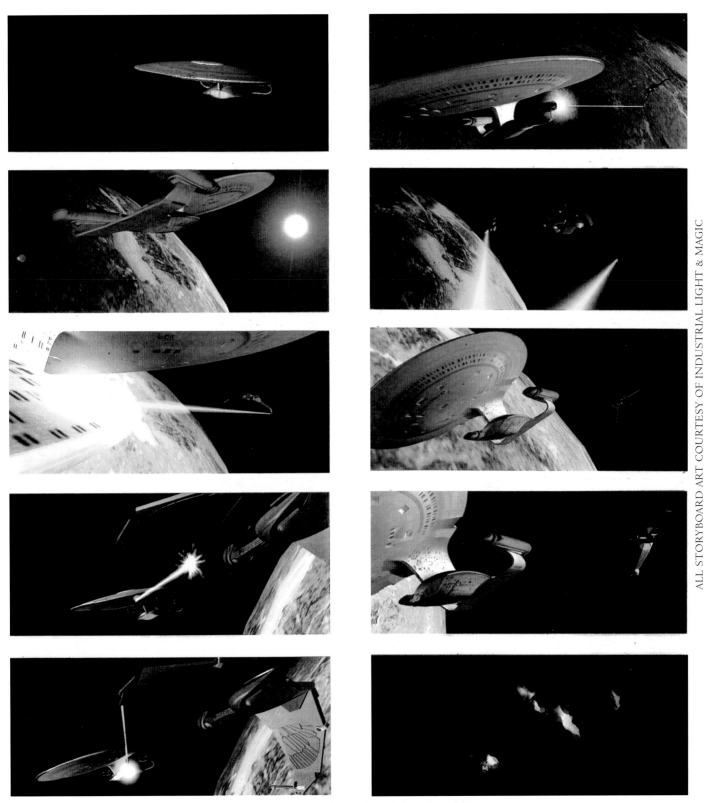

Computer-generated storyboards by John Knoll

nce again, guided by storyboards and their imaginations, the artists and technicians of Industrial Light & Magic combined live-action footage, miniatures, matte paintings, and computer-generated imagery to create these visually dynamic images, which exist only on single frames of film.

DETAILS, DETAILS...

A painting on the wall of Picard's Nexus fantasy—one of his ancestors who fought at Trafalgar

A nostalgic trophy wall in Kirk's cabin in the Nexus. The dedication plaque is a reproduction, now displayed in Herman Zimmerman's office. The crew photograph is from their last voyage together—*The Undiscovered Country*. For details on the painting of the original *Enterprise*, turn to the artwork immediately following the afterword.

A final look at a section of corridor first built for STAR TREK: PHASE II, sixteen years earlier

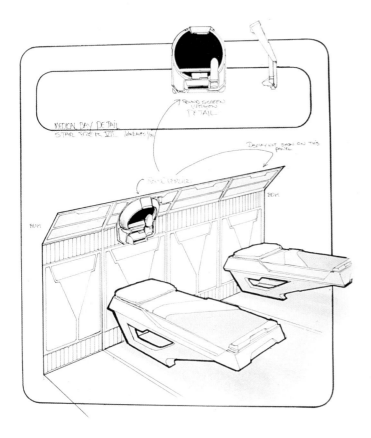

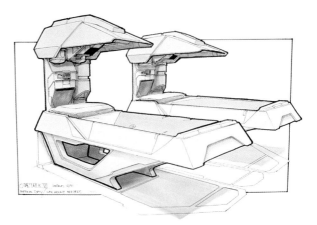

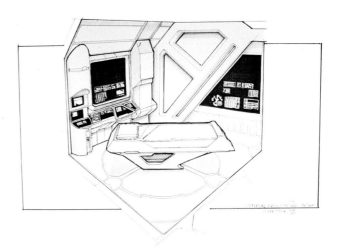

Despite these concept drawings by John Eaves, the final sickbay of the *Enterprise*-B was a redressed version of *The Next Generation* set.

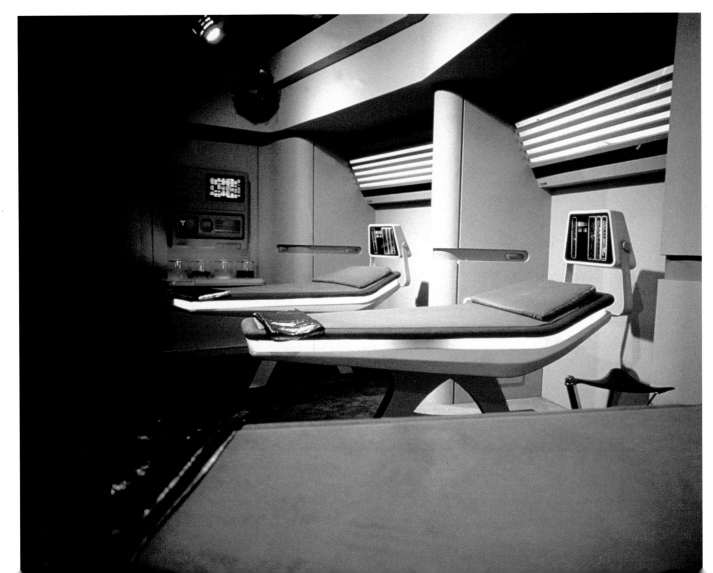

PREPARING FOR THE END

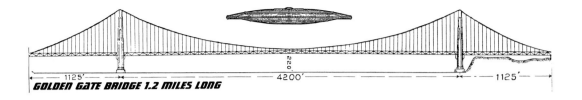

GOLDEN GATE BRIDGE 1.2 MILES LONG
1125'   4200'   220'   1125'

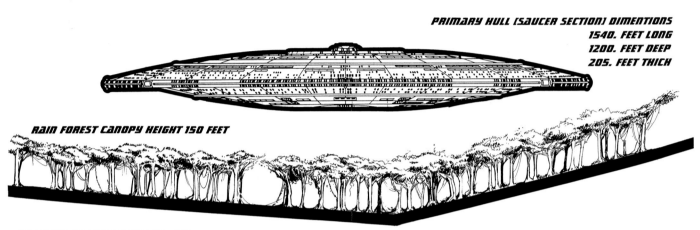

PRIMARY HULL [SAUCER SECTION] DIMENTIONS
1540. FEET LONG
1200. FEET DEEP
205. FEET THICK

RAIN FOREST CANOPY HEIGHT 150 FEET

ENTERPRISE D SCALE REFERENCE

The dramatic saucer-crash sequence in *Generations* was originally conceived of by Ron Moore, Brannon Braga, and Jeri Taylor as a possible scene for the sixth-season cliffhanger episode of *The Next Generation*. However, the visual effects required to successfully create the scene were prohibitively expensive for a television production, so the sequence had to wait until the *Enterprise*-D's first—and last—feature film.

These storyboards show the detailed planning that went into what *Generations* coscripter Ron Moore called "the big 'wow' sequence of the film."

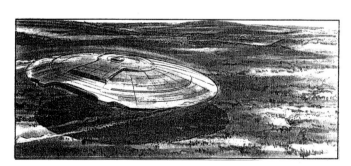

The camera follows the saucer as it skims along the surface of the forest. The saucer and its shadow move closer together.

Looking up through the tall trees as the immense saucer flies overhead, blocking out the sky. An instant later, a shock wave hits the trees, obliterating the frame with debris.

On the main viewscreen, the ground looms closer.

Close on the lip of the saucer as it plows through the trees

The saucer hits the surface, throwing up a huge cloud of dust and debris.

From a high angle, the saucer rips through the jungle.

The saucer crashes behind a hill. The crash causes a cloud of dust and debris. (During production, this shot was known as the *Lost in Space* shot.)

OVERLEAF Saucer-crash concept painting by Eric Tiemens.

COURTESY OF INDUSTRIAL LIGHT & MAGIC.

STORYBOARD ART BY MARK MOORE. COURTESY OF INDUSTRIAL LIGHT & MAGIC

Layers upon layers. Data's painting of his cat, Spot, after Picasso. Designed by Wendy Drapanas.

AFTERWORD

One of the most common questions asked of people involved in the production of STAR TREK is: Why is STAR TREK so popular?

Everyone has his or her own favorite answer. Hope for the future. Exciting stories. Intriguing characters. A dramatic metaphor for the human adventure. All are valid, but can any one really be *the* answer? We don't think so.

Because asking what makes STAR TREK so popular and so enduring is like asking what makes the space shuttle fly.

The space shuttle is the most complicated machine humans have ever built, and no one answer can explain its flight. Instead, there are hundreds, perhaps thousands of small, interconnected answers, all leading to a greater, grander conclusion.

And so it is with STAR TREK.

No one will ever be able to say precisely what makes it so popular, because its appeal is the product of a myriad of interlocking factors.

More than thirty years ago, Gene Roddenberry had a unique vision for a series of adventures set in the future. What would have happened to that vision if a designer other than Matt Jefferies had created the *Enterprise?* What if it had looked like Flash Gordon's rocket—become something we might only smile at today?

Where would STAR TREK be if NBC had bought that first pilot, without a Kirk and a McCoy, but with a Spock who smiled?

Whatever the answer to STAR TREK's first success in simply getting on the air to find its audience, through the layers and layers of contributions from hundreds of writers and producers and directors and actors and artists over the decades, there's nothing simple about it anymore.

And so it is with the art of STAR TREK, as well.

When we first began working on this project, the question that hung before us was: How can more than thirty years' worth of STAR TREK art be distilled down into a mere 320 pages?

After almost two years of research and sifting through more than five thousand sketches, paintings, blueprints, and photographs, the answer became all too clear.

It can't.

For every image in this book, two others just as interesting had to be excluded. For every artist given recognition, another, equally important, must be viewed in another, future collection.

This book, then, is just one of those small subsystems found within the mighty space shuttle. The look of STAR TREK has always been distinctive, evocative of adventure and the wonder of the future, and now, after all these years, it is warmed by a sense of nostalgia. It's not the only reason STAR TREK has become so successful a foundation for storytelling, but it does cause us to stand back and acknowledge all the other elements that have come together, blended, and evolved, just as Gene Roddenberry imagined.

That's the true art of STAR TREK, and it always has been.

OVERLEAF This final image of the original *Enterprise,* perhaps the last to appear in a STAR TREK production, was created to hang on the wall of Kirk's cabin in STAR TREK GENERATIONS.

Michael Okuda digitized a frame from a computer animation of the ship created by John Knoll of Industrial Light & Magic. Next, he manipulated the image in Photoshop to create the colorful watercolor effect.

The signature of Matt Jefferies was then digitally added to the image in fitting homage to one of STAR TREK's founding artists.